ONE LAST CONCERT

CHRISTOPHER J. HOLCROFT

OTHER TITLES BY
Christopher J. Holcroft

Only the Brave Dare
Canyon
A Rite of Passage
Finding Thomas
Time Voyager

ONE LAST CONCERT

CHRISTOPHER J. HOLCROFT

DoctorZed
Publishing
www.doctorzed.com

This third edition published 2022 by DoctorZed Publishing.

DoctorZed Publishing books may be ordered through booksellers or by contacting:

DoctorZed Publishing
10 Vista Ave
Skye, South Australia 5072
www.doctorzed.com
61-(0)8 8431-4965

ISBN: 978-0-6456195-3-9 (sc)
ISBN: 978-0-6456195-4-6 (e)

A CIP number for this book is available at the National Library of Australia.

Cover image teen boy © Nataliia Prokofyeva | Dreamstime.com
Cover image abstract hearts music notes © 25409423 | Dreamstime.com

DoctorZed Publishing rev. date: 10/10/2022

To my wife Yvonne,
for her everlasting love.

To my choristers everywhere...
the world loves to hear your songs.

"If the people we love are stolen from us, the way to have them live on is to never stop loving them"

James O'Barr

Prologue

Laughter could be heard everywhere as the boys and youth choristers started to gather at the St Dominic Savio church in Brighton, in the south of the United Kingdom. This would be the last time they would see their parents and friends before starting their whirlwind tour of Australia. The tour was part of a major concert tour being partly sponsored by local industry and the rest funded by the group's families. Six months of local concerts and fundraising throughout the adjoining villages had bought all members of the boys' choir including their concert master and musical director, airline tickets to the *land down under*. The choir had already sung with The American All Boys Choir and the Australian National Boys Choir during a British song festival and become good friends with their international counterparts.

A cacophony of high-pitched noises filled the air as the younger boys' excitement grew. Parents were becoming impatient as the bus to take the choir to the airport was now running twenty minutes late.

Musical director Bradley Worth organised for a parent to

go next door to the Rectory and make a phone call to the bus company to find out what was happening. Within minutes the parent came rushing back saying the first bus had broken down and the company was sending a second bus but it wouldn't arrive for around another half an hour. Worth was excellent at the impromptu. He organised for the older boys to line up the luggage ready to go and then shepherded everyone into the 18th Century church.

Inside the beautiful stone building, one of the youngest singers Blake Cooper knelt in prayer. The altar boy loved this church and would often be found sitting quietly in the pews seeking solace and praying. Worth quietly acknowledged him and then asked for the choir to stand in front of the altar for a few goodbye songs. He figured this would focus both the boys and their families before the expected rush onto the bus and also fill in time.

Without direction, the choir automatically formed up on the three steps in front of the altar and faced their 'congregation' not knowing which song to sing. The boys' concert master Mrs. Emily Connelly powered up the organ and started the introduction to their favourite – *The Lion Sleeps Tonight*. A hush came over the parents as giant smiles suddenly formed on the faces of the boys. A couple of the older choristers started making animal noises to set the scene of the jungle. Some of the younger ones followed suit with noises of monkeys and birds. Mrs. Connelly picked up on the melody on the organ and the younger choristers started humming the rhythm. The music and the boys' voices bounced off the church walls in an acoustic celebration for the senses.

"*Wee-ooh wim-o-weh. Wee-ooh wim-o-weh.*

Wim-o-weh o-wim-o-weh o-wim-o-weh o-wim-o-weh o-wim-o-weh o-wim-o-weh o-wim-weh" of the 1939 South African hit song echoed around the walls as the boys became animated. They loved this song as it allowed them to act out their various bird calls, growls and whistles before starting their rhythmic chant. Worth gave the signal and the animal noises stopped. The beautiful melodic sounds of the boys' voices filled the church.

The younger boys with the higher voices took the lead for the first part of the song. *'In the jungle, the mighty jungle, the lion sleeps tonight.'* They were soon followed by the older boys and youths with deeper resonating voices. *'In the jungle, the mighty jungle, the lion sleeps tonight.'* The audience clapped along to the song and could be seen rhythmically moving with the African song. The old church was built for singing. The boys' voices resonated off the walls as they put their hearts and soul into their singing. Smiles were everywhere as the choir and musical accompaniment brought the song to its natural end.

Almost on cue, Blake's father Barry came bursting into the church waving his arms and shouting.

"It's here! The bus is here. Sorry boys, but we don't want you late for your plane," he yelled out.

Mrs. Connelly nodded to Worth and the two signalled to the boys to make their way outside. A loud "Ooh!" resonated throughout the church with many parents shaking their heads as the angelic singing came to a halt. Within ten minutes the chartered bus was on its way to the airport with its precious load. Parents stood and waved as the bus with children from virtually every family throughout the district made its way out of the church grounds.

Bus driver Ian Scanlon knew he had a special cargo. Families across the district had been saving for a year; holding fetes, concerts and other fundraisers to send their boys away today. The route Scanlon took from the church to the airport he had driven hundreds of times. Today was no different except for the timings as he was running around forty minutes late. Speeding was not an option to try and make up time. He just had to hope the organisers had fudged in extra time in their planning.

Ten minutes down the main highway Scanlon started approaching a set of traffic lights. He shifted gears to slow the bus in case he had to stop. No problem, he got the green light. Scanlon started accelerating again when he noticed a truck carrying bottles of liquid petroleum gas running the red light on his right as he approached. He tried to stop the bus to avoid a collision but was too late. His huge behemoth of a vehicle slammed into the side of the truck igniting a series of gas bottles. The resultant explosions could be heard for twenty kilometres as both the truck and bus were turned into moving, flaming torches of death. The truck had been hit mid-ships by the bus. The force of the impact and the exploding gas bottles incinerated the bus and truck within minutes. Both the truck and bus drivers had no hope of escape and were immolated within seconds.

The boys on the bus driver's side saw the truck run the red light and yelled out to their mates to take cover. The force of the impact sent a gas cloud around and through the bus enveloping it in a gaseous shroud. Spark after spark from exploding gas bottles ignited the cloud superheating it and turning it into a fiery inferno of death.

The last things the boys saw were the looks of shock on each other and the windows of the bus being blown in towards their faces by giant balls of flame.

Chapter One

Present day:

John Sutton looked at the dateline of the real estate magazine. Yep, this was the latest – it had today's date. The acoustic sound engineer and his wife Melanie were keen to move to the countryside and escape the city rat race. He had been scouring the magazines for months for a disused church so he could set up a sound studio. The heavy stone-walled building would give a much clearer and crisper sound effect than modern edifices. Sutton believed he may have found what he was after. The former church in Brighton also had a three-bedroom Rectory with adjoining stables which was a bonus. The only thing Melanie would baulk at would be the small, attached graveyard containing fifteen old graves, some dating back to the 1800s. Melanie was a piano teacher who taught students from basic beginnings up to diploma levels. She also helped John with background music for his recordings.

The price was right. Sutton just had to take a trip to Brighton and ensure the buildings actually met his needs.

"Mel, this could be our big chance," John said to his wife over a breakfast cup of tea. "It looks right. We don't want anything too big to maintain …"

"Or too big to clean up on the inside. Does it show photos of the inside of the church?"

"No. Just the outside and surrounds. It has a three-bedroom Rectory which would be plenty of room for us and there's a bonus."

Mel stopped sipping her tea. "A bonus? Do they throw in steak knives?" she laughed.

"Not quite. There are stables attached to the Rectory which we can use …"

Melanie lost it. She started laughing.

"What's up?"

"Sorry John. I had this mental picture of the parish priest making a fast getaway on horseback and leaving the Church to fall into ruin for some reason."

"Very funny!"

"Come on, we'd better finish up and get dressed if we're going to drive to Brighton."

"Can't we drive there in our pyjamas?"

"No. It might scare the villagers."

John stood up and walked over to his wife, put his arms around her and gave her a big kiss. "Thank you. Who knows? This could be the very thing we are both looking for."

Within half an hour the Suttons were driving to Brighton. The large open congested highways soon gave way to the smaller unclogged arterial roads and the village laneways. The couple drove through Brighton and was amazed at the number of houses available for sale.

"This isn't a mining town is it?" Mel asked.

"No. We're too far away from any colliery."

"It's just a bit spooky to see so many houses run down or for sale."

"You're right. Ahh, there it is up on the hill."

"Typical. The Church always likes building on hills so their buildings can be seen more easily."

The Suttons drove to the entrance of the disused church and saw the For Sale sign out the front. They parked their car in the driveway, alighted and started looking around. Fine metal mesh had been sculptured around each of the stained-glass windows to protect them from loose flying rocks or other objects. The grey slate roof was covered in moss and the entrance door was locked. They started to walk to the adjoining Rectory when a car pulled up behind them.

"Hello, I'm Nigel White from White Real Estate. Can I help you?" the driver asked as he alighted from his car.

John looked at the young salesman with the three-piece suit, boyish looks, glasses and a big smile.

"Hi, I'm John Sutton and this is my wife, Melanie. We saw this old church advertised in the real estate magazine and thought we'd come and have a look at it."

"Lucky I came by when I did. I was on my way through the village to Brighton and noticed your car. This church has been on the market for some time."

"It's a beautiful old building and surrounds," Melanie chimed in.

"Yes. It would probably still be in full use today if it wasn't for the choir's bus accident about a decade ago. You know, where the bus and truck collided setting both vehicles on fire instantaneously."

John studied the agent's face for a few seconds as he tried to remember the accident. The penny seemed to have dropped. "Yes, I think I remember. Is this the one where the children were on their way overseas ..."

"Australia, I think," Melanie finished for him. "It was one of the worst accidents the UK had ever seen."

"So the kids all came from here, did they?" John asked as he looked around.

"Yes, from all around the village. Anyway, enough of that, would you like to go inside the old place?"

John looked at Melanie and they both nodded. They followed White into the building and stood there with their mouths agape. The building was in pristine condition. The pews and organ had long gone, along with the altar and any signs of devotion. However, the building was in really good condition. The trio moved into the centre of the building and looked around. White went to say something, and John put his hand up to silence him as if he was listening to something, frowned and then smiled before nodding.

"Mel, give us a few bars will you, I want to check the acoustics," John said as he looked around with a wry smile.

Melanie cleared her throat and launched into a few bars of a song she knew. The sound resonated around the building. John's eyes widened, his mouth fell open and he looked at his wife. This was exactly what he wanted. He asked his wife to sing a couple of songs while he walked around the inside perimeter of the building and smiled broadly. His eyes caught the choir loft above the entranceway and he studied it for a few moments.

"Nigel, is the loft, okay?"

"Yes. It's very sturdy. It would make a great occasional room. Come and have a look."

John took Melanie's hand and smiled broadly. She knew her husband had already made up his mind but went along for the ride. The three made their way up a circular wooden staircase at the end of the building and into the choir loft. It would easily fit up to fifty people as they sang the church service. The timber flooring was perfect – sturdy and not in need of maintenance. John asked his wife to sing for him one more time as he went back down the stairs and walked through the empty building listening to the sound effects. After a hearty rendition of some of Melanie's favourite songs John signalled her to stop. White accompanied Melanie downstairs to where John was standing.

"This place is outstanding," John said. "It gave off a fantastic pitch and range of sounds. Yes, this would be excellent."

"I think we'd better look at the Rectory and stables before he gets too excited," Melanie chipped in as she took her husband's hand.

The trio were about to exit the building when John saw a metal plaque with a photo of a choir attached to the wall and stopped to read it.

"In loving memory of the 45 members of St Dominic Savio's Boys and Youth Choir taken to God on 3 January 2003. Forever in our hearts. Your angelic songs will never be forgotten."

The plaque had a metal etched photo of the entire choir, Mrs. Connelly and Mr. Worth.

"If you decide to buy the place you can remove the plaque if you want," White said.

"This photo was taken here – well over there, actually," John said as he pointed to the front of the nave. "I think it should be a pre-condition of anyone buying this place the plaque remained. I bet the children were the heart and soul of this place."

White smiled and nodded. "I never used to come to this place to worship. However, my parents did take me along for a few concerts here. This place would be overflowing with people. Whenever the boys sang here there was always, I don't know, a feeling of tremendous warmth and peace. Anyway, I'd better show you the Rectory and stables."

John took in what White said and had one last look inside the empty building before exiting. He played with his right ear. Melanie picked up on her husband's movements.

"Are you okay?"

"Yeah, I think so. I'll tell you later."

White finished locking the door and walked the Suttons across to the Rectory. The former Priest's residence was still quite functional and in good condition.

"It's almost as if the priest had just decided to pack up and leave one day and closed the door behind him ready to return the next," Melanie said with a smile as she looked from her husband to White. "There's been no real move to take away whatever functional furniture was here. The priest could virtually come back today, unpack his suitcase and carry on. Mmm," Melanie said as she looked around the building.

"Yes, it seems the priest hung onto living here until the last minute when the Church said it could no longer support him here," White said.

"Why's that?" John asked.

"Once the choir was wiped out a lot of the families just stopped coming here. I guess they found it too painful a reminder."

"Ah, the positive side would be the lack of visitors to the place then," John said as he looked at a crucifix hanging on the wall.

"Well yes, except the few visitors who come to pay their respects to those buried here? It goes with the territory I'm sorry to say but people who want to go to the graves here must have access. Don't worry; there would be a very little inconvenience."

"Nigel, what about headstones or graves for the children from the choir, is there something here?"

"There's a sort of memorial plaque in Brighton itself where the accident happened and the plaque inside the old church you've already seen. There was nothing to bury. The whole choir sort of just evaporated in the blast."

Melanie had tears well up in her eyes as she pondered the situation. "That would be so hard for the families – not having anything to say farewell to, nothing of the boys to visit."

John put his arm around Melanie and squeezed her.

"Okay Nigel, you better show us the stables now."

The trio moved from the Rectory to the adjoining stables. John stood mesmerised as he mentally pictured what space he would need for his and Melanie's cars and equipment from his garage. He checked the walls and roof and looked at Melanie.

She winced and knew John's mind was made up back in the old church.

"When was all this built?" John asked.

"Somewhere in the mid-1800s, I believe. I can get you exact dates if you like."

"And has the church been deconsecrated?"

"Yes. The priest and bishop did a special service before the workmen came and removed the pews, and other bits and pieces. It hasn't just been abandoned."

"Let's go back to the cars so we can exchange contact details. I think Melanie and I would like to think this one over some more."

"Okay."

The three made their way back to the cars where John and White exchanged details. For White, this could be a serendipitous sale. If he hadn't decided on going to Brighton he may not have met the Suttons. For John and Melanie, they needed to look at their finances and discuss if they were really ready to give up their city lifestyle for a quieter life in the country – if the sales figures were agreeable, then the answer would be yes. The return trip home was something neither of the couple would forget.

"You've already made your mind up, haven't you?" Melanie asked.

"I don't know. It seems perfect enough."

"What was playing on your mind in the church? Whether we could make it into a sound studio and still have room for music instruction?"

"No. It was weird. I believe I heard the boys from this church

– all laughing and playing in the main body of the church when we first walked in. Later they joined you in singing."

"You heard the spirits of the dead choir boys!"

"Yes. They were definitely there. Also, there were two adults with them, a man and a woman."

"Were they the same people in the metal etching near the door?"

"I guess so. If they are Melanie, we could have some pretty interesting company."

The smile on Mel's face suddenly changed as she saw how serious her husband seemed.

"Remember when I asked you to sing a few bars?"

"Yes, to check out the pitch in the stone walls and roof."

"No. When you sang, the boys stopped playing and they listened. When I asked you to sing some of your favourite songs the church seemed to erupt into song for me as the boys joined in. It was truly wonderful. Maybe I'm losing my mind. I haven't heard spirits for quite some time – not since I was a young boy. I don't know what made me hear them tonight."

Mel looked at her husband and put her hand on his thigh. He had not sounded so earnest in quite a while. Also, John never made up stories. He had many gifts as a person, but imagination was not one of them.

"John when I sang my songs for you what did you hear?"

John pulled off to the side of the road and placed the car in park and pulled on the handbrake. He turned to his wife and had a serious face.

"At first, the boys' voices were just a gaggle of noise – like you'd hear in any playground. When you started singing *Panis Angelicus* the boys seemed to automatically have found their pitch and joined in. You were accompanied by what sounded like a ... I don't like saying it ... a host of angels."

"What about when I sang *I Have A Dream* from Le Misérables, what happened then?"

"You had the most beautiful accompaniment, but they didn't know the song – they just hummed in unison."

It was Melanie's time to be shocked. She had sung a couple of her favourite songs and had felt quite at home singing in the empty church. Usually, when she sang somewhere new she became nervous.

"You know, John, when I was singing both songs, I felt I could feel the rhythm of the usual music accompaniment not just hear it."

"Mel, there was one more thing. You remember I stopped at the plaque on the wall?"

"Yes."

"Well, I heard a boy's voice say to me '*don't tell anyone you can hear us*' – that stunned me. If I told anyone other than you I'd be considered mad!"

The pair sat in the car in silence for a full minute digesting what each other had said.

"Darling if you don't want to go ahead with buying the place I'll understand," Mel said. "It may just be too weird for us both."

"No, I would really like to go ahead and buy the place if we can talk the Church around to the right price. Even though the boys' spirits were in the church they were happy and joyous –

not evil. I think I need another visit to the church so I can run some tests with my equipment."

"Would you be okay if in fact, the boys' spirits were haunting …"

"Visiting, not haunting."

"Okay, visiting the place?"

"Yes, I think so. We both have our faith and know that if the boys are still here then there's a reason behind it. Let's see if I can have another visit to the church one night during the week."

"Alright!"

Chapter Two

John arranged with Nigel White to conduct a music test within the former church the following Wednesday night. He brought in an array of specialist recording equipment; speakers and a special compact disc Melanie had bought in London.

John was early. He sat in his car outside the darkened building for a few minutes in silence before walking around its perimeter. No, he didn't hear any angelic voices or playground-type noises, just the usual quiet of the night. He loved it. There were no large trucks or flights of aircraft taking off or landing in his direction, unlike where he lived with Melanie. John took a portable chair out of the car and sat in the dark and watched the stars while he waited for his real estate agent.

White's car could be seen entering the church grounds at the bottom of the hill. Two white lights from his headlights lit the road ahead of the vehicle in twin ribbons of light. An eerie glow emanated from the driving compartment and slowly grew as the car travelled towards John. It wasn't until White's car stopped that John had a chuckle. The glow John saw was the light from the small navigation GPS device White had attached to his windscreen bouncing off White's face. No ghosts here.

"Hi, thank you for allowing me to do a trial recording tonight," John said and went to White to shake his hand.

"No probs, John. I have to go into the village and speak with a couple of customers anyway."

"You're working late then aren't you?"

"Yes, I usually finish around 5.30 pm but a couple of the villagers are thinking of selling up and I go where the sales are."

John thought for a moment. "Are they parents of some of the dead choir boys?"

"Why yes, they are – how did you know?"

"A lucky guess, I suppose. Melanie and I saw a few houses up for sale in the village as we drove through last weekend."

"Yes. It's a real shame but ever since the choir's demise, the house sales have increased quite a bit. Do you want a hand with your equipment, or will you be okay if I open up and turn the lights on for you?"

"No probs, I'll be fine, thank you. I just need to put some equipment in the centre of the building, close up and then play some music and record its effects."

"Alright John. Come, I'll show you where the lights are."

White and John walked to the side of the building to an electrical meter box. The real estate agent used a small torch from his pocket to light the way and locate the main fuse. He replaced the fuse, turned on the switch and the lights of the former church suddenly came on. The pair then went to the main entrance door and opened it.

"This is when I leave you to it," White said. "I'll be back in a couple of hours to see how you are going."

"Thanks, Nigel, I really appreciate your assistance."

White then drove off and John took his recording and playback equipment inside. Once he closed the door John could hear every movement he made as the noise of his shoes or clothing amplified as it bounced off the walls. He imagined the building full of people. Any noise the members of the congregation made would have been muffled by the furniture, the clothes the people were wearing and the people's voices. Alone in an empty stone-walled and slate-roofed building, his movements on the wooden floors and any noise from his metallic equipment seemed loud. It took around ten minutes to set up the equipment and speakers. John walked around the inside perimeter of the former church. All was quiet – great. He played a CD of one of his rock singer clients and started recording it. The music and singing filled the church. John was confident the recording with the noise bouncing off the stone walls would give him the effect he was after. He played back the songs and sat in the middle of the church as the large speakers brought life to his recording. It was fantastic. The building had provided a beautiful harmonic not available in sound studios. He then played the compact disc Melanie gave him and he was moved to tears. His wife had ferreted around the London music stores and bought a CD of the choir who last sang in this church which they had recorded the month before they left on their fateful drive to the airport for the trip to Australia.

John read the accompanying publicity blurb as the St Dominic Savio Boys and Youth choir was heard once more in the church. The blurb said the first song, *Panis Angelicus* was originally a stanza written and set to music by Saint Thomas Aquinas, a theologian living in the 13th Century. John's tears ran freely when he read that *Panis Angelicus* means 'bread of angels' as the voices he heard accompany his wife and the boys' spirits in this building had to have been angels. Nearly six hundred years after St Thomas Aquinas penned his famous work Belgian-born César Franck set the music to voice in 1872. It gained international recognition when it was performed at the funeral Masses for both Robert and Edward Kennedy – two of the USA's most famous politicians.

John was moved to hear the 12 songs on the CD play in the disused church as he re-recorded them. It had been around a decade since the children's voices had been heard live singing the songs he was hearing now – this was an enigma for John. When he heard the boys in the church, they were pre-teenagers and teens. Had they lived, most of them would be aged in their twenties now. During the last song Nigel White quietly opened the front door and signalled to John. He gently closed the door and stood listening to the choir sing *Sanctus* as it reached its top and low notes of the beautiful hymn. Once complete, White walked over to John and congratulated him on bringing music back to the church.

"Ah, but this is not a church now – just a beautiful stone walled building with magnificent stained-glass windows."

"John, you are so right. From your professional perspective, will this building do what you want it to do?"

"I think so. I've been quite moved by the fantastic sounds within this building."

"So do you just play a recording and then re-record it using the ambient sound of the building to give some sort of special effect?"

"Yes, sort of, but I also add other sounds if the piece requires it. This is one of the things I would use the building for. I'd also like to record live as I believe this building has all the acoustics needed."

"Good. When will I know your final decision on the sale?"

"Nigel, I need to play the recordings to my studio bosses, and this should clinch the deal. I'll be ready to discuss the sale with you on Friday."

"Excellent. I saw a few people in the village tonight who are looking at selling up and they were keen to also know what you are doing."

John looked at White for a few moments. "What did they think of the notion of Melanie and I moving in here?"

"They loved it because your work will bring life back to the old building."

"That's excellent. I didn't want to get off on the wrong foot with the former parishioners. You know I wouldn't blame them for moving on either as long as they find good work somewhere."

White nodded and then helped John pack up before closing the disused church. He went back to the fuse box and removed the main fuse and closed the box before returning to his car.

"Taking no chances with break-ins?" John asked.

"It's just policy to shut all power off to the buildings we are selling in case of fires."

"Okay. Thanks. I'll be back in touch on Friday."

"Thanks, John, I look forward to it."

Both men drove off and within the hour John was home all excited. He brought in the two CDs he re-recorded so his wife could listen and give her opinion on the harmonics. John organised a glass of port for them both and they sat in their lounge room and listened to the rock singer belt out his feisty tunes.

"This is excellent John. The old building has really added a sound you can't get in a studio," Melanie said as she reached for the now empty port bottle. "I take it you played my gift?"

"Played? You had me in tears at one stage as I listened to the boys sing on their CD and read their publicity blurb. They had beautiful voices and really would have done well ..."

"Yes, if not for their early demise. Did you hear them tonight?"

"No. I didn't even feel their presence."

The Suttons worked their way through the re-recording starting with *Panis Angelicus*. Near the end of the CD, John got up to make a cup of tea for them both. In the kitchen, he heard the opening animal noises the choir made before they launched into *The Lion Sleeps Tonight*. He stopped what he was doing and went back into the lounge room. Melanie was still in her seat looking quizzical.

"How did you do that?" John asked as she heard the boys sing '*In the jungle, the mighty jungle ...*' John stood gob-smacked. He never mixed any recordings with the CD Melanie gave him. "You must have just put it on. My question is where did you get it?"

"John, I swear I haven't moved from my seat since you went to make a cup of tea."

The Suttons looked at each other and listened intently as the song continued to its final refrain '*Hush, my darling, don't fear, my darling, the lion sleeps tonight.*' When the boys had stopped singing and harmonised ' … *wee-ooh wim-o-weh* … ' A distinctive boy's voice then could be heard whispering '*Don't tell anyone.*'

Both John and Melanie were stunned. John played back the last track on the CD and turned up the volume quite loud. '*Don't tell anyone*' could be heard quite audibly.

"John the CD I gave you had 12 tracks on it. The one you brought home has 13, plus a message."

"Mel, that's the same boy I heard in the church on our first visit. And that's the same message he gave me then. The question is what do we do about this?"

"Are you prepared to work in a haunted space?"

"Haunted? Do you realise what we may have here?"

"Surprise me, because right now I could easily walk away and look for somewhere else to work and live. "What if we settle on the place and then find our work is jinxed by the boys' ghosts?"

Melanie thought for a few moments. "Will you play the last part again please?"

"Alright."

John organised the CD and fast-forwarded it to the end of the 13th track. He adjusted the controls on his playback system and turned up the volume.

Don't tell anyone was distinctly heard as if the boy saying it was raising his voice while standing within Sutton's lounge room.

"Mel, there is supposedly a phenomenon called *white noise* where recording people have heard the voices of dead people coming through their various home appliances whether it be a TV, radio or even a tape recorder but it is usually associated with static. The problem here is we had no white noise and no static. Also, the boy's voice and song are so distinct it's as if the boys are trying to tell us more than not alert anyone to them being around."

"Maybe they have no other way of letting people know they are still here on Earth and haven't moved on to heaven or wherever we all go. I want to help them if I can. You could have provided some sort of vehicle to communicate between the boys and us."

John was restless. This was the first time he had ever heard of his recording equipment as a vehicle to talk with the dead.

"Nigel wants us to give him a final answer on Friday, so we really need to think about what we are doing. If we go ahead and move into the Rectory and take over the property there is no going back. If the place is haunted, we may need some sort of exorcism to try and move the boys on."

"Well, I'm still up for it and I don't believe we need an exorcism of the place. The old church has everything we need for us to move out of this apartment and start a new life. How about we sleep on it and make a final decision tomorrow?"

"Alright Mel, let's go to bed."

The Suttons both had a restless night. Thoughts of contacting the dead; a choir wiped out in a gaseous vehicle explosion still roaming around the Earthly plane and moving house played on their respective minds. John hauled himself out of bed at the first sign of light in the sky and went to the kitchen. To his surprise, he saw Melanie sitting at the breakfast bar sipping a cup of tea.

"The jug's not long boiled if you want a cuppa."

John went over to his wife, put his arms around her and gave her a big kiss.

"I'd rather have you. Have you been up long?"

"No. My mind was racing so I thought I better get up and have a cup of tea. It usually settles me. You know I think we need to speak to someone to confirm if we have a recording of the boys or whether it is some form of spiritual mischief."

"What do you want to do?"

"Well, Nigel wants an answer on Friday – tomorrow. I'd like to confirm the voice we heard is actually from the choir."

John poured his tea and sat down with his wife.

"What are you proposing?"

"How about we see if we can contact the former parish priest here and invite him to dinner? If he's available and if he comes, we could play the last track and the message to see if he remembers the voice."

"Mmm, that's a long shot but could work. If he gets spooked, we may have to say we just came across the recording through former parishioners who have seen us here and wanted us to hear the boys."

"Done! I'll follow up with Nigel this morning from the office. Will this leave you enough time to prepare a meal?"

"Yes, but ask him what he likes so I have a few choices of menu."

The Suttons finished their teas and John showered, dressed

and went to work. He felt comfortable in his work environment where he had the latest high technical capability to record and investigate the noise. He was a sound technician at a recording studio and had helped lay many tracks for new and upcoming recording artists. John rang Nigel White and got the former priest's contact details. Father Brendan Kirby had not moved too far away but had moved in with an ailing parish priest in an adjoining parish church. Father Kirby jumped at the chance to meet the Suttons.

"Mel, our guest tonight will be Father Brendan Kirby who was the former parish priest of St Dominic Savio's," John gushed down the phone at morning tea.

"Fantastic my husband," Melanie said excitedly. "What does he like eating?"

"He's not fussed as long as it is home cooked."

"Okay, I'll organise steak and kidney pie and vegetables and a nice dessert. You get the wine."

"Thank you, my love, consider it done. See you tonight. Father Kirby will drive himself over and be at our place around 7 pm."

"Alright see you later."

Once Melanie had hung up John went back to work. He recorded *The Lion Sleeps Tonight* and the boy's message on a single CD to play for Father Kirby. Hopefully, the priest could tell him and Melanie something about the voice.

Chapter Three

Brendan Kirby was glad a young couple was deciding to live in his old church. He had been parish priest at St Dominic Savio's for fifteen years before the gas explosion wiped out his choir. This single incident was responsible for a high percentage of families in the district moving out – they wanted to escape the collective painful memory of the bus and truck accident that robbed them of seeing their children grow up. Besides, by having someone living in the Rectory and working in the old church it would again add life, albeit in some small way, to the former St Dominic Savio's.

Kirby stopped outside the Suttons' place and checked the address he had written down. This was the right place. He picked up a bottle of wine and briefcase from the front seat of his car and made his way to the couple's front door. Within seconds of ringing the doorbell, Melanie opened it. She beamed a huge smile and introduced herself when she saw the priest. He was silhouetted against the evening sun and wore black shoes, black trousers, a white shirt with gold metal crosses on the corners of the collar and a black sweater. Kirby could easily have stood in for artists if they wanted a face to depict that of Jesus Christ. He looked swarthy, dark-haired and had piercing brown eyes which lit up easily when he smiled.

"Hi Melanie, I'm Brendan Kirby."

"Please come in, John shouldn't be too long arriving."

Melanie showed Kirby into the lounge room.

"Mmm that smells beautiful," Kirby said.

"I've cooked steak and kidney pie for us – I hope you like it?"

"It's one of my favourites. Mrs. Green my former housekeeper at St Dominic Savio's used to cook it often for me. It was always a delight to come home to after working in the parish."

"Do you miss it?"

"Yeah, it was my life for more than fifteen years before attendances started dropping off, and eventually I had to close the church."

"It must have been hard for you. The choir you worked with for so long all killed in that horrific smash and then the people moved away."

Kirby studied Melanie for a few seconds before answering. It was still a touchy subject.

"Yes, I had seen most of the choir grow from babies to boys and youths. Many had even helped serve with me. Their loss has been really felt throughout the village and district."

"John and I had a look through the buildings on the weekend and saw the plaque on the wall near the exit. They were good-looking boys and young men."

"Yes, they were. They were taken before they even knew what life was all about."

The front door opened and closed, and footsteps could be heard down the hallway leading to the lounge room.

"Hello Father, I'm John," Sutton said as he introduced himself. "Sorry I'm late, traffic was heavier than I expected."

"Hi, I'm Brendan. I was just reminiscing with your lovely wife about the old church."

"It's a veritable treasure trove," John said.

Melanie stood up and said she would get the dinner organised and left the men to catch up.

"John, she's lovely."

"Thank you. It took me a while to find Mel but when we did connect it was pretty much love at first sight. This is rude of me. Would you like a glass of red or white wine, a beer or something stronger?"

"Now that would be lovely. A glass of red wine would be fine, thank you."

John stood up and went to the drinks cabinet at the other end of the room. He took out a bottle of cabernet sauvignon and showed Father Kirby before opening it and pouring three glasses.

"Mel loves this wine too so I'm glad you do. Well, we have a lot to talk about. I'm a recording engineer and Melanie is a music teacher, so we'll be filling the old church with a lot of music."

"Excellent, John – the old church was built for song and music. It has one of the best sounds anywhere in the south of the United Kingdom. Well, at least in my opinion."

Melanie re-entered the room and announced dinner would be five minutes away. She saw a glass of wine poured for her, picked it up and drank some.

"Thanks, John," she said.

"Mel was able to find a CD from the former choir for us to listen to and hear their magnificent voices."

"Don't try looking any further – they only ever made the one. The choir had so many plans for recordings and tours. I'm sure they would have made it big on the world stage. Did you know they were planning a trip to Australia when they had that terrible accident?"

"Yes, and their Australian hosts along with an American choir came and sang at their memorial service, I think," Melanie said.

"Yes, it was the biggest service attendance the church had ever known during my stay there. We even had to erect speakers outside the church so the overflow of people could hear the magnificent choirs. My boys were really loved."

"You know Brendan; my work allows me to dissect single notes and chords so they can be re-arranged for better effects."

"Your work must be very interesting, but no one will ever capture the sounds of my lost choir again."

"What if I told you I already have?"

Kirby's eyes widened as he searched his mind. He hadn't known Worth had recorded any other songs and music with the boys' choir.

"That'd be a surprise. I think the musical director Bradley Worth only ever recorded one album. What do you have?"

John reached into his briefcase and took out a CD and placed it into a player turned it on and played the second track.

Don't tell anyone clearly was heard and Kirby closed his eyes for a moment and shook his head. He looked up at John with moist eyes.

"I haven't heard his voice for so long. Can you play it again, please?"

John obliged and then sipped some more wine. "Do you know who it is?"

"Yes, of course, it's the voice of Blake Cooper, one of our youngest – correction was one of the youngest singers in the choir. Where did you get it?"

"Gents before we start having long conversations, let's go to the dining room and eat," Melanie said as she stood up.

"What was Blake like?" John asked as he grabbed the bottle of wine and showed Father Kirby into the dining room.

"Blake was very devout. He was virtually saintly in the way he prayed and the way he helped anyone and everyone. How did you get his voice?"

The three sat down and Melanie asked Kirby to say grace. The priest had been unnerved when he heard Blake's voice. He found it hard to concentrate on a prayer of thanksgiving, but he did well.

"When I went to the old church last night, I re-recorded a collection of artists' works to see what the harmonics were like," John said. "Mel had found the boys' CD and gave it to me to play. At the end of the CD, I heard some noise. Only after I adjusted a few recording levels did I hear Blake's voice. At first, I thought I was mistaken so I played the last song again and recorded it. I think the original mixer must have missed the boy talking when he made the recording. These things happen."

Mel shot John a glance but continued to eat the steak and kidney pie in front of her.

"Do you have the original CD here perchance?"

"Yes, would you like me to play it?"

"That would be really wonderful. Thank you; I haven't heard their songs for a long time."

John left the dinner table and went to the lounge room where he started playing the original CD Mel gave him before returning to his dinner.

"You know they only ever recorded 12 songs before the start of what would have been their tour down under," Father Kirby said.

"Did they ever sing *The Lion Sleeps Tonight?*" Mel asked.

"Yes, it was one of their favourites but was considered not in the same theme as these songs we're hearing now so it was going to be on their second album, I think."

Father Kirby digested what was happening with the boys' music and the message from Blake.

"John, I have the feeling you want to tell me something," he said as he sipped his wine.

"Yes, I do, but rather than tell you straight out I want to play something for you. Please bear with me and I apologise for what must seem like a game to you."

John went back to the lounge room and played his two-track CD from the beginning and returned to the dinner table. Kirby went white as he heard his boys launch into their favourite song complete with animal noises and then Blake's message at the end. He looked at John and then wiped away some tears. He took out his handkerchief and blew his nose.

"I don't know what you are doing or how you got that recording. I'm rather stunned actually. Tonight I was looking forward to meeting the young couple who are possibly about to take over my old church. I find I'm listening to voices from the grave. I don't know what to say."

Melanie reached across the table and gently held Father Kirby's hand and smiled.

"Brendan we're at a loss too and I guess we wanted to share something special with you that I came across by accident," John said. "We don't know these boys or have any untoward intent regarding the church. It's just that when Melanie gave me a 12-song CD of the boys I loved it so much I re-recorded it in the church last night to see if I could improve on any of their sounds. When I came home there were 13 songs on the second CD plus Blake's message."

Father Kirby's eyes were red and moist. He gained his composure and drank some more wine. This was an unexpected evening he would never forget.

"When you said the old church was a veritable treasure trove I took it you meant for its beauty and the various stained glass windows ..."

"Yes, absolutely. However, when I chanced on the unrecorded song I wanted to know whether it was in fact your boys singing. The next thing we have to do is find out if I can duplicate the recording again."

"What about Blake? Surely, he was trying to tell us something?" Melanie asked.

"You know, in the Church, we believe when a person dies they go to heaven; they don't linger here," Father Kirby said as he tried to rationalise the situation.

"Brendan, every Sunday Christians pray in the Mass they

believe in one God, the creator of all that is seen and unseen. Could this be part of the unseen we pray about?" John asked as his mind went into overdrive.

"I don't know. There are so many TV shows and movies around about people talking with the dead they give the impression anyone can do it at any time. The voice of Blake Cooper absolutely sent shivers up my spine. It was almost as if he was in your lounge room calling out to us."

"Brendan, Melanie and I are keen to buy your old church property, but we have to do so with our eyes wide open as to what we are inheriting. Now I know the name of the boy whose voice we have all heard it will make it easier if I hear anything else in the former church."

"You know you really can't tell anyone about these recordings," Father Kirby said. "A lot of people won't believe you. If they think the church is haunted, it could be a catastrophe for you with all the wrong people wanting to visit."

"Can we keep this between the three of us?" John asked.

"No problems with me," Father Kirby said.

"Or me," Mel chimed in.

"Thank you for this Brendan, it was very hard for us to ask you along tonight and then play the recordings. Mel and I have very open minds about these things, but we knew from Nigel White how close you were to the choir."

"I'm just; I don't know, excited but also scared to have heard Blake's voice again and also *The Lion Sleeps Tonight* – that song really got me, especially when you realise the song was never recorded by the choir and it was the last one they began to sing before they left on their fateful trip."

John looked at Brendan and took a sip of wine.

"It must have been hard for you the day the boys took their final journey."

"I'll say. It was probably the hardest in my life."

"I read the boys were in a bus that was hit by a gas truck. It must have been pretty terrible for them. Can you tell us what happened?"

Brendan wiped away some tears and took another sip of wine. He seemed to play with his glass for a few seconds.

"It was all over in a matter of seconds for all those on the bus. The truck and bus both exploded sending bits of metal; chards of glass and other debris into nearby buildings and vehicles for nearly two hundred metres.

"There was no hope of survival for any of the bus or truck occupants. The scene itself was like the images of terrorist bombings overseas on the news with large vehicles alight and giant plumes of smoke billowing into the sky.

"Within minutes every available fire appliance, police vehicle and ambulance were rushed to the scene. Hundreds of people milled around the crash site in shock at what happened. Mobile news crews arrived quickly and recorded the horrific infernos, sending satellite coverage around the globe and breaking into every TV program service in the country to detail the event. News of the bus crash quickly spread among the boys' families amid huge outpourings of grief and "no, it can't be our bus.""

Melanie gently took Brendan's hand in hers and then patted it before Brendan continued his graphic story.

"Police had telephoned the bus company for information

about the passengers. Within a short time, I received the worst news of my life from Police.

"My choir had just been entirely wiped out – before they had even boarded the plane to start their epic journey down under. I had worked closely with the choir and the boys' families, making the church available for rehearsals as often as it could be over the preceding twelve months.

"My whole parish worked hard trying to raise funds for the choir. After the Police called I had to do the worst job of my calling – offer comfort en masse to a whole community. I tell you, John, Melanie it was hard. Every family in the district had sent a son on the bus. Virtually no family was untouched by the event. Within an hour of the crash, families started returning to the church where, a short while before they had farewelled their boys. Police had set up roadblocks around the crash site and no one could get near the scene except emergency vehicles. It was very obvious from the news coverage the deaths of those on board the vehicles were instantaneous. Police Officers were sent to St Dominic Savio's to assist the families and me with what information they had about the crash.

"I greeted every family member of the choir who came to the church. Gone were the angelic voices of the boys we heard here tonight, as they imitated animals and started their beautiful rendition of *The Lion Sleeps Tonight*.

"Instead, the church echoed with the wailing and crying of families as they tried to comfort each other. The tragic loss of so many children caused a national outpouring of grief not seen in the United Kingdom since the 1966 Aberfan mine disaster in Wales in which 116 children and 28 adults died."

"What happened in Aberfan," John broke in.

"A huge spoil-tip that had built up over many years at a mine flooded down to the nearby Junior and Secondary schools trapping students and killing them in their classrooms.

"There was some joy surrounding my boys though.

"The Australian National Boys Choir, which was to be their hosts, cancelled all events for the following few weeks. The choir was sent by the Australian Government here on the first available plane to help give comfort to the families of their friends. I held a memorial service for all forty-three choristers; Mrs. Connelly and Mr. Worth a week later."

"I imagine the service would have also been hard for you, too," Melanie proffered.

Brendan winced as he looked his hosts in the eyes.

"You know, family members of each dead chorister placed a candle representing their boy around the steps of the altar and there were larger candles for Mrs. Connelly and Mr. Worth. Choirs from Australia and the United States sang songs during the service. We had to erect giant television screens outside the church so the overflowing huge crowds could view and hear the proceedings. The lawns outside the church were packed with hundreds of people who could not fit in the building.

"The following week, I held a special thanksgiving service for the boys' families. Within a few years of the service, the district surrounding my church started emptying as families of the dead boys began to move away. Eight years after the accident the Church told me to close St Dominic Savio's and place the buildings and land on the market."

Kirby stayed for around another hour, with the Suttons and

him discussing the Rectory and stables and what the couple must do when people want to visit the graves on the property.

"Thanks, Mel for a really delicious meal. John, you opened a window to a bygone time I thought was over long ago, thank you," Kirby said as he was leaving.

"Brendan it's been a pleasure meeting you and getting to know the last occupier of our new home to be. Thanks for the info on the choir. If anything unusual happens regarding my recordings I may have to call on you."

"That'll be fine, John. The choir and I had a pretty good rapport, so if you need me please call. God bless."

The Suttons retreated to the lounge room to discuss the evening.

"So you have made up our minds about buying the old church, have you?" Melanie asked John with a large smile.

"Well, I now think the place is calling to us. It's a weird feeling. I think the old church has a fantastic set of harmonics that we'll both benefit from. If I get any more recordings from the boys thrown in we'll have to deal with them as they happen. At least we know we have Brendan to call on if needed."

"He's a lovely man, a little quirky, but I like him."

"Yes, and I think we rocked his boat with the two recordings tonight. You know love; I wouldn't mind hearing the boys' album one more time tonight – maybe over another glass of port or two."

"This sounds good to me – your shout."

The Suttons sat in silence as they listened to the 13-song CD. John's mind was evaluating what he would do if he recorded other songs by the boys. Would he just compile them, try and let the boys' parents know about them or even try and market the boys' works as new recordings? How do you explain to the public you have recorded a new album with a choir that has been dead for a decade? No, this couldn't work as he would have too much to try and explain about a dead choir not having moved on after dying. This was not for him. The wrong crowds would start going to the old church in search of the boys' ghosts.

"You know, that was really interesting about how Australian and American choirs came here to sing at the boys' memorial service," Mel said as she stood up.

"Yes; our boys seemed to have really endeared themselves to our international cousins. Any youth funeral has a large service, but I guess when you have one for forty-five people you'd have to expect churches like St Dominic Savio's to overflow considerably."

The Suttons cleared the dining table and put the dishes into the dishwasher. It was time for bed. Melanie had a good night's sleep as she had worked hard the whole of the day organising the dinner and running around buying and cooking the food. John had a restless night. In his mind's eye, he could see the etched photo of the boys hanging in the church singing the songs on the CD. He heard them sing other songs, but he couldn't remember them when he finally decided he had to get up and stop being so restless. He went to the kitchen and made himself a cup of tea and worked out the program of recordings he had to make for his boss in the former church.

First, though, he had to contact Nigel White and seal the deal for the property and then arrange time off to move houses.

Chapter Four

The Suttons managed to sign on the dotted line with Nigel White and moved into the new home the following weekend. It took two removal trucks and three days of setting up before the Suttons felt comfortable in their new home. The stables now had that 'lived in' look again. Two cars occupied the building along with the usual gardening and other tools found in most garages. The Suttons renamed the Rectory 'Sutton Hall' while the former church posed a problem for the couple. They figured it wouldn't matter what they called the disused church concerning John's work, locals and others would always call it St Dominic Savio's. John had toyed with the idea of naming it '*The Choir Loft*' or something similar as a corporate name but let it go for the moment. He believed a name would come in time as he developed his work there.

John went to work the next day in the former church for his first full day. He had a busy schedule of recordings and was keen to make a start. After each recording, John would play it back to ensure he only captured the noise he wanted. Off to the side of the nave of the church at the front was the former vestry the priest and altar boys used to change into their liturgical clothes. John initially set up a large urn in there so he had cups of tea or coffee on demand as required. He decided to upgrade his water service and organised for a plumber and electrician to install an instant boiling water device mounted on the wall.

John had finished his first three hours of recording and then decided to have a break. He had an executive-style reclining leather chair and footstool. He placed the chair and footstool near the entrance to his 'tea room', sat down and began enjoying a cup of tea. A cool change enveloped him like someone standing in front of the afternoon sun casting a shadow over him and he rubbed his hands. He suddenly became aware of a spiritual presence standing in front of him.

"Will you help us?" a teenage boy said quite clearly.

John arched his back and looked around to ensure no one had entered the building while he was organising his tea.

"Blake is that you?" John steeled himself and asked the voice. He wanted to confirm it was the boy he had first heard in the church and on the recording.

"Yes."

"Thank you for the beautiful song you left me on the CD last week. Father Kirby loved it too," John said as he tried to reassure himself.

"Father Brendan was our best friend here. I'm glad you gave him the recording you made."

John was a bit perplexed. He hadn't spoken to spirits since he was a little boy and to him, they were imaginary friends.

"Why are you still here Blake? Are the other boys with you?"

"Yes – we want to say goodbye to our parents. The bus crash happened so quickly none of us could say goodbye."

"How come I can hear you and no one else can? Surely there must be local people you could have spoken to? What about Father Kirby?"

"Your mind is open to us so Mr. Worth wanted me to talk with you."

"What is it you and Mr. Worth want me to do?"

"We want you to organise one last concert for our parents."

John was rocked by what Blake said. Does he want a farewell concert for a boys' choir that died ten years ago? It couldn't be done. Anyway, all he had was one new song recorded by accident – not by design – by the boys.

"Blake, wasn't a special farewell concert held in this church after you all … well, after the accident? Why do you want another one? What happens if I organise the concert?"

"No. There was a special service, not a concert. We sang here but no one knew. If you hold the concert for us our mission here is then over."

"Does that mean you can all move on to the *light*?"

"Yes, we think so. You have to help us, please."

John shook his head. "You managed to slip *The Lion Sleeps Tonight* on a recording I did last week. Father Kirby said it was one of your choir's favourite songs."

"Yes, we all loved it. It was our way of letting you know we're here."

"If any concert could be organised, I would need new material other than just one song. Also, I would need some sort of message all your parents could hear so they knew I hadn't just made the whole thing up."

"We can do that."

"Blake, you have given me a lot to think about. I'll need to discuss this with my wife and see what can be done."

"Thank you and please thank Melanie."

The voice of the teenage boy trailed off and John then felt the warmth return to him. Wow, what a mind-blowing experience, John thought. The boys were stuck in a temporal plane and couldn't move on. He had too many things to consider. Firstly, John felt he needed to find out why his mind was open to hearing the boys and not others. John was not a medium nor were his parents. He couldn't remember ever playing with Ouija boards and summoning spirits to answer questions with groups of friends or spirits visiting him. No, he was an ordinary person. Sometimes when he was a young boy he would play and speak with imaginary friends. It was only later as an adult that he believed those 'friends' could have been spirits. John's afternoon of work had just been put on hold while he thought about what just happened. A concert for the dead? A concert with the dead? Neither thought excited him; however, he had been given a challenge of monumental proportions by a group of dead boys and teenagers he never even knew. Just for the moment, John thought, if such a concert could be held, how would it play out? He stood up and got himself another cup of tea before resuming his seat.

John thought about the mechanics of organising the concert. It would need to be arranged on a series of levels. Foremost, the boys themselves would have to help with songs he could record and then produce on CDs for each of the families to prove the boys were still here. For a weekend, the former church would have to be emptied of its equipment and seating put in especially for the parents and families. Somehow, he would have to convince the families the boys were still here so they would attend … this would be very hard unless he had another reason for the concert. Also, how do you tell the families their dead sons have been with them for ten years and not moved on? The families' religious beliefs would assist as they would understand the boys would always be with them. However, the concept in their minds would be the boys would have gone to heaven and not lingered on Earth and been with them as sort of angels or spirit guides. John finished his tea and went to walk out of the old church. He stopped at the wall plaque of the boys and looked closely at the image. Without a second thought, John went to his recording area and retrieved a screwdriver. He then removed the plaque and took it with him to Sutton Hall where he placed it on a photocopier and made a paper copy of it. John then scanned the copy and made an electronic copy of the image.

John wondered how Melanie would take the news of his discussion with Blake. He pretty well knew she would believe him and support him as they were both pretty much alike. He'd had some odd adventures before but nothing like working with a group of more than forty dead people to help them move on. Melanie still taught music in the city and had not moved her client base to Brighton. It was much easier for the children and adults she taught to go to the outskirts of the London central business district than make the haul out to the village. John needed some advice, so he reached for the telephone.

"Hi Nigel, it's John Sutton, do you have a minute?"

"Hello, John – yes, I do. How's your new place going? Settled in?"

"Great thanks."

"Do you know whether the boys' choir that was here had some sort of front man or public relations person that helped them with publicity for their events?"

"Don't tell me you're organising a new CD or something for the boys?" Nigel laughed mockingly.

"That would be hard given where they are. I'm just after some old posters and material I can put up in the former church."

"John I don't know off the top of my head but if you give me a few moments I'll ask my dad, he'll know, and I'll ring you back. Are you at Sutton Hall?"

"Yes, thank you, I appreciate your help."

John hardly had time to replace the telephone in its receiver and walk to the kitchen when Nigel returned his call.

"You're in luck. I spoke to my father, and he said the PR type person was Mr. Barry Cooper. He was one of the boy's fathers. I think his kid's name was Blake."

A cold shiver ran down John's neck and back when he heard the connection and he smiled and shook his head.

"Is Mr. Cooper still living here or has he joined the others and moved on?"

"No, he's still here. Apparently, he works from home. I'll give you the address and his phone number if you like?"

John wrote down Cooper's contact details and thanked Nigel for his help. It was too early to tell anyone what he had in mind about the boys just yet. First, he had to do his research, gather his material and then evaluate whether Blake's request could be done. John picked up the phone again.

"Hello, Mr. Cooper?"

"Yes."

"Hi, I'm John Sutton; I've just bought the old St Dominic Savio's church and property and wondered if I could come and see you, please?"

There was a pause on the phone while Cooper evaluated what John was saying.

"I'm not interested in selling, thank you."

"No, no I'm sorry. I didn't introduce myself properly. I'm a sound recording engineer and bought the old church to do my recordings. My wife Melanie is a music teacher who teaches children in the city."

"I thought you wanted to buy my property as well. How can I help you?"

The pair talked for about ten minutes before ringing off. John's afternoon of work had taken a different twist. He wanted to visit Barry Cooper and talk with him before Melanie arrived home and they had dinner.

Barry Cooper lived in the centre of the village of Brighton which was about a ten-minute walk from the old church itself. John enjoyed the walk because he could take in the sights and sounds of the village up close without the distraction of driving. The homes along the way from the old church were quaint but beautiful. There were no brand new two or three-storey monoliths. The village houses seemed untouched by time and John could easily imagine people in 17th or 18th-century clothing walking around as it would not seem out of place. He found the Cooper home and saw a beautiful stained-glass window built into the front door.

"Hi Mr. Cooper, I spoke to you a little while ago. I'm John Sutton," John said as he pushed his hand out to shake Cooper's.

"Hello John, please come in, I'm Barry. Would you like a cup of tea?"

"Yes please, if that's not too much trouble?"

"No trouble at all. Any friend of the boys' choir is always welcome here."

Cooper ushered John into the lounge room and introduced him to his wife Coral. John noticed the mantelpiece and the tops of cupboards and sideboards in the room were all adorned with family photos. The Coopers had three sons and the photos showed a history of them growing up except for one – this must have been Blake. His eyes lingered on the photo of Blake with Father Kirby.

"This was the last photo taken of Blake before his accident," Mrs. Cooper said. "He lived for the choir while my other two boys were more adventurous type people."

"He was a good-looking young man," John said. "Blake looks more like you than Barry but he, along with the whole choir had that, I don't know, angelic look about them, maybe it was the age of them. My wife Melanie and I had dinner with Father Kirby recently and he told us of the joy the boys had for their singing. It must have been a real pleasure watching and listening to them live."

"I think any choir at the age of this photo all seem like angels. Only some sing like them and some don't, ours did. Yes, it was a pure delight to watch and listen to them.

"Our boys had such a passion for their work that when they sang next to other choirs they really stood out."

Barry organised three cups of tea with a platter of biscuits and brought them into the lounge room.

"So what brings you to Brighton, John?" Barry asked.

"Well I'm a sound engineer and I record and re-record various pieces of work for studios across the United Kingdom. I've turned the old church into my sort of recording studio."

"And your wife, Melanie, what does she do?"

"Mel is a music teacher for beginners to diploma level. She teaches piano and singing for all ages just outside of London."

"You're the right people, just at the wrong time," Mrs. Cooper said. "We could have used you a decade ago when the boys were here. You two have some lovely talents I'm sure would have helped the boys."

"Mel and I have bought the old St Dominic Savio's, and I've already started recording various pieces of music and songs in the old church. The acoustics are truly marvellous which is why we bought the property."

"Yes, I think that's one of the reasons we didn't like the boys going to other places to sing as their sounds were captured so much better in the church," Mrs. Cooper said.

"Thank you for seeing me today, I appreciate it," John said as reached for his tea. "I guess I was hoping to gain an insight into the boys whose plaque is hanging in the old church. Also, I was wondering if you had any background material on the choir and the names of those who were members."

"Sure, but why do you want all this?" Barry asked.

"Well, I'm sure when people start hearing music and

singing emanating from the old church again, they will want to have a look at what's going on. I thought if I had some material on your beautiful choir, it would help answer a lot of questions by itself."

The Coopers studied John closely while he was talking and then looked at each other. John noticed a hint of agreeance between the couple with Barry nodding.

"You know I used to arrange the choir's publicity," Barry said with a large smile. "I have a lot of material on the choir so you'll have to define more what you are after. Maybe some posters and background blurbs are what you need."

"Barry that would be fantastic thanks. What about Blake, what can you tell me about him? Father Kirby said he was probably the most devout of the entire choir."

The last question opened a door for the Coopers to extol the virtues of their youngest son to someone new. The couple had not done this in a long while and it was comforting to them. John was a stranger, but he was bringing music back to the old church and Blake would have loved it. The Coopers had a good feeling about him.

"Most days Blake used to hurry home from school, drop his bag and then run to St Dominic Savio's," Coral said. "He used to spend a lot of time there."

"Singing rehearsals?" John asked.

"No, they were only twice a week plus on Saturdays. Blake would spend a lot of time just knelt in prayer or sitting in the church meditating."

"It sounds like he was either stressed out or wanting to become a priest maybe?"

Mrs. Cooper laughed. "Well, we'll never know now. He was never stressed out as he was too young for that and he was a boy full of life and energy. Joining the priesthood? Well, that could possibly have been where he was headed. Father Kirby always said he was like St Dominic Savio himself."

"What do you mean?"

"St Dominic Savio is the patron saint of choirs. He died when he was about fourteen and is one of the youngest saints in the Christian Church. Father Kirby said Blake had similar characteristics to St Dominic by the way he would sit and pray in the church for long periods and was always trying to help the other boys."

"The accident must have been hard for you and all the other families then."

Barry put his hand on his wife's hand. "It was tragic. One minute I was rushing into the church to tell everyone a second bus had been found to take them to the airport after the first one broke down. The boys got on the bus and waved us all goodbye and then minutes later they were in the accident. It was the last time we ever saw them. They were so excited about going to Australia."

John looked at the mantlepiece and saw an Australian aborigine boomerang. Hanging next to it was an American Indian dream catcher. It was a beautiful circle of wood and string web and had three sets of charms hanging from it. The Coopers followed John's eye movement.

"A boomerang was given to every one of the boys' families from the Australians. They said it would help us as the love we sent out to our boys would always be returned. A lovely keepsake to show the love the Aussies had for our boys. The dream catcher is beautiful too. According to the Sioux Indians, it catches all the bad dreams and only allows good ones through. We love them both."

"It must have been very hard for you all," John reiterated.

Mrs. Cooper looked directly at John. "The hardest thing was there was nothing for the families to farewell. All the boys and the whole choir just evaporated in the bus fire. We had nothing to bury and no final resting place to visit the boys."

"I think Father Kirby said there was a memorial concert with the boys' choirs from America and Australia to honour your lads."

"Yes, but it wasn't a concert. It was a memorial service a week after the accident," Barry said. "Members of the All American Boys Choir and the Australian National Boys Choirs came and performed at the service. It was truly remarkable."

"Were your boys close to the American and Australian choirs? After all, it was a long way to come for the other boys to sing at the service?"

Barry looked at the ground and composed himself. John felt the tension.

"Our boys had been working with the other two choirs on and off for a couple of months. The three choirs were preparing to put together a combined concert in tribute to all the service people in our armed forces.

"Were the other two choirs here in the UK working with yours for this concert?" Barry asked.

"No, they were independently doing their rehearsals in their home countries but worked closely via the internet. It was a time when our three countries had a lot of soldiers, air force people and sailors off fighting wars in Iraq, Afghanistan and elsewhere. The trip to Australia was going to be a sort of holiday for the hard work our boys had done."

"Did you record any of the songs the three choirs would have sung at the tribute concert?"

"No, not like you can. I think some parents may have had tape recordings, but this was over ten years ago, and technology has since marched on. Any tapes they had would probably be useless now."

"Not necessarily, as they could be melded with new ways to record accompanying music."

Barry looked at his wife and then back at John. "I'll ask around with the remaining parents and see if anyone has a tape of any of the rehearsals."

"Thanks, Barry, who knows we might be able to complete the work. Anyway, these are just thoughts. I think I've taken up enough of your time and I better get back home before Mel wonders where I am."

John said his goodbyes to the Coopers and walked back to Sutton Hall armed with posters of the boys, a list of all the choir members at the time of the accident, and some background material. He couldn't believe what he heard the Coopers say about a tribute concert to the armed forces. This last piece of information could be what he needed if he was to help Blake.

"I hope you were watching me this afternoon, Blake," John said aloud to himself. "I think I may have found a way to help you move on."

Chapter Five

Melanie came home from work to find John pouring over posters of the boys' choir and publicity blurbs scattered on the lounge room floor.

"Hello my love, where did you find those?"

John looked up at his wife and she knew this would be an interesting evening. She had seen that look before when John had gone on a mission with his work, whether it was to add certain backgrounds or compose arrangements for his clients.

"You're not going to believe the day I have had."

"Well, let me get a cup of tea and you can tell me all about it."

John went back to scouring the paperwork scattered on the floor he got from the Coopers while Melanie made the teas. When she returned, he told her of his morning with his re-recordings before he had a break outside his tea room. John described his conversation with Blake and then pointed the boy out on one of the posters. Now he not only had a name for the spirit he was talking with but a human face to put to it that he could show others. He explained how he had spoken to Nigel White and went for a walk to the Coopers where he got all the paraphernalia on the floor.

"Well, my love, you have been busy. At least now you have

an image of the boy who talks to you and met his parents. It's funny how the one who is most like St Dominic Savio is the organiser for our little group of spirit friends. Alright, you have all this information, now what do you want to do with it?"

"Mel, I think we can do ourselves a favour and concomitantly move the boys on and give some closure to their demise. I sort of believe now if we do the last two things we'll be left in peace and this village will prosper again."

"It sounds like a pretty tall order. What do you propose?"

"Well, a short while after the boys all died choirs from America and Australia came here to sing at a memorial service. The interesting thing is that the two choirs from overseas plus ours were preparing a combined salute to their respective armed forces who were serving in the Middle East and other places. I've asked Barry Cooper if he could shop around with the remaining boy's parents for any tapes of the memorial service or rehearsals. If any turn up that could be a basis for me to start putting together a compilation. Blake said our choir would help with more material like the little present they left us last week."

Melanie looked at John and saw a strong determination in his eyes she had not seen for some time. She knew her husband was now on a mission and she could only support him until he reached his goal or found he could not continue.

"What about work? If you concentrate on doing your compile and associated work for Blake and the boys, how will you do the re-records?"

"I know this work for the choir is not something I asked for – it sort of fell in my lap. I have no idea why you or others can't hear Blake. It would make it easier if you could, as it sounds like I'm on an imaginary mission of sorts."

"Darling both of us are very open to a lot of things. Maybe the universe helped bring us together with the boys by assisting you to find this church in the first place. Think about it. Who else could put together the boy's songs? And you'd be doing it in their former playground of sorts, somewhere they would feel comfortable."

"I think you're right – especially about the universe reaching out for us both. Come on, we'd better get some dinner, you must be starved."

Melanie smiled as she joined John in walking to the kitchen to start preparing a meal. The couple had been married for only a couple of years and both had a love of children. They held off starting their family when they lived in their apartment as it was too small to bring up children. Both wanted a couple of boys and a girl and were keen to start trying in earnest when they settled in their new home. John was still very excited about his project and over dinner kept throwing about ideas he had for how he could use any music or songs from the boys if Blake or the parents came through for him.

"Whatever happens, my sweet," Melanie said deliberately over a glass of red wine during dinner. " ... once this project is over, I think it's time you and I thought about starting our own family."

John refocused and realised he had been excited about events around him but had been neglecting his wife. He got up from the table walked behind Melanie and put his arms around her.

"You're right my love. Sorry, I've been neglectful. We really should start tonight, you know."

John started kissing his wife slowly around her neck and up the side of her face. His hands moved slowly and rhythmically up and down the side of her chest. Melanie's breathing changed as she was massaged. The amorous advance meant the washing up would be done in the morning. John lifted his wife from her seat, embraced her and began kissing her on her lips and down her neck. Their eyes met and Melanie saw and felt a passion in her husband she had not experienced for some time.

"I'll bet this has been a first for the Rectory," Melanie laughed.

"Well you'd hope so," John said as he too laughed. "However for those living at Sutton Hall, welcome to normal couple relations."

"So I'm just a relation, am I?" Melanie asked as she rolled over on top of John.

"No my love, you are the love of my life."

"Don't you forget it!"

John had his cue from Melanie and started caressing and kissing his wife again. Melanie was the first to get up and sat quietly with a cup of tea in the kitchen. It wasn't long before she was joined by John. He had nothing on and went straight over to his wife and put his arms around her, kissing her gently on the side of the face and then mouth.

"So what's on the agenda today my lover?" Melanie asked.

"I have to finish the re-records and compilation from yesterday and then I'll start nutting out a plan for our choir to see if we can actually help them."

"Good, but remember work for us must come first. The boys have been stuck here for a decade so a few more months or so won't hurt them."

John agreed and Melanie finished her tea; showered and dressed for work. This was going to be a full day and John wanted to make the most of it. After his beautiful lovemaking with Melanie, he had lain awake thinking of his conversation with Blake and then the boy's parents. He hadn't asked Nigel White for Blake's parents' contact details and yet somehow the connection had been made. John smiled as he thought it funny he had been contacted by Blake who was acting as the PR-type spirit for the boys and his father was the front man for the choir when they were alive. It was nice to keep the profession in the family. He made some toast and another cup of tea while ideas of working with the boys' choir flooded his mind. Melanie walked back into the kitchen and kissed John goodbye. She had to catch a bus to London for an early appointment with a diploma student. Her smile gave way to a giggle as she took in the sight of her husband sitting naked at the breakfast bar eating toast. The image would be with her all day.

John reached for the telephone and was about to contact his mother when he realised he was still naked. Some things are better done with clothes on, he thought. John smiled as he replaced the handset and had a shower and dressed – now he was ready for work. Phone calls to John's parents had to be made once you had a cup of tea in your hand as the calls were never short. John chatted to his father and mother for around thirty minutes and updated them on life at Sutton Hall and invited them over in a few weeks once he and Melanie had settled in better. He asked his mother whether she remembered him talking to imaginary friends or spirits when he was younger. The reply was quick. Yes, he had had several 'imaginary friends' when he was a little boy and then grew out of them. No, he had never spoken to her of ever seeing the spirits of dead people. John tried to allay his mother's concerns by saying he sometimes heard weird sounds in the old church when he did his re-records.

"Surely you don't think there are spirits in the old building trying to contact you?" John's mother asked.

"No, of course not," he lied. "Sometimes when the wind picks up outside during a recording it sounds like voices talking and I have to muffle the sounds. It's all probably to do with the acoustics of the building."

The pair rang off with John promising to get back to his mother soon with a date for lunch so his parents could have a good look around the property. John then went into the lounge room and picked up his briefcase plus the papers and posters Barry Cooper had given him before making his way to his 'office' in the old church. Opening the side door he made his way into the building and put the papers and briefcase to one side before going to his recording console and noticing it was still turned on.

This is strange, John said to himself as he cued the second last song for replay. He always made a point of turning off all electrical input into his equipment when he finished work for the day. It was a habit he had been taught long ago. He played the song back through his large speakers and nodded with the rhythm and then realised he must have miscalculated. The last song he played was supposed to be the final song of the album he had been working on for his main office yesterday. The end song on his compile then started to play and he sat riveted to his console. The voices of two pre-teenage boys rang out most beautifully as they sang *Panis Angelicus* with piano accompaniment. The song brought tears to John's eyes as he shook his head in wonderment. Melanie had sung the song as a test runs for acoustics in the old church when the couple investigated the building with Nigel White. It was also on the original CD Melanie had bought John. Now, somehow he had a second, more clear recording of two boys singing the song which is usually sung in large cathedrals to gain the advantage of the acoustics and harmonics of the larger spaces and building constructs. John replayed the song and turned up the volume as loud as he could without distortion. He walked around the inside perimeter of the old church as the boys' perfect pitch could be heard everywhere. The song was better than the one on the 12-song CD Melanie had given him.

"Thank you, Blake," John said aloud as he composed himself. "This is absolutely marvellous."

John went back through his recordings and found *The Lion Sleeps Tonight* the boys had left for him before. He added the new song and then recorded it on CD before deleting it from his rock group's album. This called for a cup of tea. John went to his special tea room, made a pot of tea and brought it outside to his main working space. He then played the two songs at almost full volume while he sipped his drink. The music seemed to mesmerise John as he took in the beautiful singing.

It's not every day you hear songs sung by real angels and have the proof, he thought to himself.

He was lucky. Work was light at the moment from his main office. Until he was contacted by his boss he had some spare time. John went to his computer desk and interrogated a search engine for details of the American All Boys Choir and the Australian National Boys Choir. He sent both organisations a long email each describing how he and Melanie had moved into the former St Dominic Savio's and how boys from both choirs had sung at a memorial service for 'his' choir. John was keen to touch base with any former members of the choirs who could help him with some research on the service and also the work the three choirs were doing as a salute to their respective armed forces before the St Dominic Savio choir was wiped out.

John's requests had hit the right chords with the right people. Within a short time replies from both choirs arrived detailing what information they had about the memorial service and some contact details of former choir members. John was in luck. A number of the former members of both the American and Australian choirs were in the Army. The exact detail of what each former member did in their respective service was not known. John wrote to them anyway as emails and letters. He walked to the Post Office and posted the letters. Village life agreed with John as everything seemed within walking distance, unlike the suburbs where most amenities were accessed by transport and were so impersonal.

A car slowly came into view and parked outside the old church as John walked up the winding path. Standing next to the vehicle was Cooper.

"Blake, I think you are going into overdrive," John thought to himself. "First you leave me some songs, and then I obtain contact details for former members of choirs who sang here – now your father is anxiously waiting to talk to me. I get the message and I'm working as fast as I can for you."

"Hi Barry, a great day for a drive," John said as he approached Cooper.

"Hello John, it certainly is. I have some good news for you." Cooper broke out in a smile and studied John's face.

"I've tracked down a copy of a recording of one of the rehearsals the boys did for the armed forces concert! It's not well recorded but at least it will give you an indication of what they were singing. I haven't heard it yet so I'm only going on what I've been told."

John shook his head in disbelief and smiled broadly.

"Well done. This calls for a cup of tea. Come on in."

The pair went into the old church with Cooper stopping just inside the side door. He looked directly at the plaque of Blake's choir John had reaffixed to the wall and then the sound recording equipment now occupying space where pews once stood. John stood motionless as he watched Cooper take in the surroundings.

"It's slightly changed since you were here last, I imagine," John said to break the silence.

"Yes, it has, but progress is important for us all."

"Come on into my tearoom and we'll get a cuppa before I start explaining what everything is for."

Both men went into the former vestry where John made tea for them both.

"Many times I used to come in here and help Blake and the other boys get dressed into their gowns either before Mass or their various concerts," Cooper said as he drank his tea. "I never quite imagined this area as a tearoom but I'm glad it is."

John took Cooper back into the main room and over to his recording panel. Cooper gave John a tape cassette and watched while his host turned on a series of dials and switches before pushing the tape into a slot.

"Barry, take a seat near the tearoom and I'll bring this old church back to life for you."

Cooper made his way over to the entrance to John's tearoom and sat down. John watched closely as Cooper relaxed into the soft chair. He put a pair of headphones on and started playing the tape all the while adjusting a series of dials and switches.

"This sounds good," John eventually said. "I just cued the tape and adjusted some of the sounds to try and bring them out more for us. Here we go."

John pressed a button and the old church again came to life as the sounds of a small orchestra started to fill the air and the tape began to roll. He adjusted another sliding switch and took out some of the bass tones. When the boys started singing John turned up the volume. He then left the console and went to the rear of the building under the choir loft before slowly walking down to where Cooper was sitting.

"This is beautiful. Who was the orchestra?"

"I'm not sure as we used to use several community groups to help out."

John listened intently to the songs and watched Cooper's face. Blake's father was sitting quietly enjoying the singing when he seemed to shiver for a moment and then looked around. Cooper smiled and resumed his position in the chair before taking another sip of his tea. John nodded quietly as he realised Blake may have been trying to communicate with his father. The tape lasted around fifteen minutes and had four songs on it.

"Well it's been a long while since I heard that rehearsal," Cooper said. "Your recording equipment and speakers really make the sounds quite pleasant to hear."

"Yes, this is what I do for a living. I help clean up the sounds of recordings before the final disc is pressed into CDs by music companies. I'm like the final checker or gatekeeper. I noticed you got a bit cold during the performance, are you okay?"

"I'm fine thanks. I sort of got a tingle up my spine when the boys were singing. It was almost like old times when the boys were here. They were pretty good in their day and they sound just as great now."

"Do you mind if I borrow the tape for a few days? I'll see if I can clean it up any further, so you have a better copy."

"That would be great, John. Coral will be so pleased to hear it."

John got them both another cup of tea and re-joined Cooper.

"Do you mind me asking, when the boys' memorial service was over, did the LPG Company whose truck ran the red light in the first place, ever put up money for a memorial?"

"No, you're okay. Please ask any question you like. The LPG Company ceased to exist not long after the accident. The local council didn't want to help with any funding saying they were cash strapped. In the end, the parents agreed on the plaque you have near the side entrance here and a similar one at the accident scene."

"You know I was told I could remove the plaque if I bought the property."

Cooper's eyes widened and he was about to say something when John continued.

"I told the real estate agent it should be a condition of the sale of this property the plaque must remain here."

"Thank you, John, I know the other parents would agree with me when I say that. The boys meant a lot to us all and had such a bright future ahead for each of them. To have it all taken away in a matter of heartbeats was just unbelievable."

"I just want to let you know I've written away to a couple of former members of the American All Boys Choir and the Australian National Boys Choir to see if they have any material they can help me with."

Cooper stood up and grabbed his empty teacup. "You know they'd be in their mid-twenties now."

"Yes, but they may have some recordings their folks did."

"Good luck with your project. Please don't forget my tape."

"No, I won't. Just one last thing; who was the duo that sang *Panis Angelicus* from our choir?"

"That was Blake and his best mate Richard Worth – the musical director's son, why?"

"Oh, nothing, I was just trying to put names to faces to voices, so I know who was who."

"Okay, good luck."

John walked Cooper to his car and waved him off before returning to the old church.

"Alright boys you really have some work to do if we are to get a concert off the ground," John said to the empty old church. "This recording Mr. Cooper brought over is good, but I know you can do better."

John sat at his controls and played the tape again noting each song. He then started a search in his electronic music file on his computer for orchestral pieces for the songs. It didn't take long as military Remembrance Day concerts abounded. He found the pieces he wanted and saved them to a special concert file. John then set to work to record the tape Cooper had given him and to try and scrub the music from the background, so he was left with just the boys' voices. Easier said than done, he thought. An hour later a huge cry echoed in the old church.

"Yaaay! Okay Blake we're on the right track now. What do you think of this?"

John had married the boys' songs with the new orchestral pieces and played them back. To the untrained ear, the songs and accompaniment were quite reasonable. The music was crisp and clear and the boys' voices were nice to hear.

"Blake, if you can hear these songs you'll find this recording is okay but your voices are too far away from the microphones to give a good recording sound," John said to the empty old church. "The music sounds great but it's hard for me to get your voices any better when they're mixed."

John made a CD with the new songs and closed up his office. Melanie would be home soon and it was time he started thinking about cooking a nice meal for his wife.

Chapter Six

John was quietly excited. He had started to collect a series of songs from the boys. If he had another six, he could make a CD for the families. What if he was able to make a CD and sell it on the open market? What would he do with the money? There was no thought of keeping anything for himself. He pondered the question while he prepared dinner. Melanie arrived home with some books under her arm.

"Hi love, what are those?" John asked as he kissed his wife.

"It's exam time again and I have to mark the work of my up-and-coming students as I prepare them."

"Are these public exams?"

"Yes, I prepare the students and then they book and take a public exam to move them up the rankings. It's good because it also gives credence to my teachings and confirms my standing as a teacher and their work to move them up the rankings. Did you have a good day?"

"Yes, not bad at all. Let's have a glass of wine while dinner simmers and I'll tell you all about it."

"Why do I have this feeling I'm about to hear something new about our boys? Mmm"

The look on John's face said it all as he poured Melanie and him a glass of wine. He started detailing his day when the telephone rang. John picked up the handset and then heard the international beeping sounds.

"Hello, John Sutton?" a broad accented voice asked.

"Yes, who is calling?"

"Hi John, I'm Robert King, the musical director of the Australian National Boys Choir. I got your message this afternoon and I know you've been given Phillip Boyce's contacts, but is there anything else you need?"

"Hello, Robert. Thanks for your call. I've written to Phillip and one of his American counterparts asking if they had any material on their work with the St Dominic Savio's Boys and Youth choir."

"I started work with my choir after yours met its demise, but I can tell you they were well thought of here in Australia."

"Thank you. I understand your boys came here to be part of a memorial service ..."

"Yes, the government had been good backers of my choir and was quite keen to foster bilateral relations with the United Kingdom. We were billeted out with families of a local school to help defray costs."

"Did you keep any recordings of the Memorial Service perchance?"

"After I read your email, I went searching in our archives and haven't found anything yet but I'll keep looking. Are you thinking of having some sort of anniversary service for your boys?"

"No. I think it's time for a concert as this will help the boys in several ways. You saw from my email my wife and I bought the old church the boys sang in after it was decommissioned.

I'm a sound engineer and my wife Melanie is a music teacher. A number of the families of the boys' choir have started to move out of the village and district here and this whole area is quite depressed. I've been able to find two beautiful songs the boys recorded, and these would be great for a new release. Four others arrived today but will need more electronic scrubbing to enhance them."

King and John talked for some time about possible opportunities before ringing off. The tom-toms were working overtime or maybe it was Blake and the choir, John was sure it was one of them.

"Sorry darling, the call was too good an opportunity to miss," John said to Melanie as he joined her for dinner.

"That's okay, my love. I had to grab dinner, or it would have been cooked to death. So that call was from Australia, I take it?"

"Yes, I started to tell you about how I emailed both the American and Australian boys choirs that sang at the Memorial Service here for our boys. Well, that was Robert King the musical director of the Aussies. He thinks his choir is coming here to the UK in November as part of our Remembrance Day service. If we held any concert for our boys in November, he may be able to swing it so his boys can come along."

Melanie saw in John's eyes that a fire had been lit with his project of checking out the feasibility of some sort of memorial concert for 'their boys' choir'.

"What about the Americans? Any word from them yet?"

"No, but the way things have been moving I don't think it will be long."

John started detailing to Melanie how his day unfolded when he stopped and stood up.

"I nearly forgot I have some new material for you to listen to. See what you think of this."

He went to the lounge room and played the CD with the songs by his boys' choir. The military salute the boys had performed consisted of a series of songs with one from each of the armed services. Also, included were *Bless Them All* and *Pack Up Your Tro*ubles.

"Where did you get these from, they sound terrific?"

"Well, after I went to the Post Office, Barry Cooper dropped them around on a tape. I scrubbed them up and added some fresh orchestral background to see what could come of them."

"These are great. This now makes six songs from the boys. How many do you need for a concert and when you hold it what will you do with the profits?"

John looked at his wife and gave a half-smile and nodded. The pair was well aligned in their thinking.

"I had the same thought this afternoon and I think it would be great to have some sort of headstone or memorial sculpture here on the grounds, but on top of the hill outside the old church. It would give relief to the boy's parents and allow them something tangible to visit away from the accident scene or inside my workspace."

"Well, now that pushes the boundaries. I see where our boys are taking us now. They're not after recognition of their work or anything as vain. They're after two things – somewhere their parents can be comforted about their loss, and for them to move on. You wouldn't read about this sort of stuff, would you?"

"No, you're right. I think all the pieces are starting to fall into place. I checked with Barry Cooper as to whether the LPG Company or the local Council had been approached about any memorial for the boys. Apparently, the gas bottle company no longer exists and the Council got out of helping the parents ten years ago by saying it had no funds."

"So you want to raise the funds through a concert for the boys?"

"Yes, I think we could do it, especially seeing the boys themselves are helping."

"You should contact Father Kirby again as priests usually have contacts with stonemasons and he could probably help you."

"Good idea."

It was John's turn to be up early as he watched the sunrise from the kitchen window. The old church and Sutton Hall had good views of the surrounding countryside. One of the side benefits of buying the property for the Suttons was that no houses were directly next door to their living quarters. There was plenty of space around Sutton Hall to enjoy. A shrill whistle disturbed the peace and John turned off the stove, picked up the steaming kettle and poured its water into the teapot. John looked out the window again. The first vestiges of light were reaching over the horizon turning the scene from an eerie dark blue top and black bottom to a lighter blue with a slow-growing wafer of red reaching to the black ground. John made his tea and continued to watch the sunrise. It was beautiful. Slowly the sky started turning a grey as the red wafer centralised and shafts of yellow punched through from the black earth. The first cup of tea was beautiful as it awakened John's mind and body. He savoured the moment as the red wafer fully in the sky disappeared and was replaced by a golden yellow arch of light on the horizon. It would be a hot day today. The grey sky slowly gave way to blue and the first fingers of daylight began to melt away the night as the shapes of houses and buildings became slowly discernible.

"Brendan must have truly loved this place," John thought to himself. "Where else would you see such a beautiful light show and all for free."

Melanie padded her way to the kitchen in her dressing gown and stood watching the sunrise for a few quiet moments. She too was struck by nature's light show.

"I hope the pot is still hot," Melanie eventually said as she went over to her husband and pinched him on his bottom. The pair kissed and Melanie made her own tea.

"I just saw a beautiful light show as the sun came up. It was pretty nice as the colours all changed across the landscape. It was like watching a slow-moving movie without the music. I can see why Brendan really liked this place."

"Well, he probably didn't see too many sunrises. I'm guessing his work in the parish would have kept him busy during the day and all odd hours at night leaving him little time to watch sunrises."

"Yeah, you're probably right. Sleep well?"

"Like a log and you?"

"Excellently, it all has to do with your beautiful rhythm."

"What do you mean?"

"Well, when you fall asleep you have a lovely cadence with

your breathing, and I find it easy to sleep. It's when I'm away I miss that, and I find I can't sleep too well."

"It's the same for me. I never sleep well when you're away either. I guess it must be the same thing. Anyway, what's on today for you?"

John sat at the breakfast bar and joined Melanie. He told her about how he would try and see Father Kirby and get some ideas about stone monuments for the boys.

"That is of course if I don't have any new work from head office."

"It goes without saying, doesn't it?"

"Yes, I think so. What about you, what's on your agenda today?"

"I have two more students to do dummy tests for and another three to work with on their recital pieces."

"Well, that should keep you busy."

"I'll say. My work is quite full-on at present, so I'm looking forward to a break at Christmas."

"So am I, as this project with the boys should be well and truly finished by then."

Melanie finished her tea and left the kitchen to shower and dress for work. John went to the lounge room and played the songs from the boys to get him in the mood for the day. The songs were uplifting and left him with a sense of achievement and purpose. Melanie was out of the shower, so he went for his. The pair worked in tandem depending on each other's needs. She had to get to work first and needed the shower first. If he was travelling or had to go to work first, then Melanie would adjust her timings for getting ready for work.

"Okay love, see you tonight," Mel said to John as she kissed him goodbye. She would have breakfast at work.

"Bye."

John got dressed and walked to work. This was probably one of the most exciting things he looked forward to daily, walking from Sutton Hall to the old church. He no sooner entered the building when he felt a chill come over him and heard a voice he knew was Blake's

"John, you've been busy for us, thank you."

"You're welcome, Blake. I have seven songs you recorded but I will need more somehow to make the concert happen," John replied without even flinching.

"Have to trust us, John, we'll come through for you."

"Do you mean you'll leave me some more presents on my recorders?"

"Please trust in us as we are with you."

"Alright, I will. I'll be talking to Father Kirby today to see if I can get something of a memorial organised for you all."

"Yes, he is the one to see. You are on track John. More help will come to you."

"Blake, when your father was here the other day with me playing the tape of the memorial rehearsal of your choir, did you come by?"

"Yes I was here and he felt my presence, but he can't see or hear me like you. This is why the concert must take place, so they can all hear us."

"You know I have contacted both the American and Australian choirs you worked with to seek help?"

"Yes, and you will get it soon."

John went to ask another question but stopped as he felt the chill leave him and a warmth return denoting the teenager had left him. His audience with Blake was at an end. The teenager's conversation was very uplifting to John. He went to his control desk, picked up the telephone and held it mid-air as he thought about what was happening. A special group of dead boys had enough trust in him to communicate with him from another realm. John had become an earthly channel for forty-five people and he wanted to carry out their last wish to the best of his ability. He replaced the handset, picked it up again and dialled Brendan Kirby.

"Hi, Brendan, it's John Sutton, how are you?"

"Hello John, good thanks. How's your project coming along?"

"Pretty good thanks. I now have seven songs the boys recorded."

"Seven ..." The phone went dead for a few moments while the priest took in what John said.

"Fantastic, where did you get the other five or shouldn't I ask?"

"Barry Cooper found a tape of a rehearsal the boys did as a salute to the military for a Remembrance Day concert."

"Excellent as those songs weren't on their first album either. How can I help you?"

John asked Kirby about the stonemasons and what sort of memorial would be fitting for the boys if the parents agreed. He then outlined his plan to hold an anniversary concert for the boys to raise funds for the cost of the memorial. Kirby gave John the contacts for a couple of stonemasons.

"You realise, Brendan, if this all comes together you will have to officiate at the unveiling of the memorial," John said.

"That would be a huge honour, but you have a bit of a way to go before we start thinking of any unveiling."

"What time was the bus accident, do you remember?"

"I'm pretty sure it was around 3 pm as they were rushing to get aboard the 4 pm plane. Why do you ask?" Brendan said.

"Just fitting the pieces together in my mind, thanks. I'll get onto the stonemasons and see where this takes me."

"John, I understand what you are doing and if nothing comes off from your efforts then you would've earned some good brownie points for another time regardless."

"I have it on good authority the boys will come through for me and help make this all happen."

"You do? If you need to talk to anyone about this let me know."

"Thanks; but I'm fine for the moment."

"Well good luck."

John rang the first stonemason and he wasn't interested in helping as he was too busy and understaffed. The second stonemason Peter Brown took a different tack. He was keen to help but didn't have anything suitable for a special memorial to suit the choir. It would have to be sourced from overseas. John said he would get back to him and rang off. He got up and walked to the tearoom and made a cup of tea. Sometimes just a short walk helped John think more clearly. He picked up the phone and rang Barry Cooper to arrange to drop off the CD of the tape he made for him. Before he could make any further calls, the phone rang.

"Hello, is this John Sutton?" a voice with an American drawl asked.

"Yes, speaking."

"Mr. Sutton my name is Andrew Jackson and I used to sing in the All American Boys Choir a decade ago."

"Oh, fantastic! Did the choir contact you about me?"

"Well yes and no. They sent me an e-mail saying you were looking for some help regarding the St Dominic Savio's Boys and Youth Choir. Also, I got your message via the US Army email system."

"Andrew, I'm so glad you responded, thank you. You'll find I followed up with a letter too."

John explained to Jackson he wanted to put together an anniversary concert with a salute to the armed forces of America, Britain and Australia thrown in. All proceeds go towards a special memorial for the choir.

"Well, it's amazing how God works. Not only am I a former member of the American choir that sang with your boys, but I am also a Captain in the US Army Band as a musician and singer," Jackson said.

John was gob-smacked. "Do you have any recordings of when you worked with my choir?"

"No, they would all be gone by now. When are you looking at holding the concert?"

"Well I thought it had to be on a significant day, so I was thinking of Remembrance Day here ..."

Jackson chuckled.

"You're not going to believe this. My band from Fort Worth and I will be in London to celebrate the day at several British services on that morning. Maybe we can work with you. I'll check it out."

"Do you know or remember a Phillip Boyce from Australia?"

"Yeah," Jackson laughed. "The good Captain Boyce and I have kept in touch over the years, and we swap music and recordings."

"Great, as I have put the feelers out to contact him too."

"If you can snare him, it will be a miracle. He is pretty popular and in good demand on the Aussie military circuit."

The pair rang off with John promising to send Jackson copies of the various songs he had managed to record so far. John needed a second cup of tea. Blake and the boys were pulling things together. If he could stage a concert there was a strong possibility the US Army Band could play. What a draw card! John turned on his computer and checked his emails. Sitting second from the top was one marked 'security unrestricted'. He opened this one first and sat back in his chair shaking his head with delight before leaning forward again to read the message.

Dear Mr. Sutton,

Robert King from the Australian National Boys Choir has been in touch with me and I also received your email yesterday.

I sang soprano with the boys choir here as a teenager, and after school finished I joined the Australian Army as a musician. Now I am a Captain with the Australian Army Band in Sydney and travel all over the place.

I went to the UK after your boys died and I stayed with a family from one of your local schools for a week.

Together with the American All Boys Choir and my choir I sang at the memorial service. I don't have any recordings from the service or the singing the Australian National Boys Choir did with yours. However, if there is anything I can do to assist please contact me directly on the numbers below.

It was an honour to sing with and for your boys. Don't hesitate to contact me.

Your friend,

Phillip Boyce

CAPT – Australian Army Band

John was taken aback. He noted the time and calculated when it would be best to contact Boyce. There was a time difference, so he left the call until dinner time. He finished his tea, rang Barry Cooper and arranged to drop the CD off in the next half an hour. John locked up his 'office' and walked to the village.

"Hello John, come on in," Cooper said as he opened his front door.

"Hi Barry, thanks for seeing me. I think we have a few things to talk about with regards to the choir."

The pair went into Cooper's lounge room and sat down. John gave Cooper a CD plus his tape recording of the boys' five military rehearsal songs.

"John, do you mind if we have a listen to your CD, please? I'd really like to hear the difference with the tape."

"No, please put it on."

Cooper played the CD and was astounded as he heard

John's enhanced version. His eyes moistened as he listened to his boys' voices backed by stronger orchestration.

"You've done a lot with this. It sounds great, thank you."

"Barry, I'd like to hold a sort of farewell concert for the boys at the end of the year."

"A farewell concert? The boys have already had a memorial service. What is there to gain by having this concert?"

"I'd like to hold the concert to raise funds for a memorial to honour the boys. It could be built in the old church grounds."

"You own the grounds now."

"Yes, but not the graveyard. If a memorial was built in the graveyard area out the front of the old church, it wouldn't matter who owned the place as it couldn't be removed."

"I was wondering where you were heading with your work with the boys. Where would you get enough material to stage a concert? The boys can't record anything anymore."

John looked directly at Cooper and smiled.

"If I had around 12 songs – this would be enough for a CD release and also a concert. I've spoken to the Australian National Boys Choir musical director Robert King and he may be able to assist me."

"How could he help you?"

"Well, it seems his choir may be in London in November for Remembrance Day service. If his tour comes off they may be available to perform here."

"Having the choir here would be fantastic but you have a lot of *ifs* there."

"Well, there are a couple of more pieces in the pipeline. Firstly, Andrew Jackson used to be a singer in the American

All Boys Choir and is now in the US Army Band as a Captain and singer. I've spoken with Andrew, and he says he may also be in London in November for the Remembrance Day service too. If he is, he could be at our concert in the afternoon."

"I'm impressed, but you've added more *ifs*."

"Yes, and there is more. I've been in email contact with Phillip Boyce who used to be a singer with the Australian National Boys Choir. Like Andrew, he's also a Captain but in the Australian Army Band. He's keen to assist and I'll be phoning him tonight."

It was Cooper's turn to study John as the newcomer to the village excitedly told of his contacts. A small nod took place and John knew he had Cooper hooked.

"This will mean a meeting of the parents – wait – what am I saying? At another time we would have held a parents' meeting to discuss the concert and memorial in detail. I guess with a number of them leaving the district and the boys no longer here this would be implausible."

"I'm probably not ready yet for a meeting with the boys' parents. I still need more information about what would be available for a concert. However, I want to solve the problem of the memorial itself. Do you know anyone that could help with some sort of design?"

"Yes, I think I do. In the last couple of years, a female artist has moved into an old property not far from here."

"Do you know her name or contact details please?"

"Yes, I wrote them down somewhere as one of my clients wanted some stonework done for a commercial building. I'll just check my office."

"It's nice to work from home, isn't it?"

"Oh yes, I'm semi-retired now and I use what was Blake's bedroom as an office. It's fine."

While Cooper went to his 'office' John walked around the lounge room and viewed the photos on the various shelves and cabinet tops. He saw the Coopers at play in all sorts of various poses. He focused on one with Blake dressed in an alb and cincture holding a songbook in the church.

"That's one of my favourite photos of Blake. He was just about to sing solo for the bishop," Cooper said as re-entered the room.

"He looks to have been a very determined young man."

"Yes, especially in all things church-related. I found the artist's name and details. Who knows she may be of some help?"

"Barry, if you see any of the other parents I'd appreciate some feedback about what I'm trying to achieve and see if I have their blessings."

"I don't think you would have any problem with that; however I'll bring it up with any parents I come in contact with. If – there's that word again – it all comes off, our boys will have a good send-off and we parents a place to visit and remember them collectively."

"While I'm at Sutton Hall, there will always be a welcome cup of tea for any parent of the boys, please tell them."

"I will."

John walked back to his office and checked for work from his head office. There was none, so he interrogated a search engine on his computer to find the artist. Her name was

Caroline Bailey and she was a painter and sculptor. She had won a series of awards for her work in stone and was keen to start an artists' collective on her property. John rang the artist and was surprised to have her answer the phone on the second ring. He introduced himself and explained what he was trying to achieve.

"Mr. Sutton I may be able to help you. I'm glad you didn't leave it any longer as sculptures take a while to design and complete."

"Fantastic, when would you like me to drop by and talk in detail about the project?"

"Well, I'm free this afternoon or first thing in the morning."

"How about 2 pm this afternoon?"

"Alright, see you then."

John realised what Bailey was saying was right. If he left his run any later trying to organise something of a sculpture for the boys for Remembrance Day, it could be too late. He needed to stretch his legs, so he walked out of his office to the graveyard at the front of the old church and took in the fresh air. The graves dated from the mid-1800s with the writing on the headstones almost hard to discern because of the wear caused by the weather. The youngest was a man who died in 1830 in a cart accident. John walked back into Sutton Hall and retrieved his camera. He took a series of photos of the gravesite and church. Next, he photographed some of the promotional posters in his office Cooper had given him. John laughed when he saw the image of Blake on one of the posters – it was the same as the one he had seen in his father's house earlier that day of the youth dressed in an alb carrying a songbook. He transferred the images onto an electronic memory stick so he could take them with him to the artist's place and then went to Sutton Hall for lunch.

John reflected on what he was doing. He had the impression both Cooper and Kirby thought him daft for attempting his "project". Yet they would be among the beneficiaries if his work succeeded. Dealing with the spirits of people that had not crossed over didn't really faze him either. This was an interesting challenge, and he was keen to step up to the plate. It was time to go to the artist's home.

The drive to Bailey's place was enjoyable for John as he took in the beautiful countryside and revelled in the lush colours of the meadows and dales he passed. It was easy to find the artist's place – it had a large modern-day sculpture at the road entrance that acted as a mailbox. John inched his way up the tight driveway to the main entrance to the house. It was set back from the road and had a large glasshouse attached to the side. No sooner had John alighted from his car when a voice called to him from the glass house.

"Hello, Mr. Sutton?"

John studied the woman before him. She had long black hair tied back in a bun, large brown eyes and was wearing a thick apron.

"Hi Miss Bailey thank you for seeing me so quickly, I appreciate your time."

"Please call me Caroline and come on into my studio."

"Thanks, Caroline, I'm John. I've brought some images on a memory stick you may want to see as we discuss the project and whether you can help."

"Good, this will make it easier."

Bailey showed John into her studio. Gone were the long tables that would have held plants and the various watering systems in the days when the building was used to grow a myriad of plants. In front of John was a very modern workspace with several completed and half-completed sculptures; a series of paintings hung on the wall and an easel with a table full of paints sat in a corner with a half-finished painting of a man in red robes with a mayoral chain around his neck. Bailey watched John as he cast his eyes around the studio.

"Welcome to my workspace. You can see I have a series of works on the go at any one time."

"It's fantastic. I haven't been in an artist's studio before, so I feel privileged. Who's the man on the easel?"

"Oh him, that's Graham Butler the Mayor of Brighton."

"Ah, the local Mayor, now there's someone I'm yet to meet. I'm glad I came here so I could see his likeness. I've got the memory stick if you want to have a look at some images while I talk you through what is needed. By the way, would you like to listen to some of the songs from the boys while we view the images?"

"Sure, why not? It will give me a couple of ways of connecting with the boys while we talk."

Bailey connected John's memory stick to her computer and started playing the songs. She then brought up the images John had captured and looked at them in detail.

"What beautiful voices! It would have been a very sad loss to the area when so many angelic voices left this world."

"Apparently so; my wife Melanie and I have only moved

into the district recently, so we never knew the boys or had even heard of them."

John looked at Bailey as she seemed to gaze above the computer while listening to the singing. She hardly blinked. When she refocused and looked at John her eyes had narrowed and a look of heavy determination was set on her face.

"Do you speak with the boys?"

Now it was John's turn to be amazed as he tried to work out what the artist was trying to say.

"What do you mean? They've been dead for a decade?"

"John, I have this overpowering feeling the boys are still here. Do you talk with them?"

"Caroline you must be psychic or something." John thought about what he was about to say and then watched the artist closely. "When Mel and I first went to the former church and were being shown around the place I believed I heard one of the boys talking to me."

Bailey went through the images of the boys slowly and stopped at the photo of Blake and the bishop. She lingered on the photo and then started tapping it.

"Was it this boy?"

John's eyes widened in disbelief as Bailey poured over the image.

"One of the things I have learnt to develop over time is my power of reading people and art. It sort of gives me an insight into people so when I capture them in paint or stone I have the right feeling they want to convey. Along the way, I've become very intuitive spiritually. I have a feeling the boys have been reaching out to you."

"Yes, they have."

John then detailed how he had first heard Blake and then the boys singing. He told Bailey of the two songs left by the boys for him and then the find by one of the parents of the five songs of the rehearsal.

"I'm impressed. If I come across something like this most people don't want to talk about it in case others think they are barmy or even in cahoots with the devil."

"I wouldn't have said anything to you about them ordinarily, but you showed an insight I guess I was looking for in someone else."

"John, this boy with the bishop; is he the one who talks to you?"

John felt he was being read by a clairvoyant – he was astounded. "Yes, that's Blake. You'll hear him sing a duet with the musical director's son with *Panis Angelicus*."

"He's a handsome young man. Well enough of him, what do you want to actually do for the boys?"

"I want to do three things. First, hold a concert in their honour on Remembrance Day so their parents can hear them sing one last time. Secondly, I want to have a memorial the parents can visit when they like and thirdly, I want to help the boys cross over."

"I think we can achieve all three. Have you told anyone else you talk with the boys?"

"Only the former parish priest – but we promised not to tell anyone else."

"That makes sense as anyone else you spoke to would think you're hearing voices in your head or maybe possessed after moving into the old church grounds. Okay, let's work through this and see what we can both come up with."

Bailey and John went through the images on the computer and discussed what sort of things really portrayed the boys. The artist then printed an image of the graveyard and the front of the church. She took her sketch pen and drew a sketch of a boy singing dressed in an alb and holding a hymn book in his hands. Bailey painted the sketch and then held it up.

"Is this the sort of thing you were thinking of as a memorial?"

"Yes, I guess so. This would be a traditional way of looking at the boys. I know you can't do an image of the lot of them so a symbolic one would be great."

"I think you're right. It would also only capture one age of the boys. Let's try that again."

Bailey then printed out another copy of the graveyard and church and set to work. Within a couple of minutes, she gave the finished sketch work to John and then watched his face light up.

"Fantastic; this would be so much more in keeping with modern times and allow the parents to connect with their boys. I think you have nailed it on the head," John said as he studied the sketch.

Bailey had drawn a large, curved park bench with its back to the old church and overlooking the district below and the nearby graveyard. At either side of the bench seat was a sculpture. On one side was a young boy and on the other a taller, older youth. Both were in poses of singing.

"The parents could come and sit down on the bench, enjoy the view and feel one with their boys – this is brilliant. The problem would be money and maybe the cost of the work. What do you think something like this would cost?"

"Normally I would say a lot. However, as I can see you are driven out of respect for the boys and not for profit, I may have a way of having someone else pay for it."

"What do you mean?"

"Well, you saw the painting of the mayor over in the corner of the studio. Butler is also a member of the local tourist association and is looking at possibly setting up a museum, I think."

"A museum? What's so important around here that I'm missing? You know the Council rejected any funding requests a decade ago so why would they help out now?"

"Ten years is a long time, John. You might find the Council has more money now and if the local tourist association backs the plan the work could be made as a grant. Museum-wise, I don't know. It's some sort of secret project Butler is working on."

"Secret project, eh? Well, no doubt it will run its course. Would you have enough time between now and November to make the sculpture? Regardless of who pays for it?"

"Yes, I would. I could work with a stonemason to complete the sculpture."

"Thank you, Caroline, you have made my day. Can I have a copy of this sketch, please? I want to start gaining support from the grassroots level for the project."

"No problems. The mayor is due here tomorrow to finish posing for his painting so I'll talk to him about the work. I'll then ring you and let you know what he thinks."

"Thanks, Caroline – I'd appreciate it."

Bailey photocopied the sketch and gave it to John. He thanked her for her input and started to leave.

"John, the boys will be alright. I believe you're on the right path to set them free and don't worry, they'll move on when they have accomplished whatever they need to do."

"Thanks, Caroline, I'll be in contact again soon."

John drove back to Sutton Hall totally impressed. He had a quick artist sketch of a proposed memorial for the boys that he felt would be very inclusive for the parents, locals and tourists.

Now he had to work on how to pay for the memorial and find out whether the boys' parents would like it.

Chapter Seven

Melanie was quite excited about the boys' project and the speed that it was coming together. It was good for John to have some extracurricular projects to work on but this one had a momentum she had not seen before. She arrived home to again find John halfway cooking dinner for them both and engrossed in conversation on the phone about the boys. Melanie kissed John gently on the cheek and took over the cooking. Finally, John got off the phone.

"Hi love," John gushed as he got his thoughts together. "This has been another big day for the boys, and it all seems to be coming together well. I'd better start with the phone call. That was Phillip Boyce from Australia, you know the one that's in the Army Band and used to sing with the Aussie National Boys Choir. Well, he's quite excited as he's being sent here in November for our Remembrance Day. He wangled the trip because the Captain due to come here is now being deployed to the Middle East and he's replacing him."

"That's great love. What about Boyce, is he likely to be deployed there also?"

"No, he's not long come back from there and needs to start some more study next year to progress to being a Major.

Anyway, the interesting thing is he's not being sent here to be with any Aussie contingent."

"Now don't tell me he's coming here to be with the Household Cavalry and sing at Buckingham Palace?"

John winced at his wife's retort. "No, he's teaming up with his friend Andrew Jackson from America as a sort of Allied military support act."

Melanie was astounded. It was as if the gods were playing with the earthlings as puppets and orchestrating events surrounding the boys' send-off.

"John, that doesn't make sense. How can the Australians be sending Boyce here to act as support for the Americans? Our Memorial Services are pretty sombre affairs, yet you make it sound more like a concert tour."

"Apparently the Americans requested that Boyce and a couple of other Aussies join them to give some combined recitals at a series of diplomatic events."

"Well, this really is a coup for the two men who once sang in our former church to be reunited. What's the likelihood of them actually coming here?"

John's face lit up and a broad smile enveloped his face. "Both have blanked out a three-hour block in their diaries for the afternoon of Remembrance Day. They'll be here with a band!"

Tears formed in Melanie's eyes as she listened to her husband detail the mechanics of what the two former choristers had gone through in their respective military services to arrange the double act at the former St Dominic Savio Church. Over the years both men had been in touch on an irregular basis and had exchanged songs and music. However, when John put out his feelers for information from the two men about when they were teenagers singing with the St Dominic Savio Boys and Youth Choir the communication between the two army officers took on a new emphasis and direction. They both felt they had to complete something by performing at a concert for the choir that had evaporated. Now John had a major reason to help stage a concert for his boys and for the band to perform at it.

Melanie served tea and the couple started eating when John suddenly stood up.

"I almost forgot. I have something to show you," John said as he darted out of the dining room and into the lounge room to retrieve his artist sketch.

"You know how we want some sort of memorial here for the boys?"

"Yes."

"What do you think of this as a concept? I went and saw Caroline Bailey, the artist Barry Cooper recommended, and she drew this sketch for me. The seat would be positioned on the land overlooking the graveyard but with the view down the valley."

Melanie studied the photo and sketch.

"This is it. The seat looks like it is meant to be there. I think it would be a very welcome addition to the property and also give the boys' parents some comfort. The only thing missing is something to detail what the seat is all about. It needs some sort of metal tablet somewhere detailing what happened to the boys. You know, some sort of plinth."

"Yes, you're right. Mmm, I'll think about that and see what can be done."

"Now my darling, are there any other surprises or can we have some sweets?"

John got out of his chair, walked to where Melanie was seated and put his arms around her. He gave her a series of kisses on her cheeks and down her neck.

"You're my dessert. However, to satisfy the inner woman, would you like some chocolate ice cream?"

"Now that's my kind of man."

The following morning John went to his office as usual and made a cup of tea before he began work. He had a piece of poster-sized cardboard Melanie had given him and he stuck it up on the wall behind his control panel.

"Okay boys this is the state of play," John said to the empty workspace. "We have a place to hold a concert." He then stuck a photo of the old church on the cardboard. "Outside we have a suggested memorial your parents could use with joy. I'm still working on this." Next, he stuck his photo with Bailey's park bench sketch on the poster. "Now the coup de grace is the US military band with two singers you know. I'll just draw a couple of little rectangles here so I know where to place some photos of Andrew Jackson and Phillip Boyce. Okay, guys, I'm about done. We need confirmation about the memorial and for your parents to come along to the concert."

John turned on his work computer and searched the internet for information about Jackson and Boyce. He found images of them singing at various military shows; printed them out and stuck them over the rectangles he drew earlier.

"Okay guys here are some pix of Andrew and Phillip as they are today. They'll be here for your send-off." John then listed the names of the seven songs he had for the concert so far. "Now I have some real work to do," he said as he checked his emails and saw several requests from his main office.

John was playing and re-recording a piece of music when he looked up and saw Father Kirby standing at the doorway. He cut the music and asked the priest to enter.

"Sorry Brendan, I didn't see you. I sort of get engrossed in my work. It becomes my world for the duration of the track."

"Good morning, John. No problems, I do the same sometimes. It was a pleasure to drive up the hill and hear music coming from this old girl again."

"Actually I'm glad you're here as I have some fantastic news for you. I was leaving it until lunchtime to contact you but you must have been reading my mind. Come and have a look at this and tell me what you think."

John showed Kirby his poster and explained what it all meant. The priest studied the photos but was drawn repeatedly to the sketch of the park bench seat.

"John, this is fantastic, it really is," Kirby said as he ran his fingers down the list of songs and then across to the park bench. "You've come a long way with your project."

"Well, I try my best. We nearly have all the pieces ready for the concert. We have the venue; the band and singers, and the memorial still in play."

"Have you given any thought to how you will play with your presents left by the boys?" Kirby asked as he pointed to the song list.

"No, this one sort of eludes me. I guess in the back of my mind I was going to ask the American band to play the music and then I play the boys singing."

"Yes, well there's the problem. Who would believe the boys could leave you anything – they're dead."

John studied Kirby and tried to work out where he was going. "I'm pretty open to suggestions."

"I've been thinking about it for a while and may have a solution for you."

"I'm listening."

"Two of the schools I visit as a pastoral carer have burgeoning boys' choirs. What if they performed here for you with the American band?"

"But then we'll hear this new choir singing and not the one we're trying to send off."

"Ah yes, but there's more. What if this choir mimed or hummed some of the songs but joined in with others?"

"Am I hearing you right? Your combined school choir would be prepared to assist by miming and humming some of your dead choir's songs and then join in as a sort of duet in real time?"

"Yes. Now that a concert is going to take place, it would give the new choir some exposure at a major event and help our boys too."

John thought about how it could be done and then had a brain snap. "Okay, let's go to the end of the nave," he said as he walked with Kirby. "If we had the US band positioned here along with Andrew and Philip and the boys in the choir loft, what do you think?"

"I believe it could work."

"This would allow the schoolboys to be seen from a distance and allow our parents to know it is not really their boys singing, as such."

"Yes, that would work."

John looked at the choir loft and then where he was standing and nodded. I thought you didn't believe in what your old choir was trying to do?"

"No, I didn't quite say that. The church is faced with mysteries every day. There seems to be too much happening to write it all off as a new owner of a defunct church wanting to have a concert to farewell the boys who once sung here. You've come a long way John and I'm sure all the parents will be thrilled when they realise what you are doing."

"My problem is, I can't tell them why I am doing it so this way I keep my promise to Blake."

"I am sure he will really appreciate you doing that. However, you can tell the parents a couple of former singers in choirs that attended their memorial service are holding a one-off concert here for their boys. When you throw in the US Band and the memorial, who could stay away?"

"What do you think of the proposed memorial?"

"I am really impressed with the sketch. It looks like the memorial has always been here. The artist has captured the emotion well by making it a bench parents and others can sit on and take in the views. They can commune with each other and with their boys."

"Caroline Bailey will be seeing the mayor today about a portrait he is having done and will press him for help."

"That's interesting, as I'll be seeing his mother in hospital today on my rounds for the sick. I'll mention to her the great work you are doing and see if we can evince some action from both the Council and Tourist Association."

"I knew there was a reason for you being here today rather than just dropping in. Would you like a cup of tea?"

"I thought you'd never ask."

The pair went to John's tearoom and made a pot of tea. Kirby was amused with John's improvement to his old vestry. The two men sat outside the room in John's recreational space to enjoy the brew.

"John, have you got a copy here of the songs the boys left you?"

"Yes, would you like to hear them?"

"That would be great thanks."

John went to his control panel and cued the songs. He looked at his computer and saw an email from Robert King. The current director of the Australian National Boys Choir wanted to know how John was going with his project. Also, what was the latest news with Phillip Boyce and Andrew Jackson? John pressed the play button on his control panel and walked back to his tea area to join Kirby for the boy's singing.

He was about to say something when he noticed Kirby was sitting with his eyes closed. John resumed his seat quietly and sat and watched Kirby as the songs filled the old church. John saw Kirby move his shoulders and then rub his hands slowly as if a breath of winter chill had washed over him. John smiled as he realised the boys were playing games with their former parish priest. He poured Kirby and himself a second cup of tea in silence.

"Welcome back Brendan," John said with a smile as his guest opened his eyes a few moments later and re-focused when the singing stopped.

"Sorry John, old memories are hard to die. It was almost as if the boys were here. With my eyes closed, I could virtually feel their presence."

"You looked cold Brendan. Do you feel a draft here?"

"Well, this place was always cold, especially in winter. No, I don't think I felt a draft as much as goose bumps on hearing the boys sing here again."

"They had the same effect on Barry Cooper when he was here the other day."

"Yes, they would. Barry did a lot for the choir and was always fussing about them. The boys appreciated what he was doing for them. John, I'd better get back to my rounds. I have to see Mrs. Butler and a few other old dears before lunch."

"I'm glad you dropped in. Having your current combined choir here I think would be fantastic. I'm pretty sure the parents of our choir would appreciate it too."

"Alright John, thanks. I'll sound out the choir and their teachers and see what they think."

"Brendan, I had contact with Robert King the current director of the Australian National Boys Choir. He said he thought he might be bringing his team here for Remembrance Day. Somehow, I think your lads would fill the bill better and achieve what we need."

"That's some replacement! Let me know if you have any problems with the Aussies."

"Thanks, Brendan."

John walked Kirby out of his office and waved him off. The local combined choir would be a good choice as they would bring a familiarity to the concert rather than a group of international lads. John laughed as he re-entered his office and walked to his control panel. It was good to see both heaven and earth working to achieve something together. In this case, the goal was the local Mayor and the Tourist Association. John loved the pincer movement in play to snare support from Graham Butler with the artist in one ear and Mrs. Butler in the other. He'd love to be a fly on the wall in the mayor's home tonight!

John re-read King's e-mail and replied thanking him for his support and advising him of his contacts with Jackson and Boyce. He also sent a copy of each of the songs he had captured so far. John then went to his project board and wrote 'Local combined boys choir' and circled it. The rest of the morning was spent working on material sent from his head office.

Chapter Eight

Graham Butler was a man keen to capture his time in history. He had been Mayor for less than a year but was keen to have his portrait painted as soon as possible and hung in the Council Chambers for posterity. Butler was president of the local Tourist Association and was keen to push activities that brought visitors and commerce to Brighton. He had pioneered some good innovations in the district. Butler had been overseas several times and was always impressed with being able to pick up a telephone at an airport and dial a hotel for free to arrange discount accommodation. One of his innovations to his sleepy district was to install a free telephone with a bank of accommodation sites listed so visitors could book their stay in Brighton from the tourist information centre. The phone set-up was a small step with progress for some places but a huge one for Brighton.

Butler was an amateur archaeologist and had found what was believed to be Saxon jewellery and remains of cooking pots on his property. If the finds were authenticated, it would be a tremendous boon to the museum he was trying to set up as a paying sideline on his property. Butler drove up the tight driveway of Caroline Bailey's home and parked his car. No sooner had he started to alight from his vehicle when he was met by the artist.

"Good morning your Worship, did you have a good drive here?" Bailey asked with a smile as she moved forward to greet him.

"Good morning, Caroline, yes thanks. I always love this part of the district; it's so rich in colours."

"Ah, then you will probably like where I am up to with your portrait."

"Have you started painting it now?"

"Yes. I think today should finish your sittings and you should have your painting by the end of the week if you are satisfied with where I have gone with it."

"Now you have me excited. I'm keen to see your lovely handiwork."

Butler reached into the rear compartment of his car and took out a thick suit bag before joining Bailey as the couple went into her studio.

"Okay put your robes and chain on and then we'll have the first viewing," Bailey said as she walked forward to her easel.

"You certainly are a temptress, Caroline. I thought you'd have it already on view for me."

"No, there has to be an unveiling so I can gauge your reaction."

"Okay, thank you."

Butler rushed to don his official mayoral gown and chain of office. He then walked over to the easel with widened eyes like a child about to receive a present. Bailey asked him to stand back a bit and then slowly lifted the cloth covering her painting. Butler was amazed at the vibrancy in colour and the good likeness of him Bailey had captured. The artist watched the excitement in Butler's face and knew she had pleased him with her work.

"This is fantastic Caroline. The lines, the colour, and the detail are magnificent. Well done."

"Thank you, Mr. Mayor, but you can see I still have some detail I need to capture this morning to add life to the portrait. It shouldn't take too long."

"I'm really impressed Caroline, thank you."

"Thank you. It's always good to hear a client is happy with my work. Okay, if you are ready I'll get you standing over here again and I'll start work."

Butler moved to a marked spot on the floor and resumed his pose. Bailey adjusted his robe and hands to fit the image on the canvas.

"That's it, thank you."

Bailey picked up a paintbrush and dipped it into some paint, squished it a bit on her pallet and then started stroking the canvas slowly with it. Butler stood still as he was now well used to holding the pose. However, his eyes wandered around the studio and settled on a poster behind Bailey. He winced as he struggled to identify what was wrong with the poster. The photo had been taken looking up the slight gradient from the graveyard leading to St Dominic Savio's. A beautiful, curved, stone park bench sat at the top of the rise. At either end of the bench were ornate sculptures – one end had a young boy and the other an older youth – both in singing poses.

"How long has the bench seat been at the old church?"

"It's not there yet."

"It looks like it has been there for some time."

"Thank you. It is a project I'm thinking of taking on."

"Caroline from here it looks as if the bench has always been there. I couldn't figure it out at first as it looks as though it belongs in the setting. What's the story?"

"Do you remember the choir of St Dominic Savio's that was vaporised in that horrific bus crash ten years ago?"

"Who could forget?"

Bailey laughed as she stopped painting.

"Apparently the Council has, and no one has come forward with any memorial for the boys until now."

"That's up to the parents surely, not Council. Anyway, hasn't the old church been sold to a musician or something?"

Bailey walked over to the poster and pointed to the bench.

"A young couple has bought the former church with the husband using it to re-record music and songs for record companies. His wife is a music teacher in London."

"Oh, that's nice. At least the building will be used to good effect."

"Ah yes. The new owner of the place, John Sutton approached me to see if I would design a sculpture to remember the boys who died on that bus."

"That's nice of him. Is he paying for the bench seat?"

"No. He said your Council had no money to assist the parents a decade ago when their boys died. Your Tourist Association was only in its infancy then also and never helped. When he found out about the boys Mr. Sutton came to me to design a sculpture for the site. I guess he'll soon be on your doorstep asking whether your two work areas can assist."

"The seat is a problem for the boys' parents, not Council or the Tourist Association. Anyway, who would commit money to private property at the old church site?"

"Of course, you would be right if that was so. However, Mr. Sutton's proposal is for the seat to be built within the graveyard area so it can never be removed by successive owners of the church."

"This sounds nice of him."

"Well, he thought this out, as the seat overlooks the valley and surrounding district. It can't be built out and there is guaranteed access for visitors. The bench would serve as a memorial to the lost boys' choir from this district and as a tourist attraction because of its uninterrupted views of the area."

"What does Mr. Sutton get out of all of this? Does he sell music or something to visitors?"

"No. He is a sound engineer and has no dealings with the public. Mr. Sutton said the only recognition of the boys' fate were two plaques – one affixed to a power pole at the crash site and the other inside the old church."

"Well, it sounds like a pretty good project. What would it cost for the seat and your design work?"

"I'd do the design work for free in recognition of the local boys and their families. The stonemason has told me he would be willing to make a deal too as he knew some of the boys."

"I just can't make decisions about these sorts of things. They would have to come as a formal request to Council or the Tourist Association for consideration. Are you seeing Mr. Sutton soon? If so, get him to submit a proposal and I'll ask both bodies to consider it. I can't guarantee anything after all the boys have been dead for a decade and public interest has died down."

"Mr. Mayor, I'll be in touch with Mr. Sutton this afternoon, so I'll give him your message. Thank you. Now straighten up your right arm, please. We have some more work to do."

The posing lasted another hour before Bailey was happy with her progress. Butler rushed around to the front of the easel to look at his image. He was really impressed with this newcomer to the district. Her work was a standout. After the Mayor had disrobed his Mayoral gown and Chain of Office and put his 'party clothes' back in his suit bag Bailey then walked the mayor to his car.

"Caroline thanks for the beautiful work. I am sure Council will really appreciate it."

"As long as you do Mr. Mayor – that's what matters."

"Thank you. Don't forget what I said about Mr. Sutton."

"I won't, thank you."

Butler drove to work at his Tourist Association. He had a staff seminar to conduct and was keen to complete it so he could then go to the Council Chambers.

* * *

Brendan Kirby had been parish priest to three of the four people on his sick list for more than two decades. The fourth was a ring-in after only being around for 15 years. Every couple of days he would drive to St Michael's Hospital to visit his sick parishioners. Today was no different. He visited the first three people, a male and two women; sat, talked and prayed with them for a short time each. These people were lonely as they were senior citizens whose families were busy working with little spare time on their hands for hospital visits. The older folk loved to hear the latest news about the district and Kirby was a good communicator. But he saved his energy for his visit to Mrs. Veronica Butler, mother of the mayor.

"Hello Veronica," Kirby said as he entered Mrs. Butler's ward.

"Hello Brendan, thank you for coming to see me today."

"That's alright Veronica. I'm here doing the Lord's work."

Kirby sat down and talked with her for a few minutes before breaking into prayer. After a few moments of silent prayer, he launched into a new conversation.

"Well there is a lot of movement at the old St Dominic Savio's," Kirby said.

"What do you mean? Is the old church being knocked down?"

"No, no, far from it – a young couple has bought the property and is breathing new life into it."

"That's nice. It would be a shame to see the old church go. It's been around for so long it's a landmark for the district."

Brendan saw his cue and launched.

"I'm glad you see it that way. The owner of the old church is a sound engineer, and he re-records music and songs for a record company in it."

"What does his wife do?"

"Oh, she's a music teacher in London. Anyway, the owner is a man called John Sutton and he's taken our old choir to heart."

"That would be hard; the boys have been gone for so long now."

"Yes, I agree, it's been ten years since they went to God. Anyway, John read the plaque in the church about the boys' accident and decided to hold a concert for them."

"A concert? For our boys?"

Suddenly clarity started returning to Mrs. Butler's eyes.

"Yes. Apparently, he has an American military band and two former boy singers who sang at the memorial service going to stage the concert."

Mrs. Butler reached for her tissues from the side table and wiped her eyes.

"No one cared for the boys once they were gone. A bit like us oldies here and our families. When is the concert?"

"John is going to hold it on Remembrance Day, in the afternoon, which is why the American band and the two singers can be there. They'll all be in London at various services in the morning and then at St Dominic's in the afternoon."

"Oh, this is really good news. Why does he want to hold the concert? What does he hope to gain from it?"

"John became upset when he realised there was no memorial for the boys except the two plaques. He wants to hold the concert to raise funds for a special sculpture in the old graveyard."

Kirby enthusiastically detailed John's proposal for a

sculpture in the form of a park bench as a lasting memorial for the boys. Mrs. Butler wiped more tears from her eyes.

"You know Brendan; I can't remember how many albs I made for those boys and even those serving Mass with my son Graham. I still think of them all as my boys."

"So do I; it's like it was only yesterday the boys were running around the church or singing in it."

"Does Graham know about the concert and sculpture?"

"No, I don't think so. John's only just put together the ideas and started to make it happen."

"Graham will be excited to know there will be a special concert in the old church. The bench seat outside will be absolutely marvellous for the boys' parents and other visitors."

"When the Church built St Dominic's it picked the highest ground."

"Yes and with the best views of the district and this Mr. Sutton's seat will be the icing to the cake. Well, you are full of good news today."

"Alright Veronica, I must be going now as I have more work to do."

"Thanks for coming Brendan."

"God bless."

Kirby felt he accomplished his work of sowing the seeds of support for John's work. He knew Mrs. Butler would be enthusiastic and was like a terrier with a bone when she started on a project. He drove back to his own Rectory to check on his housemate priest who was recovering from a long illness. Veronica Butler mulled over what Father Kirby told her. A special concert at the old St Dominic Savio's and a new tourist attraction!

Surely her son would love to know this. She picked up the bedside phone and called her son.

"Hello Mrs. Butler," the receptionist said. "Mr. Butler is in a seminar and won't be out for another hour."

"Thank you. Please get him to call me as I have some pretty exciting news."

"Will do, I'll let him know you called."

The pair rang off. It was a bit too much for Mrs. Butler to hold inside herself. She had to tell someone about her news. It was just too good. She rummaged through her bedside drawer and picked up her contacts book. Within seconds she had started a ring around of her friends.

Graham Butler finished his second speaking part in the seminar and checked with his receptionist for any calls for him. The receptionist said the phones had hardly stopped ringing after his mother called him. She gave him the message and watched her boss. He nodded slowly and smiled.

"I'll bet I know what it's about," Butler said aloud.

"Has your mother's condition worsened Mr. Butler?"

"No, but I think she has somehow got wind of a new tourist project I heard about today regarding the former St Dominic Savio's. I can't believe how quick the message is getting around. If my mother rings back, please tell her I'll call her this afternoon after the next session."

"Alright, Mr. Butler."

Butler smiled and re-joined his seminar. He wasn't in a position to start the return phone calls yet as he was co-chairing the next session and couldn't pull out.

At Sutton Hall, John had worked his way through several

re-records and was happy with the results. Buying the old church was probably one of the best things he had ever done, besides marrying Melanie. He could do his work from home and had one of the best sound studios in the country. Everything seemed close at hand – from the workplace to shopping and transport. The burgeoning problem was the village life. John loved working with people, but they sometimes forgot he had to work too. He finished a re-record and went to his tearoom to get a cup of tea and have a break. No sooner had he sat down to enjoy the quiet of the workspace when a figure filled the doorway and then knocked.

"Oh, John, sorry to interrupt," Barry Cooper said as he took off his hat and entered the building. "I'm getting messages and enquiries from all over the place about your concert and memorial and thought we'd better catch up with each other."

John stood up and greeted Cooper. "No problems Barry. You must have smelt the pot of tea. Would you like a cup?"

"Yes thank you, I'd love one."

John gestured to Cooper to sit down while he went to the tearoom and retrieved a second cup and saucer and some milk.

"Okay mate, what's happening?" John asked as he poured Cooper a cup of tea.

"I've had at least four calls today saying you were putting on some sort of concert."

"Word seems to be spreading. Who's making the call around?"

"I don't know but there seems to be a lot of activity among the senior citizens here."

"What do you mean?"

"Coral got the first call this morning from her mother who is in a nursing home. She said a lot of the patients had started asking their families to book them out for Remembrance Day and not to return until after your concert."

John started laughing and nodding. He knew there was mischief afoot.

"It sounds like it started with someone's parents and then with their children your age."

"Yes, what about the memorial? How would they know anything about that?"

"Well, only a few people know I have been working on that project. Wait on, Father Kirby was in here earlier and said he was going to visit the Mayor's mother today as part of his rounds of the sick."

"Yes, that would do it. Veronica Butler was a mainstay of this church. She would help make all the albs for the altar boys and organise the various social functions. She was a woman always on a mission. Have you been in touch with her son Graham as yet?"

"No, I had some real work to do today here so I've been busy."

"Mmm, all roads seem to lead us to Graham Butler."

John thought about the situation for a few moments while he sipped his tea. He looked at Cooper who seemed very intense. John wondered whether he had slipped into a very quiet semi-retirement after the boys' demise and was then forced to arc up when he and Melanie arrived.

"You know we could either take on the village tom toms directly by inviting the local newspaper here to do a story or let the drums keep beating. What do you think; you were the boys '*public relations person*?'

"This is like viral marketing where word of mouth advertising is ahead of the game and outsiders are used to publicise an event. The only problem is you have no control over it. I'd suggest now is the time to start bringing some control to the situation."

"Well, I think I have enough information locked in to allow the Media to start running with it."

Cooper's eyes widened and John could see he was waiting for an invitation.

"Barry, you're a PR man, aren't you?"

"Yes. I was the boys' PR officer and am currently in semi-retirement. This concert of yours would be just what the village and district needs."

"Why?"

"Well, as you know a number of the boys' parents have left the area. The whole place is so quiet there's no recognition it even exists anymore. That was one of the reasons this church went up for sale."

"So it was the boys who really put this village and district on the map?"

"Yes. They were renowned for their singing and people used to travel from adjoining areas to come here where we're sitting now just to listen to the boys."

John poured them both another cup of tea and thought for a few moments. He looked around his office space and mentally asked: *Well, Blake, are you and the boys ready for us to start the publicity about your concert? Will you stay the course?*

The answer was swift. The light in the tearoom flickered and John heard a loud *Yes* in his head. *Okay let's go for it*, he replied.

"What was that?" Cooper asked as he noticed the flickering light. "You might need a new bulb in there."

John laughed as he thought about Blake playing games in front of his father.

"Yes, I'll look at that later. Okay, what do you suggest we do? Butler is a key here but I haven't contacted him yet in either of his roles."

"Butler can wait a bit while we gather more far-reaching support. I think it's time we held a parents' meeting to alert those left to what you are doing and to introduce you to them. Support will then start to steamroll. Our next step would be to contact the Brighton Post and have it do a story."

"Where would you hold the meeting?"

Cooper looked around at John's working space and smiled. "Here of course."

"But I don't have enough chairs."

"Leave that to me. I'll ask them all to bring their own."

"Alright. What about the newspaper?"

"I'd suggest we alert the parents first so they have no surprises coming their way and then we start our PR campaign in earnest."

John could see Cooper was now literally on fire. His eyes had widened, his speech had picked up in speed and he seemed more animated. He was a man on a mission and John was his driver.

"Alright, Barry let's go firm and start the wheels really

moving. Would you be prepared to help out with the rest of the concert publicity?"

"Yes of course."

"Now we have the Americans locked in and Boyce from Australia coming, it should encourage a lot more people to come here."

"John there is a lot to organise in respect of far-reaching Media to run stories on your project. I'd suggest this place of yours will be overflowing with people for the concert and we may need to think about how we want to handle it."

"Well, this is where I retreat into my music world and leave the PR details to the expert. Oh, by the way, I forgot to tell you something."

"What?"

"One of the reasons Father Kirby was here was to tell me he thought he could possibly get a combined choir from two local schools to sing for the concert."

"I thought you had the Australian National Boys Choir coming here?"

"Well, that's not definite. However, Father Kirby's choir may be an alternative. He's going to check it out."

"Either way it would be fantastic to have a boys' choir here singing again. Well, I'd better start cracking and get a public affairs plan drawn up so we have a road map of what to do and when."

"Thanks, Barry – I knew it was important you came here today."

The two men laughed as John walked Cooper out of the former church to the graveyard and then waved him off. John spent a few moments at the site where he would like to see the boys' memorial erected and then returned to his office. He went over to his poster and added the words 'PR campaign' and circled it.

"Well boys, this will be a pretty good concert and I am really looking forward to it," John said out aloud.

"Mind you, I'll have to re-arrange my workspace. However, because of the importance, I won't mind. I never knew you but already I can feel I'll miss you. Melanie will be surprised at today's events."

Chapter Nine

John was preparing dinner when the phone rang. A Mrs. Fogarty wanted to book tickets for her family to the upcoming Remembrance Day concert. She was the first of three people who had heard about the concert and rang the Suttons to make bookings. John was flabbergasted. He told the callers to watch for information in the local paper about the concert, when to ring and what number. John stopped making dinner and gave Melanie a full briefing after she arrived home in time to hear him with the last caller.

"You've had a busy day again by the sounds of it," Melanie said as she opened a bottle of white wine and poured them both a glass.

"Cheers, thanks, love. Yes, it's been an interesting day. The best thing about it is the proof that village life is not dead."

"What do you mean?"

"Think back to the lovely suburb we just came from. There's no way the locals would engage like this after hearing unsubstantiated conversations about a major event."

"No, you're right. They'd go to an online ticket agency and book their tickets. However, this couldn't happen until after there was some kind of publicity about the event."

"Well, Barry Cooper now has this in hand. I'll ring him tomorrow and ..."

The phone rang again. Melanie picked it up.

"Hello, Sutton Hall."

"Hello, this must be Melanie. I'm Barry Cooper, is John home please?"

"Hello, Barry, nice to meet you, well over the phone anyway. I'll pass you to John."

"Hi mate, you must have ESP or something."

"Hi John, what's this about me having ESP?"

"I was just telling Mel what's happened today. In between, I've already received three phone calls asking to book tickets for the concert."

"Don't worry John; this will be sorted out in the next few days as the Post gets a hold of the story. Nearly everyone here reads it."

"Excellent. So what's the latest?"

"I've managed to have all the parents of the boys still living here contacted and also a couple who have moved to adjoining districts. They're all very keen to meet you and hear your proposals. Would tomorrow night be alright, say 7 pm?"

"You don't waste time, do you?"

"I had the spare time this afternoon and the old phone tree still works very well."

"Phone tree; what's that?"

"Oh, this is where I call one person and they call the next on the list and so on. The last one rings back to me to confirm the message. It saves cost and speed."

"That's great news. Just hang on a tick Barry and I'll check with the lady of the house. Darling are you free to attend a meeting of the parents in my office at 7 pm tomorrow in Sutton Hall?"

Melanie's face lit up and she laughed and nodded.

"Yes, Barry that will be fine. I'll organise tea and coffee. About how many people should we be expecting?"

"Probably around forty people, if that's okay."

"Yes, that will be fine. See you then."

Melanie looked at John and handed him his wine.

"So we have our first parents meeting tomorrow night. This should be fun. What do you need to do to prepare for it?"

"Barry has organised them to bring their own chairs, so I need only supply the teas, coffees, milk, and biscuits."

"You will need to work out how you will seat them and what you are actually going to say. Also, you will need some sort of update from the artist ... is it Caroline Bailey?"

"Yes."

"I guess the all-important question on their minds will be the memorial and any update concerning the Council or Tourist Association."

"You know, I was going to ring Graham Butler today about that but got caught up in too many other things. I'll contact him tomorrow."

"Well, I'd suggest you ring Caroline tonight and see if she is free tomorrow night."

"Thank you, my darling, I knew I married you for something else besides love ... it's your expertise at organising things."

John kissed Melanie and then picked up the phone and rang Bailey. The artist said she wasn't surprised at how quick the parents and the village folk were responding. She said they were a tight bunch of people who didn't want to miss out on anything happening in their locality.

"I've got a clear night in my diary tomorrow night and will be there," Bailey said to John.

"I wouldn't mind coming over earlier if that's alright so I can see the actual space you have earmarked for the memorial and also see the inside of the old church."

"Thanks, Caroline. How about joining Melanie and me for an early dinner and then we'll do a tour of the place?"

"That will be lovely thank you. I can then update you both on what the Mayor said about the project."

The pair rang off and John found Melanie had already served dinner. He walked around to her chair and kissed her.

"What's that for?"

"For just being you; I love you."

The pair relaxed in front of the TV for the rest of the night. John was a morning person and drew his energy from the pre-dawn while Melanie was a night owl. She could stay up quite late after a hard day while John would be asleep after the main movie finished on TV at night. In the morning Melanie awoke to find John at the breakfast bar jotting down notes for the parents' meeting while drinking a cup of tea. It was a cloudy morning and still dark outside. No glorious sunrise today. She walked over to John and kissed him before pouring herself a cup of tea.

"Good morning, my sweet. I thought I'd make a start now and jot down some notes of what's happened and why we'd like to hold a concert for the boys."

"What's your reason for the concert?" Melanie asked in an official sort of tone of voice.

"Well, the answer for the parents will be to raise money for the memorial and create a tourist attraction they will all be proud of having."

"Good, don't mention the boys' presents and presence."

"No, my push will be to have the memorial built in the graveyard. It will be nice on a clear day to sit there and view the district in the quiet."

"Sounds like you want it for yourself."

"No. If we had kids and one of them died in a bus crash like these boys I'd want somewhere to commune with him. I think the seat is a brilliant idea. Imagine if a small sculpture or cross was placed at the accident scene. Parents wouldn't feel comfortable stopping on the side of the road, given they could find parking, and trying to talk, pray or commune with their loved ones. It wouldn't be the same."

Melanie smiled. "Nice argument Counsellor – use it tonight."

John looked at his wife and realised what she had done with her prompting. He tweaked some of his notes while he sipped on his tea and smiled. It was hard to get uptight with his wife, she was too beautiful.

"I'll take our extra collapsible chairs from the stables to the old church in case someone hasn't one."

"Good. Don't forget to get a couple of sleeves of disposable cups and you might want to look for an oversized teapot or two for the refreshments."

"Yes. I imagine Brendan had all that for church socials and other functions. Never mind, I'll hit the shops today and see what I can find."

"You know my darling, for the oversized teapots I'd try the bric-a-brac type stores as they are more likely to have them than the modern supermarket chains."

"Anything else you can think of?"

"No. They were just the immediate things that came to mind. I'll pick up something nice for sweets for our dinner with the artist."

"Alright; I'll organise the rest. Don't be late for work."

Melanie smiled, got up and placed her teacup and saucer on the sink. She kissed John on the side of his face and continued to the bathroom to have her shower and get ready for work.

John stopped writing his notes for the meeting and composed a to-do list of jobs for the day. He was going to be busy. John had been in sports clubs as a teenager and attended numerous parent meetings. This would be his first as an adult and having to run it. He was looking forward to the challenge. However, he knew he had to get it right. He had promised Blake and the boys that he would hold the concert and he was not going to renege on it, so everything had to be right. Melanie went to work and John showered and dressed. His first task was to get the four collapsible chairs in the stables and take them to his office area. The good thing about Sutton Hall was the space, there was lots of it. Everything was easy to find in the garage as he hadn't had time to fill it with junk. John gathered his chairs and went to the old church hall.

No sooner had he entered his office space when he felt a chill.

Thank you, John, we appreciate what you are doing for us, John heard a young teenage boy say.

"You are not Blake. Who are you?" he asked calmly as he looked around.

I'm Richard and we're all happy with the way you are putting things together for our concert.

"Hi Richard, are you Mr. Worth's son?"

Yes, Blake and I would sometimes sing duets together.

"Do you like the artist's drawing for the memorial to you boys?"

Yeah, we all do. When our parents come to visit here they can sit outside on the lovely bench and talk to us. Thank you.

"Richard, Father Brendan is looking at having two local choirs come here and possibly mime some of your songs. What do you think of the idea?"

We know our parents will love to hear the boys and we'll help them.

"Okay, thank you."

Warmth re-enveloped John as his workspace went quiet and Richard moved on. His conversations with the boys were pretty short, but at least he knew he was on track from their perspective. John felt uplifted after speaking with Richard. He placed his chairs around the nave and knelt down.

"Dear God, thank you for the gift you gave given me to hear and feel the boys' presence," he said in audible prayer. "I don't know why you chose me for this work but I will stay the course and see this project finished."

He stood up and turned around to go to the tearoom when he noticed the light flicker several times and then go off. John checked the switch and saw it was in the off position and turned it on. There was no flicker now. He took it as a sign the boys were happy with him and he smiled and nodded. John walked over to his workspace and checked his e-mails. There were none from his head office but one from Robert King.

Hi, John,

I hope this finds you well. Thank you for the songs you sent from your boys. They are really impressive. I've attached the music for them in case you ever need it.

I'm sorry to be the bearer of bad tidings as it is now clear my choir will not be in the United Kingdom for your Remembrance Day. Our sponsors have asked us to film a major promotion video in November to be shown on planes across the globe. We couldn't turn down their request.

I know both my choir and I would love to have been with you for your special concert and I ask you please send our best regards to the boys' families. Also, please keep me updated on how you are going with the project. If there is anything I can do to assist from the land Down Under, please don't hesitate to call me.

Your friend,

Robert

John laughed when he read the email. He quickly replied to thanking King for his assistance and telling him of Kirby's offer of a combined choir. John then printed out King's email and posted it on his project board.

"Well boys, it looks like Father Kirby gets his way with the local choir. Let's hope they're up for it."

John picked up his phone and dialled Graham Butler to discuss his project.

"Hello Mr. Butler, I'm John Sutton the owner of ..."

"Mr. Sutton, it's a pleasure to hear your voice. I've heard a lot about the new owner of St Dominic Savio's."

"Hopefully it's all been good, Mr. Mayor?"

"Oh yes; however I had a mini-crisis yesterday when all my phones were tied up answering people's enquiries about a concert you plan to stage."

"News travels fast. My apologies for any problems as a story won't be appearing in the Brighton Post until the next edition, however, I wanted to talk to you about some proposals I have in mind."

"Mr. Sutton are these proposals about the memorial you are planning and the concert?"

"Yes."

"For the memorial, you'll have to make an application for a Council grant and there's no guarantee you'll be successful as funding is pretty competitive. I saw the mock-up of the park bench at Caroline Bailey's place and it looks pretty good. I think the bench concept is excellent rather than a statue of a boy singing or something similar. Where are you looking at building it?"

"Thanks. Yes, Caroline has done a great job with her mock-up. It seems to capture the essence of the boys' choir that used to sing here. My idea is to have the bench built within the graveyard area so it can't be touched by successive owners of the property down the ages."

"Good. I like your idea of the parents being able to visit the old church area and sit down on the bench."

"And don't forget, the bench would also be a tourist attraction to the district."

"How would it be?"

"Well if the bench was situated on the high point of the graveyard grounds it has unsurpassed views of the district. It would be a fantastic place for people to visit, take photos of the landscape and rest."

"Won't any visitors get in your way as a commercial enterprise?"

"No. I would signpost the entrance to the property and the side entrance of the old church alerting visitors I have a working recording studio in operation."

"Mr. Sutton, why do you want to do this? You were not around when the choir was alive. Do you know any of the boys or their families?"

"Firstly, your last questions are immaterial. I am a citizen who sees a need and through this need a way for the district to be recognised and a lot of healing to take place. I gain nothing out of this. I don't have products to sell to the public. My work is organised and distributed through major record companies not direct to the public like a backyard charlatan."

"Sorry, Mr. Sutton I needed to see why you were doing this

and whether you stood to gain anything from it. What about this concert of yours? Won't it interrupt your workspace?"

John felt like he was going a few mental rounds of boxing with the district's community leader.

"Yes it will; however, I can't see how the full price of the memorial can be paid. The concert will be self-paid for with the artists from America, Australia and the local schools donating their time for free. I'm guessing when tickets go on sale; I won't have any problem filling seats. The real question then is does your Council and the local Tourist Association want to come aboard and be part of history?"

"You drive a hard bargain."

"No. I understand before you were Mayor your Council flatly refused to help the parents of the dead boys with any grants. Your Tourist Association didn't quite exist then. However, now we have new times with a new Mayor and a new body looking for places for people to visit. I can help put Brighton on the map with this concert and the bench will stand in memoriam long after we're both gone. The question remains as to whether you want to come aboard or be left out as both projects will go ahead one way or another?"

"Mr. Sutton you have some compelling arguments. You quite rightly say the Council refused requests for grants from the boys' parents. It was a time of financial problems across the whole of the United Kingdom."

"Yes, and the answer helped drive people from this district. I understand more people want to leave as there is nothing to hold them here anymore. The memorial I propose would give them a purpose to stay and also attract others to visit the site."

"What about the concert?"

"I have the US Military Band led by a former member of the All American Boys Choir that sang here for the memorial service coming here as the main attraction. They'll be joined by a Captain from the Australian Army Band who was a member of the Australian National Boys Choir and also sang here for the memorial service. Father Kirby is organising two school choirs to combine to sing here. This place will be packed to the rafters. Will you come aboard?"

"When will it be held?"

"The concert will be held at 3 pm on Remembrance Day so the Americans and Aussie can attend services in London first."

"I'm very impressed with what you are doing and why. You'll have to put an application into Council and I'll bring up your suggestions at the Tourist Association."

"Mr. Mayor come to Sutton Hall tonight at 7 pm and meet some of your constituents. I'm holding a meeting with the parents of the boys still living in the district to explain what I've just told you. My next move is to go to the Chamber of Commerce and the Media seeking help if Council and the Tourist Association don't back the boys this time around."

"Mr. Sutton I'll be at Sutton Hall at 7 pm."

"Thank you, Mr. Mayor. Oh, by the way, please bring a collapsible chair as I'm short on seats."

The two men rang off. John slumped in his chair for a few moments to think about the conversation he had just had. Typical politician – fill in this form or that – no affirmative action. John picked up the phone and dialled Peter Brown, the stonemason. He wanted him along tonight to explain the cost of the stone and the work involved. John punched the air in delight when Brown said he would be happy to attend. John swivelled his chair around to his poster and wrote the words "Mayor" and "stonemason" and then circled them. It was time for a cup of tea – he had earned it.

John poured himself a cup of tea and sat in his breakout area. He was happy but disappointed. Happy both the mayor and stonemason would be along tonight to talk to the parents, but disappointed because he had no definitive agreement with the mayor. John believed his concert would set some things right. First, it would allow the boys to move on – how, he wasn't sure yet. Secondly, it would allow the parents of the boys to complete their grieving. Thirdly, the memorial would give the district a new tourist attraction and the boys' parents somewhere to commune with their dead sons in a familiar setting.

John returned to his workspace and rang Barry Cooper to apprise him of the latest news.

"That's sort of good news John," Cooper said slowly as he thought about what he had just been told. "If there is a hint of conflict between the Council, the Tourist Association and our boys' parents then we have a top story ready to be printed."

"I was thinking more of the ballot box if Council refused a grant this time around."

"Yes. The mayor was elected on a slim majority but could easily be defeated in Council if there was enough community support for the Opposition and Independents. That's great news about the stonemason – he's a lovely man who has always helped out when needed. I'm putting the finishing touches to my public affairs plan and will bring you a copy tonight. Have you spoken with Father Kirby about your latest developments?"

"No. He's next on my list."

"Well ring him and let him know what Butler said. He has some good contacts in the district."

"Okay, thanks, Barry."

John then rang Kirby and updated him on what was happening. Kirby listened intently and then started laughing.

"Sorry John, but you have to love our parents, don't you?" Kirby asked.

"I'm not with you."

"Remember I said I was going to see Mrs. Butler and several sick people the other day?"

"Yes, now that you mention it."

"Well, I planted the seed with Graham's mother Veronica about your concert and memorial. She was quite taken by your proposal. Veronica used to make the boys' albs including Graham's when he served with me."

"That explains why he was questioning my motives. What about the calls both the Tourist Association and I received for concert tickets? Did you do a ring around?"

"No; but I bet Veronica started to marshal her friends to come aboard and assist. They've probably got your number from directory assistance. Don't worry; I'm pretty sure Graham will come around."

John gave Kirby the green light to organise his combined choir. The priest said he would be at both schools that day in his secular role and would alert the choir masters.

"Would you mind if the boys and their respective teachers went to your workspace a few times to rehearse? It would also allow them to familiarise themselves with the old church?"

"No, that will be fine. Let me know the times and days and I'll ensure I'm here to open up and be here."

"Okay, thanks, John. See you tonight."

Tonight was shaping up to be an interesting affair. It was time for John to escape his workplace and go to the shops. He drove down to the village and scoured a couple of second-hand furniture places. It was in the second shop he found what he wanted – two very large metal teapots. They once belonged to a Scout group that was now defunct. He completed his shopping and returned to Sutton Hall. John unloaded his booty into the old church and then retrieved a collapsible table from the stables. He went to his home and found a tablecloth and some paper napkins. Now he was ready to set up. He went to his tearoom and cleaned the two teapots until they sparkled. John put the tablecloth, foam cups and teaspoons on the table. Milk, coffee, sugar and biscuits he would leave until the last minute to keep their freshness. He was ready for the meeting and returned to his home to make some lunch.

When the Suttons moved into Sutton Hall, they had a dual telephone line to John's workspace and the home installed. This way, John wouldn't miss a call. The phone rang while John was making a sandwich.

"Hello, Sutton Hall."

"Hello, Mr. Sutton?"

"Yes."

"Hi Mr. Sutton, I'm Albert Miller from The Brighton Post. I'd like to talk to you about your upcoming concert and the special memorial you have planned."

John laughed in his head. Things were moving quite rapidly.

"Hello Albert, how can I assist you?"

The pair talked for about ten minutes with John outlining what he had planned for both the concert and memorial.

"This is fantastic news Mr. Sutton. You will certainly put Brighton back on the map. Have you got a copy of the planned memorial?"

"Yes. Albert, what are you doing tonight?"

John invited Miller to attend the parents' meeting so he could gauge for himself how the parents and Mayor felt about his plans. Miller said he would check with his editor but would try and make the meeting. John finally made his sandwich and a cup of tea and was seated at the breakfast bar when the phone rang again. He was just about to flippantly say "Sutton Hall concert enquiries ..." but held his tongue when he heard one of his work colleagues.

"Hey John, it's Mitchell. I'm looking for some words to help describe the last band you re-recorded for us. I need it for its album cover and Media Release."

Mitchell Coppock worked in the publicity department of John's main office area.

"Hi, Mitchell. No probs. What would you like to know?"

John worked with Coppock for a few minutes to describe the music of the band and the types of songs he had recorded. The penny finally dropped with John about his concert.

"Mitchell, seeing you write a lot of the PR blurbs for our

company you must have some reasonable current contacts with the metropolitan and national Media?"

"Yes. I work with a lot of the music industry Media. What did you have in mind?"

John outlined what he was doing for the boys' concert and memorial and asked whether Coppock could help place some material with the major Media outlets.

"Yes, I can organise what you're after and also work with your local contact. Let me know when you're ready and I'll move on it for you. Your concert may be something the nationals are looking for at the moment with all the doom and gloom around. I remember reading extensively about the boys and how they all died in that terrible bus crash. This story of yours could give the nation a lift. Let me know when you're ready."

"Thanks, Mitchell, I will."

John was chuffed. He couldn't remember when a project of his went so well with virtually everyone pulling for him. The proof came within thirty minutes of talking to Coppock. John's recording boss Peter Allan rang him rather excitedly.

"Hello John; Mitchell just told me of your little project at Sutton Hall. I think what you are doing is excellent. Have you thought of involving us at all?"

"Hi Peter; absolutely, but I have to get all the pieces in place first, which is why I hadn't said anything to you just yet."

"I know your work is primarily with tomorrow's recording stars today, but it would be great to record this concert of yours. It would give our company the depth and reach we need. The publicity generated on a national and international basis would be fantastic not only for us but also for the families of the boys killed in that horrific accident."

John thought for a moment and decided to strike swiftly with his boss.

"You know, the reason for me holding this concert is to help raise money for a memorial for the choir."

"Okay, how can I help?"

John outlined the costs of the memorial seat and the fight that seemed to be brewing with the Council and Tourist Association to have something erected in memory of the choir. Allan was quick to respond.

"I think what you are doing is pretty noble. I know for a fact you didn't know any of the boys, so what you are doing is driven by community interest."

"Peter, how do you know I'm not related to the boys in some way?"

"Easy; I'm Bradley Worth's brother-in-law and helped put together their only CD a decade ago!"

It was John's turn to be shocked. He had worked with Allan for more than five years and his boss had never mentioned anything about the St Dominic Savio's choir or any other boys' choir.

"It's amazing how coincidences work Peter. Mel brought home the boys' CD just recently so I could hear them sing. I didn't see our company trademark or label anywhere on it."

"No, and you won't. I had my private recording label I used for love jobs and did the CD as a special for Brad. I married his sister Heather and used to attend the boys' recitals and concerts – they were great. It was me who talked Brad into recording his 12 songs. We had plans for a second CD when the choir returned from their visit to Australia."

"Peter, do you have any songs left over from the album?"

"Yes, I think I have one left over. It didn't fit in with the CD so I kept it for inclusion in their second album. Ahh, yes, I remember now it's a song of peace or something. It's called Soldiers Cry and had a Jewish subtitle in it ... got it. It was called *Soldiers Cry Oseh Shalom*."

"You mean you've got the boys singing a military song?"

"Yes, you sound quite surprised."

"Peter, it's just amazing how many connections these boys had and who is coming out of the woodwork. I was hoping to find some sort of military connection to draw on with the boys because of the Aussie and Americans coming here to help out. You've just blown me away. If you find the copy, would you shoot it over to me, please? Also, for me to record this concert properly I'll need some extra equipment on the day."

"No problems. Consider it my contribution. I'll send you the copy of *Soldiers Cry* once I find it. The rest we can talk about as you work out what you need."

"Thanks, boss. This will mean a real lot to the parents and the local community."

"Okay, no problems. Watch your emails."

John couldn't believe the conversation he had just had. In his mind, he had started mapping out what recording equipment he may need for the concert and how he would approach his boss to have the song compilation pressed into CDs. Now his boss was approving what he had planned and was asking what John needed to complete the task. This had to be some sort of divine intervention! He jotted down a list of equipment he would need. This included extra microphones; cables, an amplifier, and fold-back speakers for the artists to hear on stage. The list also included a compressor for his mixer so he could amplify the quieter sounds of the artists and outside broadcast public address speakers. John wrote an email to Allan using his laptop thanking him for his support and outlining what equipment he forecasted he would require for the concert. He then wrote 'concert recording equipment' on a sticky note ready to post on his project wall, circled and ticked it. The front door opened and Melanie entered Sutton Hall with a few grocery bags under her arms. John went up the hallway to meet his wife and help her with the groceries.

"Hi love, have a good day in London?"

"Grrr, the traffic was horrendous. There must have been some international congress in the heart of the city or something. I wouldn't mind moving my work to here and save all the time and frustration of being in the city."

John laughed as he helped unpack the grocery bags. The thought of Melanie working in Sutton Hall while he worked in the former church was attractive. The problem was the clientele she attracted in the city could afford more for her services than the nearby villagers. He could see eventually Melanie would split her time between working at Sutton Hall to cater for locals and London for others.

Melanie filled the kettle with water and started organising a pot of tea for them both. This was her calm time and she needed to relax before starting to make dinner for the pair of them and Caroline Bailey.

"What time is Caroline due?" Melanie asked.

"She should be here about 6 pm so we can have a walk around the graveyard and see where the memorial could be positioned."

"Okay, I'll finish this cuppa and start making dinner. So what happened today?"

John felt he was adding to a continuing soap opera but wanted to ensure his wife was up to date with all that was occurring with the concert. Melanie chuckled when John told her about the stonemason, the reporter and his boss. She sneered when he mentioned the mayor and his official response.

"Well, you must have felt quite chuffed when Peter Allan told you he was married to the sister of the boys' choir director?"

"I nearly fell off my seat when Peter described his connection. This concert has had more twists and turns in it yet everything is pushing for it to happen."

"Well in a sense, I'm not looking forward to the post-concert time."

"Why not?"

"Well, hopefully, the boys would have moved on and this place will revert to what it should have been, just a quiet area on top of the hill."

"When this is over, I think it will take me a little while to come down from all the intrigue. I believe I have spoken with spirits before but not like this. I've never worked for spirits either or watched them pull things together to make an event happen. It's just an eye-opener."

John went over his notes for the night and printed off a

checklist of items to talk about. He knew he had some control over the meeting, but side issues would come up and could possibly divert his attention – hence the notes to keep him on track. He started walking into the kitchen to assist Melanie when the doorbell rang.

"Hi John," Caroline Bailey said. "I hope I'm not too early."

John looked at his watch and then realised the time had gotten away from him. It was now 5.50 pm.

"Caroline, no problems at all, please come in and meet Melanie."

Bailey made her way into the kitchen and met Melanie. She gave the couple a bottle of white wine and showed them her completed sketch of her proposed memorial seat.

"Caroline, this is fantastic," Melanie said. "John told me he was really taken with your proposal and initial sketch, but this is just fantastic."

"Thanks, Melanie, I guess the real proof will be how the parents of the boys receive it."

"I understand your point, but regardless, I think your whole concept is nothing short of fantastic."

"Thank you, I do my best to please."

John put the wine in the fridge and then looked from Melanie to Caroline.

"Okay, I think I better show you around while Mel gets our wonderful board of fare underway."

"Thanks, John," Mel said as she went back to peeling some potatoes.

John walked with Caroline to the graveyard where the pair took in the view.

"What a wonderful sight," Bailey said as she took in the vista. "This will be a really nice area for the seat."

"Yes, I think so too. It's almost as if there is no other place than here for the seat or memorial."

"I think you're right. The other sides of the old church don't have the views. It's funny how the living saves some of the best views for the dead."

"Yes. I've seen several graveyards that have tremendous views of the ocean or valleys. The living would pay handsomely for the same privilege."

"Well yes John, but I'd rather be alive. If you're okay with here for the seat, do you mind showing me around the old church please?"

"No, I was about to take you in any way. I've had a pretty busy day today and there are a lot of things to tell you. One of the most important is that a second boy spoke to me today."

Caroline stopped walking and looked at John. "Was he scared or anything?"

"I don't think so. He introduced himself as Richard, the son of the musical director. Richard said he and the first boy I spoke to, Blake, used to sing duets together."

"Did he have a message for you?"

John was slightly taken back by the artist's question. "Yes. He said the boys were all happy with what I have been trying to organise for them."

"Good. This all bodes well for a successful concert."

John then detailed what Richard had said and how the rest of the day had panned out. He took Caroline into his workspace and showed her the plaque on the wall.

"What a handsome lot of boys! They would brighten any place they sang just by their smiles. I'm looking forward to hearing them sing."

John gave Caroline a tour of the old church including his tearoom and the 'faulty' light switch. The artist made her way to the chairs John had already set up and stood in silence. She closed her eyes; slowed her breathing and raised her hands in front of her. John watched intently as Bailey seemed to be gently nodding her head as if in conversation with someone. A large smile enveloped Bailey as she opened her eyes and focused on John.

"The boys are very happy with you and all the work you are doing for them," Bailey said. "They told me they are really looking forward to the concert as it will be the first time since they died all their parents will be together."

"Who spoke with you? How were you able to do that?"

"A couple of the boys and a lady – a Mrs. Connelly, I think she said. She apparently used to be the Concert Master here. One of many traits is that I can sometimes reach out to the dead as a Medium. It has helped me quite a bit with my paintings."

"That's fantastic, thank you, boys. Thank you, Mrs. Connelly."

"They said you should play the song your boss left you."

"What the …? This would be the song left off the boys' CD my boss told me about this afternoon. See, you can't put anything past them, can you?" John laughed.

"No apparently not."

John walked over to the computer on his workbench

and logged on. He had an email from Peter Allan with an attachment. He read the email aloud to Bailey.

> *John,*
> *I found the song we talked about. It was first recorded by a Canadian choir. I checked out Oseh Shalom and it means something along the lines of 'A prayer for peace.'*
> *I hope you enjoy it.*
> *Peter*

John opened the attachment and found the *Soldiers Cry (Oseh Shalom)* song by Jeff Klepper. He put on his earphones, played a portion and adjusted his sound levels.

"This sounds really good. I'll put it on speakers while I record a copy."

John joined Caroline who was sitting in one of the seats ready for the meeting. When the music played and the boys sang, both John and the artist found it hard to contain themselves. They both shed tears as the six-minute-long song was played. Caroline took out a handkerchief and wiped her eyes. John used his hands to clean his eyes.

"I haven't heard such a moving song for a long time," Bailey said.

"Me neither. It will really fit in well with the style of the concert I'm thinking about – especially with two Army Captains harmonising it."

"Yes. It has a lovely dual meaning."

"What do you mean?"

"The song is like a double entendre in which it can be

understood a couple of ways. It is about the ongoing troubles in Israel and Gaza but could also be our boys asking for their eternal peace."

"Well, this will certainly stir the hearts. Maybe once the mayor hears it he'll quite willingly come aboard the project."

"I'm surprised he's not already. When he saw the initial sketch of the seat in my studio, he seemed quite pleased with the concept. He probably just needs a good outpouring of community spirit."

"Caroline, I think you're right. Maybe tonight he'll get it. We better head back to Sutton Hall or Melanie will be wondering where the hell we are."

"John thanks for showing me around. I enjoyed the tour and especially talking with Mrs. Connelly and the boys."

"No probs."

"Goodnight boys."

The light in John's tearoom flickered on and off. John laughed as he realised the boys were all ears.

Chapter Ten

B arry Cooper was the first to arrive for the meeting. He met John, Melanie and Bailey inside the old church and had a folder full of papers in one arm and a collapsible chair in the other. John made the quick introductions all around.

"I have a public affairs plan for you to have a look at and some flyers I did up using Caroline's sketch. I hope you don't mind?"

"Barry, that's great, thank you. I hadn't thought of any flyers. I've been too focused on tonight and the actual concert. I did have some good luck this afternoon though," John said.

"What was that?"

"Well I understand my boss Peter Allan is Brad Worth's brother-in-law."

"Yes. He married Brad's sister Heather. Their son Adrian would have been a cousin of Richard. I didn't realise your connection, sorry."

"Connection? Peter has given me the song not included on our choir's first CD and also said he will give me the equipment needed to record our concert as a CD."

"Excellent. What song?"

"It's the Soldier's Cry one."

"Ah yes, it's a very moving song. We laboured over its inclusion on the CD, but as it was reflecting military tones from overseas we decided not to include it."

"Well, as the concert is set for Remembrance Day it now would be quite fitting, don't you think?"

"Yes. All things change and I think you'd be a winner with it. Any chance of a copy please?"

"No problems Barry, I'll organise it tomorrow for you."

"Thanks. Well, we'd better go over anything you want to discuss before the others arrive."

Within minutes ribbons of light could be seen forming down the valley as cars started filling the roads leading to the former church. The car park had never been so full since the Suttons took ownership. Voices began echoing outside the stone building as parents and relatives of the boys and youth choir started arriving. Each person had a collapsible chair and all were keen to look around John's workspace and meet both him and Bailey. The artist had placed a large copy of her sketch on a wall for all to see and groups of parents milled around it, pointing to it and nodding with approval. The stonemason Peter Brown, Father Kirby and the Brighton Post reporter were the last to arrive.

"Brendan, should we wait for the mayor or make a start?" John asked.

"It's been five minutes since he should have been here, we should ..."

"Hi everyone; my apologies for being late," the mayor blurted out as he stormed into the former church. "I got caught up on Council business."

Butler looked around the crowd and saw the Brighton Post reporter taking notes and went red-faced. He had received a drubbing in the paper recently over some of his Council's proposals and plans. Now they'll probably report he couldn't be on time for this meeting, he thought. Butler shook a few people's hands and then sat down on his collapsible chair.

John took centre stage and introduced Melanie and himself. He outlined how he bought the former church and was quite moved when he saw the boys' plaque on the wall. Several parents instinctively turned their heads to where the plaque was affixed. John said he realised there was no memorial for the boys and youths who had died on their way to tour down under and wondered what could be done. He outlined how he had linked up with Father Kirby; Cooper, Bailey, the mayor, and Peter Brown, to discuss an actual memorial. John had set up a projector screen and using his laptop and a data projector showed the crowd images of the outside of the former church and graveyard.

"You'll see that from this high point there are beautiful uninterrupted views of the district," John said. "It's quiet and not disturbed by overhead aircraft, heavy traffic or neighbours. If Caroline's memorial bench was agreed to and placed here within the graveyard it means no one can take it away and also you can visit any time you wish. I know there is a lot to think about, but I come to you with solutions, not problems."

An enthusiastic round of applause erupted as parents looked at each other and nodded. John then detailed how he had been in touch with choirs from America and Australia and his intention to hold and record a concert on Remembrance Day in the former church. All funds received would go towards the memorial. Another rousing applause echoed in the building as parents and relatives stood up en masse and cheered.

"The Mayor has gone into great detail with me about how I must submit particular forms to gain permission to build any monument outside in the graveyard. Thank you, Mr. Mayor."

Butler went to stand up to acknowledge John but when a cacophony of jeers started rising from the crowd he sat back down. John jumped in to assist Butler.

"However, it all comes down to you as parents. You know I did not know your sons or any of you really until tonight. However, we have a chance to correct the situation if you want to. It's up to you!"

John introduced Bailey and Brown to discuss the memorial in detail. He then did a head count and found he had sixty people at the meeting. Again, when Bailey and Brown spoke about the memorial the building broke into applause and cheers. John believed he was a winner with his project. Several parents stood and introduced themselves and gave their unqualified support for the memorial and concert. A couple thought a memorial should be built at the accident site, however, they stopped pressing their point by the time it was quite clear the majority of parents were behind John.

Father Kirby stood and gave his unqualified support to John and detailed what he was proposing for the concert with the two school choirs combining in support of the American military band and the Australian singer. Again the old church echoed with cheers and applause. John then called on Butler to address the group.

"Thanks, John, for a fine presentation and for allowing us to meet in your workspace," Butler said. "I think many of us have had a huge shot of nostalgia tonight when we entered what used to be the church we either served in or attended. This was the place where we welcomed our little ones into the world and sent others on their journey back to God."

Butler paused as he looked around the stone building and gathered his thoughts.

"I first saw Miss Bailey's proposed memorial sketch in her studio when I had the last sitting for my Mayoral painting. I can tell you, I was quite taken aback when she explained what it was proposed for. Then within a short time, my Tourist Association and Mayoral office phones rang off the hook about enquiries for Mr. Sutton's concert. I hadn't even met the man, yet I began fielding enquiries for him about a concert he had not spoken to me about. I've had some Councillors also contact me about the upcoming concert and give their support. When I told them about the memorial they were ecstatic. Now I've got the full information I can advise them."

Applause broke out along with people voicing "here, here." Before Butler could continue Cooper asked the mayor whether the Council or Tourist Association would fund the memorial. He said there was still time for the memorial to be built before Remembrance Day and it could be officially dedicated on the day of the concert. The parents cheered and clapped enthusiastically in support of Cooper.

"Thanks, Barry, but I need to have the Council and Tourist Association formally vote on the proposal," Butler said "Also,

Mr. Sutton will still have to submit his proposal and plans, so I have something tangible to give both organisations."

A thick-set man with a large, booming voice then stood up and introduced himself. "Mr. Sutton, I'm Neville Davies – my son Paul sang in the choir and died in the accident. I know we'll never bring our boys back, but it is really gratifying to know someone who never knew our sons wants to champion their cause. Thank you. I'm a former Council officer and would be very pleased to help you submit any forms the mayor needs."

Davies went over to where John was sitting and shook his hand to heavy applause. He was quickly followed by several parents who wanted to thank the Suttons and Bailey for their work. The meeting broke up pretty quickly with the parents wanting to talk to the Suttons, Bailey and Brown.

Cooper asked John if would play the boys' CD during supper. John agreed and went to his console. He found the choir's original 12-song CD and started playing it. Within seconds the hubbub died down to quiet tones as the parents listened to their boys sing as they continued their conversations. Melanie, Bailey and a couple of parents assisted in pouring teas and coffees and cutting and serving the various cakes people had brought along. John watched for a while as both Father Kirby and Butler worked the crowd. He then went outside to get some fresh air and saw several parents standing in the graveyard. Emotion boiled up inside him as he saw three couples standing quietly where the memorial was destined to be positioned. From a distance, the casual observer could have been easily misled into thinking the couples were admiring the view. In reality, they were communing with their dead sons.

"John, please don't go away," Elspeth McCready said as John turned to leave the parents in peace.

"This will be a wonderful place for a memorial to our son. We're all so pleased you organised tonight and we're looking forward to the concert."

"Thank you," John said as he wiped away some tears. "I am too."

"You know, we hadn't thought of a stone bench seat," Mrs. McCready said. "After the accident, we all went numb for a while. When conversations came up about a memorial, we parents could never really agree."

"What was the sticking point?"

"Some people wanted a series of statues depicting the boys but then it came down to how many boys, who will be the model for the faces, that sort of thing. Eventually, it all became too hard. Then when the Council wouldn't help, we just shelved the idea. Eventually, people started moving away."

"I'm sorry to hear that. This would have been a beautiful church in its day."

"Oh, it was. However, you have to be a realist with the number of people that could support it."

"Well, I can assure you the memorial will go ahead one way or another and so will the concert. Your boys will have one last hurrah before we leave them in peace."

Mrs. McCready stepped closer to John and hugged him. He saw the tears rolling down her cheeks as she gave him a mother's embrace with trembling arms. Her husband Robert then shook his hands before wiping tears away from his eyes too.

"Bruce would be happy with all this. He was our son and was only twelve when he died in the bus. Soon we'll be able to sit in the quiet here where he used to sing and practice and talk with him in the beauty of our valley. This is a special time for us all."

John blew his nose and nodded. He then walked back inside the building.

"Are you okay?" Father Kirby asked John.

"Yes. I guess I'm just seeing the human side of all this for the first time."

Father Kirby put an arm on John's shoulder and nodded. "Welcome to my world."

Bailey and Melanie joined the two men after they had cleaned down the last trestle table.

"What do you think? Are you happy with how tonight turned out?" Melanie asked.

"I am ecstatic how well the whole concept was received," John said. "The parents were really keen; I now have help with the forms to submit to Council and I know we have excellent support for both the memorial and concert."

Bailey nodded and a huge smile engulfed her face as she looked around. "I'm really glad John. The whole project is positive, no one can really lose."

"Well, I guess it's time you completed your artwork for the bench so we can give it to the stone mason to start work."

"Who will fund it?" Kirby asked.

"The stone mason said he would complete the work and wait for payment after the concert, so we actually had the finished product to launch on the day."

"That's good John. Now I need to get some choirs here for practice. Will next week suit you?"

"That's fine by me. I won't be going anywhere. Caroline when do you think you'll have your finished artwork to the stone mason."

"By the end of this week," Caroline said as she looked at her diary. "I have a gap in appointments and will have the time to complete the work then."

"Thank you. Well team this should be another great week."

Both Kirby and Bailey drove off leaving John and Melanie waving after them. The couple returned to the inside of the former church to ensure the place was ready for John to use the next day.

"You know love, I'm really looking forward to us having our own kids," John said as he hugged and kissed his wife.

"What's brought this on?"

"Watching the beautiful love the boys' parents showed for their children tonight. In a sense, I'll miss the boys when they go."

John smiled and then spoke loudly. "Well boys, I hope you all enjoyed tonight. I know you believe I'm on track with things, but I hope you enjoyed seeing the parents here."

Both Melanie and John chuckled as they headed out of the building. Before they reached the door the light in the tearoom went off and on a few times. The couple then burst out laughing. John raised his right hand, closed his fist and gave the thumbs-up sign.

Chapter Eleven

Neville Davies kept to his word. The former Council Officer rang John the morning after the parents' meeting and asked to see him. Davies arrived at the former church a short time later with a series of papers for John to sign.

"What's all this Neville?"

"I went to the Council Chambers this morning and picked up the papers the mayor wants you to sign and submit to Council for the memorial. It won't take you long to sign them. I'll take you through them first so you know what they're about."

"Neville, thank you – I really appreciate the effort you have made for me. I didn't have a clue what papers the mayor wanted and he wasn't exactly forthcoming with the information either."

"Yeah well, he's like that. The mayor likes to hold things close to his chest."

"Would you like a cup of tea?"

"Yes. I'd love one thanks."

"Follow me into my tearoom and I'll make us both a brew."

Davies stopped and took in the space leading to the tearoom, smiled and shook his head.

"What's up?"

"My family and I used to sit about here when this place was

a church. Every Sunday we'd be here in the second seat on the right from the front."

"Sounds a bit monotonous, doesn't it? The same seat every week?"

"Well, that's the way we did things around here. We didn't quite see it as monotonous as just knowing our place I suspect."

Both men laughed as they realised the folly of how things were done in the former church.

"You know, John, this place used to really sound fantastic when the organ was being played and the boys were in full voice. A pin could have been heard dropping between notes."

"Neville, you know the reason I bought the property was because of the beautiful harmonics in this building. I imagine it sounds a lot different to you now compared to when this place was packed?"

"I don't know. I heard you play the boy's CD last night, but it was at a low level – you know, like dinner music."

John went to his control desk and flicked a few buttons. He looked up at Davies with an impish smile.

"Okay Neville, you forced me. Would you like to hear the boys at a much more intense level?"

"John that would be fantastic thanks."

John started playing the boys' CD loudly and then joined Davies in the breakout area outside his tearoom. Davies sipped his tea slowly and took in the boys singing, seemingly hanging off every note. John saw Davies flinch a couple of times as if something unknowing had touched him, but said nothing to distract him. He wondered whether Davies's son Paul had touched him to let him know he was still around.

"You have the sound organised so it's almost like the boys are still here. It's an amazing feeling hearing their songs with such good speakers and playback facilities."

"Well, you'd only get this system if you were working for a record company. Believe me; I couldn't afford it for myself otherwise."

The pair enjoyed listening to the boys' CD and refilled their cups. At the conclusion, Davies stood up and John noticed the man's eyes were moist.

"Can I ask one more favour, John?"

"Sure Neville, ask away?"

"Will you show me where the memorial bench will be placed, please?"

"Step right this way sir, and I'll give you the grand tour."

John took Davies out to the graveyard and showed him where he suggested the bench be placed. Davies stood motionless on the spot and closed his eyes. John recognised the same posture as the McCreadys and some other parents who wanted to feel what it was like on the mound. He knew he had made the right decision to help the boys by the way the parents were acting. John watched quietly as Davies stood still, clutching the Council papers in one hand. Slowly the big man opened his eyes and then wiped away some tears that had welled up.

"This is a beautiful spot John," Davies said. "It sure beats having it in the old church or on a street corner. At least here, parents can come in private and take in the surroundings while thinking or talking to the boys and not disturbing anyone. Thank you."

"No probs Neville. If I didn't believe in the project, I wouldn't do it. Consider it my community service as a newcomer."

Davies chuckled and shook John's hand before driving back to Council to lodge his forms. John went back to work. He wrote on his board 'memorial forms lodged' and then circled and ticked it. He then rang Bailey to alert her of the submission.

"Hi Caroline, it's John Sutton, how are you?"

"Hi John, I'm fine thanks. What's up?"

"Excellent. I just wanted to let you know Neville Davies was over here earlier with the forms for Council. We've filled them in and he's now on his way to actually submit them for us."

"That's good news, John. What did you think of the meeting last night?"

"I thought it was great. The parents seemed to like it. We had the mayor and the local paper there so I think everyone was happy. I took a few parents outside to where the memorial will be built and the raw emotion that came from them was something else. These kids were well loved."

"Yes, they were and still are. During the talks last night I spoke with Richard and Blake and they were overjoyed with what you had organised."

"Fantastic. Do you mind me asking, do you hear them in your mind, or do you see them?"

"I hear them in my head as plainly as I am hearing you, but I can't see them. Sometimes I have seen spirits, but I don't see them all the time. My mother is a medium and she sees them all the time."

"Well, that would have been interesting knowing you were surrounded by spirits as you were growing up. When you hear the boys do you feel any sensation?"

"Yes, mum attracts spirits for some reason; and yes, when I hear spirits I feel a cool shiver up my neck. Both Blake and Richard said they were looking forward to the new boys singing in the church."

"Brendan will be organising that today so I should have an answer possibly tonight as to when they will start practice." John paused for a moment. "Caroline, how will the boys move on?"

"Well, they've told you they can't move on until you hold a concert for them. This means that whatever feelings they had for people here still bind them to Earth. These should be released on the day of the concert. This will then allow them to move on in their spiritual journey."

John thought for a few seconds and took in what Bailey had just said. "We often hear people talking about spirits seeing the light and then going towards it. Is this an urban myth? What will happen with the boys?"

"No, it's not a myth. Once they feel you have completed all you said you agreed to do, it should almost be automatic. A wall of light should appear where the boys are currently and once they go to it all their cares will be over and their bonds to here broken – except when they want to return to visit people."

"Will we see the light?"

"No, only the boys will see it."

"Mmm, then we should have a great concert organised. Thank you for the insight. I'm sort of in two minds about the boys leaving. With the boys around, so many positive things have happened. I don't know what will happen when they go."

"I'm sure you'll find other positive projects to keep you busy – you're that sort of man."

"Thanks, Caroline."

The pair rang off and John went back to work re-recording a few pieces of music for his company. There was a lot to think about. If the concert didn't go ahead and the Americans pulled out what would happen? How would the boys move on? Would this cost him eternal damnation when it was his time to die? Phew, the ramifications of the concert falling through were many. He got through his workload and sat back at his desk to think about the concert. A small light blinked on the bottom of his computer screen to alert him of an incoming email. John opened his screen and saw the American singer Captain Andrew Jackson had written to him.

Hi John,

Thanks for sending over the material from Robert King. My band and I have tried it a few times and believe it will really work at your concert. We've tweaked some of the material to make it fit better and I'll send over an electronic demo recording shortly for you to hear.

Let me know how the new boys choir goes and what they intend to sing so we can organise some melodies. I've called Phillip and he's pretty keen to join us too and is also busy rehearsing.

Andrew

John smiled as he re-read the e-mail. He held off on replying as he wanted the latest information from Father Kirby. John started to relax and map out his work schedule when there was a knock at the door.

"Hi, Mr. Sutton?" a middle-aged bespectacled man asked as he viewed John and started to walk into the workplace.

"Yes. Who are …" John started to ask as he stood up but was cut off.

"Sorry to come unannounced. My name is Robert Kitchen. I'm the owner of the bus company whose bus crashed into the LPG truck carrying the choir that used to sing here. If you have a few minutes, I'd love to have a few words with you about your concert."

"Hi Robert, nice to meet you," John said as he shook Kitchen's hand. "I'm John. How can I help you?"

"Several employees told me today about the meeting you had last night with the parents of the dead boys and how you are trying to raise money for a memorial."

"Robert, let's go over to my breakout room. Would you like a cup of tea or coffee?"

"Yes, thanks, tea would be nice."

"Well yes, I had a meeting last night with the boys' parents to work out what we can do. How did your workers hear about it?"

Kitchen looked at John and laughed.

"No big meeting can be hidden around here. The village and surrounding district are eager for news of any sort and yours is everywhere today."

"Excellent," John said as he poured two teas and sat down. "I wanted to gauge their reaction before I put anything fully into motion."

"Do you mind me asking why you are doing this?"

"When my wife Melanie and I moved into this old church we saw the boys' plaque over there near the exit and made some enquiries. There was never a monument organised for the boys even though so many died at once."

"Yes, it was a bone of contention between lawyers, the government and this community for some time and it all seemed to die down. Maybe the Government was hoping it would all go away. However, I'm glad you have decided to do something about it and I'd like to offer some help."

"Thanks, Robert. What did you have in mind?"

"Well over the past decade my company has expanded, and we now have a reasonable fleet of vehicles spreading out through several communities and on to London. Maybe I can offer buses to pick up and return people from some central points to come here for the concert."

John sipped his tea for a moment and thought about buses. He figured the buses could do more than just transport people.

"Robert, do you have the buses that seem to kneel to allow wheelchair people and those with prams access through the front door?"

"Yes, I have around six of them, why?"

"Well, I was just thinking. So far I have been concentrating on what happens in this building – the concert. I haven't thought about outside."

It was Kitchen's turn to study John while he sipped his tea

and thought about what was just said. He then gave a slight nod.

"Robert, it would be fantastic if your company helped out by ferrying concert goers to and from here to a series of collection points. I'd take your advice on that."

"What about the *kneelie* buses?"

"Oh yes; they would be fantastic if they could be possibly lined up on either side of the roadway leading to this building. What we need is a parade to lead into the building! Your *kneelie* buses could play a good part in this without having to drive anywhere."

John talked through a series of concepts with Kitchen with both men agreeing to give further thought to the use of the buses. The two then went to the proposed site of the memorial. John showed Kitchen where he wanted the special stone seat and then bounced some more ideas off him about the buses. It wasn't long before Kitchen returned to his car and drove off.

"Well boys, there's your transport for people to get to and from here," John said aloud as he re-entered his workspace. He went to the board next to his desk and wrote 'buses' and 'transport'. He circled each and ticked them.

"Okay let's think about the outside of the old church," John said as if he was speaking to someone in front of him. "We'll probably have an overflow of people from in here. Where to put them and how do they take part in the concert? How do we fully utilise the fact the concert will be held on Remembrance Day – a national holiday?" John picked up a foam stress ball from his desk and started playing with it while he pondered his questions. His mind was racing as he thought through some scenarios. He completed a few more pieces of music for his work and was adjusting the sound controls on his desk panel when an unexpected voice rang out.

"Hi, darling – everything okay?" Melanie said as she walked into John's workspace.

John seemed to do a double take when he looked at his watch and realised the time. His day was virtually over and night had descended.

"Hi, honey. Have a good day with your students?"

"Yes, mine was nice. I had a few good wins with some of the younger students being able to complete their pieces almost perfectly. It's a nice feeling. What about you? How did your day go?"

"I've had some good wins too but I think it would be better to discuss all this over a nice bottle of wine and a lovely dinner."

The couple locked up the workspace and retreated into Sutton Hall. Melanie had brought some fish and chips on the way home and the meal's aroma filled the kitchen. John reached into the fridge and retrieved a bottle of white wine.

"You know love I think I'd like to eat outside tonight. It's not too cold and it would be good to just sit and view the district from our hill. What do you think?" Melanie asked as she grabbed two wine glasses from the cupboard.

"I think you're right as usual and I'll grab our chairs from the stable."

"Done; I'll get our jackets just in case it gets a bit fresh outside."

The couple split up and then met outside the old church

where the memorial seat would be built. The sky was cloudless and small zephyrs could be felt coming over the hill in bursts. Darkness filled the void between the old church and the road below leading to the district's residences and village shops. John placed the two camp chairs down and opened them up. Melanie placed their jackets around the top of each and the couple sat down to enjoy their dinner. John opened the wine and poured two glasses while Melanie opened the fish and chips.

"Mmm, that smells delicious. Thank you my sweet," John said as he took a handful of chips. "We should do this more often."

For the next half an hour the couple regaled each other with what had happened in their respective days. Twice the conversation stopped as one of them pointed to the stars to watch a falling star or space debris ignite into a speck of flame and then dip into the night sky horizon like a tiny match being waved by an invisible entity before being extinguished.

"I'll be glad when the memorial seat is built so we can come out here anytime we want and have a readymade place to sit," Melanie said.

"Well, it won't be long now."

"You'll have to give me the measurements so I can buy a couple of cushions."

"Cushions? How come?"

"Well these seats are nice but the memorial seat will be like a stone lounge so therefore it will be cold and hard to sit on for long periods. If we have our own cushions, it will save us getting cold and uncomfortable."

"I'll see what I can do. Actually, that's a great idea as we can tell the boys' parents and they can also buy some to take with them for their quiet moments here."

Melanie chuckled as she saw the concern John was showing more and more towards the choir. She knew he wouldn't rest until the concert was over and the boys had moved on. Over time Melanie had learned to leave John to complete the projects he set for himself and to offer him as much encouragement as she could. The rest would just happen as he was an organised person who would see through what he began and seek counsel on the way.

A shrill beeping sounded as John's mobile phone sounded.

"Hello Brendan, how did you go with your new choir?" John asked once he checked the front of the phone and saw Father Kirby's image light up the small screen.

"Great John. We're all set for tomorrow afternoon and will be at your place around 1 pm," Kirby said. "They'll have their music with them and will arrive in two small buses and a couple of cars."

"Don't forget to ensure they bring a chair to sit on as the last tenant cleared off with all the furniture."

The two men laughed.

"Have a guess where Mel and I are now?"

"By the sound of the background, you are outside somewhere. Maybe you're both on someone's verandah?"

"Close; we're sitting in the graveyard on the hill where the memorial seat will be built. We've just polished off a lovely round of fish and chips and a nice bottle of wine while we watched the night skies."

"Well done. I often used to stand out there and do my thinking as I found it so peaceful."

"Okay mate, I look forward to meeting the new St Dominic Savio choir tomorrow."

"Ahh yes – but these boys have decided to call themselves the Brighton Boys and Youth choir so there's no connection to our other boys."

"Well done. I'll see you tomorrow. Bye."

John replaced the phone in his pocket and looked at Melanie.

"Well, the concert is well and truly rolling now. Our guest boys' choir will be here at 1 pm tomorrow."

"That's good news. I hope you haven't got too much work on at the moment."

"No, and I'm looking forward to seeing the faces of the new boys. It will sort of give me an idea what our boys would look like."

"Come on my husband, I think you're becoming melancholy – we'd better pack up and go inside."

"Thank you for the lovely restaurant you chose tonight and for ordering the beautiful food. We can dine at Chez Suttons anytime."

The couple packed up their chairs and headed back to Sutton Hall with their arms around each other's waists. It was great to do something different together and share the experience.

Chapter Twelve

The first media call came at 6 am. John was roused from his sleep by the loud ringing of the home telephone. Today was publication day for the Brighton Post newspaper. However, the paper had arrangements with its parent company to send it a copy of the edition before full publication. Copies of any national stories from the Brighton Post were usually placed on the parent company website.

'*Bus Tragedy Choir's Memorial*' was the banner headline for the Brighton Post and its parent company carried the same heading for its first prominent national news story on its website. Reporters from other news houses usually trawled each other's websites looking for different stories to follow up in case one had a scoop on the other. Jamie Longford was no different.

"Hello, Mr. Sutton? I'm Jamie Longford from British wire services. Your story on the memorial for the boys' choir is set to get a lot of attention today."

"What the …? Sorry would you repeat what you just said please?"

John was instantly awake when he realised he was talking to a journalist who would be putting his comments on a story that could be seen internationally. Longford interviewed John for nearly fifteen minutes. John reiterated the history of the St Dominic Savio's Boys and Youth choir and how they were all wiped out in a horrific bus and truck accident. Also how he and Melanie had taken ownership of the former church and wanted to do something so the community could remember the boys who so tragically lost their lives in the fiery inferno truck crash. Also, so the parents would have a place to sit quietly and commune with them.

Longford asked about the American Army band that would be playing at the concert.

"This will be a 20-piece band led by Captain Andrew Jackson comprising trumpets; trombones and saxophones with these players doubling up to play flutes and clarinets," John said. "Other performers will include a pianist, guitarist, and percussionists who also play keyboard and glockenspiel. Captain Jackson and at least three others will also sing."

Longford queried John on the glockenspiel.

"This is a fantastic instrument the Americans will be bringing. It comprises a set of graduated steel bars mounted on a steel frame and struck with hammers.

"Captain Jackson was a former member of the All American Boys Choir who sang here at a memorial service for the St Dominic Savio's choir. He'll be joined by Australian Army Captain Phillip Boyce who also sang here for the memorial service when he was a member of the Australian National Boys Choir.

"Don't forget we'll have a new choir singing here from two local schools forming the Brighton Boys and Youth Choir!"

Longford was gobsmacked with the talent John had lined up for the former church.

"I guess the real question people are asking is why are you organising this concert and not the boys' parents, the Local Council or Tourist Association?"

John had read through the public affairs plan Barry Cooper had produced for the concert which had a series of key messages in it. During the interview with Longford John had got out of bed and gone to the lounge room and retrieved the plan so he had the right messages to say. It was great to have a radiotelephone in the house as it saved being restricted by short cords.

"Melanie and I are new to the area, and once we saw the plaque of the boys in the old church we wanted to do something for them."

John took Longford through a series of other key points before the pair rang off. He told Melanie he was about to have a busy day as his Brighton Post article had already started to attract major Media players. Before John could organise breakfast, he fielded three other Media calls, all from the radio. All had wanted to obtain voice grabs to run in their news bulletins throughout the day. John rang Cooper and gave him an update on his Media calls so far.

"Don't be surprised if the major daily newspapers and TV stations don't send out crews to see you too," Cooper said. "Do you want me to spend a few hours with you and help field calls?"

"Barry that would be fantastic – thank you."

"I'm on the way. Ensure the tea is ready."

John no sooner replaced the phone's receiver when Melanie kissed him goodbye. She didn't want to get caught up with the Media, this was John's project. John quickly showered, got dressed and made his way across to his workspace. He no sooner opened up and turned the lights on when Cooper was knocking at the door.

"Hi John, I knocked out a draft Media Release last night in case you need it for any Media that come in cold and want information."

"You're a champion, thank you."

"I took the liberty of quoting you a few times using the words you said at the parents' meeting. I don't think you'll find anything untoward."

John quickly read Cooper's Media Release and broke into a huge smile.

"This is fantastic. Thank you. I think it calls for a cup or three of tea."

The pair started laughing as John went to the breakout room and made the pair a pot of tea.

"You know John since you and Melanie came on the scene you have really stirred up emotions within the district."

"Positive emotions, I hope?"

"Yes; the boys' parents were at a stage of letting go of their memories of their dead sons. There was also a sense of pervading anger because there was no memorial built for their boys. You arrive and re-kindle our love for them and yet you never knew them."

"Thanks, Barry. I'll let you into a little secret. Melanie and I have been trying for a while to have our own children, which is one of the reasons we moved here. You know it is an emotional journey and when we saw the plaque of the boys our hearts just melted. We really felt we wanted to help them."

"How could you help the boys? They've all moved on." Cooper stared at John's eyes intently.

John was now in a quandary. Should he let slip what he knew about the boys?

"Ah, I've made a slip of the tongue. Once Mel and I saw the plaque we started making enquiries and then we found out you as parents really only had two plaques to commemorate the lives of your boys. I guess this depressed me to the point where I thought about what I would want. The rest, they say is history."

Cooper nodded and raised his cup of tea in salute.

"John, the parents are all so thankful for you and Melanie being here and helping out the way you have. Your reward will come at another time."

John smiled as he returned the salute by raising his cup of tea. "Barry, Mel and I seek no reward for anything we do. We're helping a great bunch of kids by assisting their parents. All we're after out of this is a happy district and village and a beautiful seat outside this old church to view the landscape and that no one can pull down."

Just then the light in the break-out room blinked and both men turned towards it.

"I'll have to get that fixed one day," John lied as he turned his head towards his computer.

"Must be the wiring or a faulty globe," Cooper said. "Do you want me to get a ladder and have a look?"

"No thanks Barry, I'll get to it soon enough," John said as he lied again to Cooper. He had no intention of fixing the light while the boys remained Earthbound.

The two men's repartee was cut short when there was a knock at the door. Both Cooper and John swung their heads around to see a young man in his mid-twenties dressed in a blue suit with his tie undone holding a notebook and pen in his hands. Beside him was a woman in her late twenties wearing slacks and a blouse and carrying a backpack. Cooper and John stood in unison to meet the pair.

"Hello, I'm Aaron Parnell and this is Bernice Ramsay. We're from The Sun newspaper and would like to speak with Mr. Sutton please."

"Hi Aaron, Bernice, I'm John Sutton and this is Barry Cooper, father of one of the boys who used to sing here. Would you like a cup of tea?"

"Yeah, that would be great – thanks it's quite a drive from London."

John made the newcomers a cup of tea each while Cooper spoke to the pair about the St Dominic Savio's Boys and Youth Choir. Once John returned to the break-out area Parnell trawled in his right suit pocket and retrieved a digital voice recorder and placed it on the coffee table. Cooper looked at John and did the same. Parnell interviewed the two men for around twenty minutes and then Ramsay took some photos of them and also John separately. The four went outside and John and Cooper were photographed where the stone memorial seat was scheduled to be erected. The Sun team then made their way to their car and drove off.

"I'm glad you had a digital recorder on you," John said. "I would never have thought to have had one for an interview."

"The Media interviews are my field. You have to have a digital voice recorder these days, so you have an exact copy of what the reporter has. Also, you have to let them know you have a copy so they know they can't quote you out of context. If you like we can quickly download a copy of the interview to your computer, so you have your own copy."

"Barry, that would be great, thanks."

The pair made their way into John's workspace and Cooper downloaded the audio file onto the computer.

"While we're here, have you checked out the online edition of the Brighton Post yet?" Cooper asked.

"No, I didn't know they had one and I haven't had time to go to the village and pick one up."

Cooper interrogated a web search engine and brought up the electronic version of the Brighton Post. He began to laugh as he pointed to a photo of John and Bailey with the artist's sketch of the memorial seat.

"This is a pretty good likeness of you two!"

John looked closer and smiled. He was achieving his aim to help the boys and had secured several helpers along the way. John read the story and laughed.

"Well we couldn't have got a better story printed about the parents" meeting and the memorial seat if we had paid for it," John said. "But there's only one thing ..."

A heavy knock sounded at the door and a woman in a two-piece skirt suit and two men in shirts and jeans stood in the doorway.

"Hello, we're from BBC1 TV and would like to talk with John Sutton please," the woman said in measured tones.

"Hi, I'm John Sutton and this Barry Cooper, one of the fathers of the boys who used to sing here."

"Mr. Sutton, I'm Monica Ryan and this is my sound recordist Andrew Gallard and my cameraman Keith Hay. Do you mind if we interview you about your upcoming concert and battle to get a stone memorial for the boys?"

"No, it would be a pleasure. Would you like a cup of tea?"

"No thanks it's a long way back to London and we have another job to do on the way."

Cooper briefed Ryan and her team on what John had been doing for the memorial; gave her a Media Release and showed her a copy of Bailey's sketch. Ryan was impressed. She asked for Sutton to be filmed re-recording some music as background overlay and then to go outside where the memorial was to be erected for an interview.

John chose to play songs from the boys' CD Melanie had bought. Hay filmed John placing his CD into the player and pressing several buttons to activate the various levels and sounds he wanted. While this was happening, Gallard recorded the various sounds he made and the resultant singing from the boys. John then walked outside to the graveyard and was interviewed by Ryan. Cooper stood to the side with his digital recorder in his outstretched hand and recorded the interview.

After Ryan had finished interviewing him, John wanted to know why such a small gesture as he was trying to do would have BBC TV wanting to film him.

"Well that's pretty easy," Ryan said. "This is one of the

biggest stories involving a mass group of people who have died since the 1966 Aberfan mine disaster. Although the boys have been dead for around a decade there continues to be a fight over some sort of memorial for them. You may have just solved it in one go."

"Thank you, I hope so," John said nonchalantly.

The BBC team packed up their gear and drove off in their station wagon.

"What do you think Barry? Am I pushing the right messages to achieve our aim?"

"I think you're a natural. It's a pity you weren't around ten years ago when the boys died. That interview should go over quite well – it has all the right ingredients including you at your normal work and the sound of our boys. You really couldn't ask for more."

John looked at his watch and winced.

"Well Brendan and his new choir will be here soon so this should be a fun afternoon."

"What time are they due?"

"Around 1 pm so they had plenty of time to finish lunch and organise themselves before being bussed here."

"Okay, well you have probably done all the interviews you'll have today. I'll go back home and send you a copy of the last interview's audio file."

"No probs thanks, Barry."

Cooper hesitated, seemed to bite his bottom lip and then looked at John.

"Do you mind if I come back this afternoon and film the rehearsal please?"

John realised the import of Cooper's question and how hard it was for him to ask it. He put a hand on Cooper's shoulder.

"It would be a pleasure to have you here. I'll bet Brendan needs a hand with handling the choir. After all, this is your forte too!"

The pair laughed and then Cooper drove off while John went back to his computer. He wrote on his folder next to his desk 'Media interviews' circled the words and then ticked them. Next, he checked his emails – none. This gave John some breathing space to clean up his tearoom and break-out area before the boys arrived.

Thirty minutes before the boys' choir was due to arrive; Caroline Bailey rang John with some heart-wrenching news.

"John, I'll bet you've been busy today?" Bailey asked.

"Just a wee bit. What's happening?"

"I spoke to my mother about the boys and what I told you about you completing your promise to them and then they could move on."

"Well, at least it sounds pretty simple."

"Yes – but there's more to it than I knew."

John detected nervousness in Bailey's voice. Almost as if she was scared of something. "You seem worried, Caroline."

"I guess, like you, I want to ensure we do the right thing and move the boys on."

"Okay, so what are you proposing?"

"I'd like to visit your workspace with my mother Margaret if that's alright? She can tell us more in detail about the multi-step plan she says we have to go through so the boys will move on spiritually."

"A multi-step plan eh? Sounds like a weight loss program. Caroline, virtually any time that suits you and your mother to come over please do. I'll be here every day this week."

"Thanks, John, I'll tee it up with mother and get back to you."

John now became perplexed as Bailey may have thrown a spanner in the works. He was dedicating a lot of time and energy to organising the boys' concert. The last thing he needed now was some small hiccup that could see the boys stranded between heaven and Earth.

Chapter Thirteen

John could hear the bus making its way up the hill to his workspace the moment it turned from the road onto the path leading to the former church. The cacophony of the children's voices rose like a freight train nearing a quiet suburban rail station. John went outside and saw Kirby alighting from his vehicle and then a male teacher stepped out of the bus.

"Hello, I'm John Sutton – welcome to Sutton Hall," John said as he went to shake hands with the teacher.

"Thank you, I'm Ken Duggan, Form Master for Brighton High School. This is a lovely spot. What great views!"

"Yes, and generally they are only for my wife Melanie and me – however, I am really keen to meet your boys."

Duggan called for the boys to alight from the bus and make their way into the former church. The boys were of varying shapes and sizes. The first lot wore long pants; short sleeve shirts and ties while the second wore short sleeve shirts, shorts and long socks. All had mops of hair that curled in some way across their face above their eyebrows. The earlier raucous noise on the bus died down as the boys entered John's workspace and the boys took in the sights of the building. Father Kirby introduced John to the boys as the new owner of the former church and then gave a rundown of what St Dominic Savio's used to look like. John made his way over to the second teacher and introduced himself and Barry Cooper who had arrived with a movie camera to film the rehearsal.

"Hi I'm John Sutton and this is Barry Cooper, a father of one of the St Dominic Savio boys."

"Hello John, Barry, I'm Ron McCrea, the Deputy Headmaster of Brighton Public School. Thanks for letting us practice here."

"Ron, you're most welcome," John said.

The boys were shown around John's workspace with explicit instructions not to touch his desk or recording equipment. Two boys went to the bus and retrieved a keyboard and stand while another two got collapsible chairs for their teachers. McCrae set up his keyboard in front of John's desk and plugged it into the power sockets. John looked at the keyboard and went back to his desk. He rummaged in a drawer and then retrieved a lead which he plugged into the rear of the keyboard and his amplifier. The moment McCrea tested the keyboard silence fell. It was the first time the boys had heard the keyboard so amplified before.

Duggan lined the boys up in front of John's breakout room where the altar once stood and arranged them in their various coral divisions – the sopranos and altos to the left and the tenors and bass singers to the right. Kirby sidled up to John and asked whether he could play *The Lion Sleeps Tonight* so the boys could hear how his former choir performed. John cued a CD and then played the song. He adjusted the volume and watched the boys' faces as the jungle noises could be heard and then the young choristers, followed by the older ones. Throughout the song, the Brighton boys nodded and mouthed the words in unison to the song as they had been learning it over the last week.

Once *The Lion Sleeps Tonight* had finished a cheer and a round of applause rang out from the Brighton boys as they acknowledged the St Dominic Savio's choir. Cooper stared at the boys from near John's desk and smiled. His eyes had begun to well up as tears formed.

"Okay, boys it's your turn. Let's show how we can breathe more life into this old building," Duggan said as he raised his hands ready to conduct them.

McCrea played the intro to the song and the boys mimicked their own animal noises in rhythm before they broke into the song proper. Cooper wiped his eyes with his handkerchief and then set up his movie camera and filmed the boys as they went through their various iterations of the song. The choir was good but needed a lot more practice. Duggan asked two boys to perform a duet and sing *Panis Angelicus*. All adult eyes were on the two boys – one aged twelve and the other fourteen, as they stepped forward. The mop-top haircuts were brushed to the side of their foreheads. The younger boy was wearing shorts and long socks while the older boy wore trousers. They readied themselves and watched Duggan for the cue as McCrea cranked up the keyboard. The moment the boys started singing emotions came to a head for Father Kirby, Cooper and John. The boys' voices were truly angelic and when the rest of the choir harmonised with them it was a feast for the ears. For Cooper and Kirby, the boys' voices morphed into their choir who once stood and sang proudly on the same spot. They listened in awe as the boys reached their high notes. John tweaked his left ear, smiled broadly, and nodded. An unseen choir had joined in unison with the Brighton Boys. For John, the whole of the former church was now reverberating with joyous song.

"Thanks, boys," John said quietly to himself. "You add tremendous energy and harmony to these other boys. I think they will do you proud."

At the end of the song, all the adults clapped and cheered and the boys took a bow.

"Bravo boys, bravo," Duggan said excitedly.

"Well done fellows, that was truly fantastic," Kirby said. "Is it time for a bit of fun?"

McCrae and Duggan smiled broadly as they knew where Kirby was going.

"This concert will be a salute to the armed forces of three countries and there'll be soldiers from each country playing and singing here. Some of the common songs for all the soldiers are in the medley you've been working on from the Second World War."

"Okay boys, let's let our hair down and put some fun into our soldiers' salute," Duggan said. "Take up your positions ..."

On cue, McCrae ramped up the keyboard and started playing *Bless Them All*. The boys began play-acting some of the lines with one lying down as if he was in bed and another about to bark imaginary orders as the Regimental Sergeant Major. Their skit was hilarious and had John, Cooper and

Father Kirby laughing haughtily. The boys rehearsed several other songs for more than an hour and a half before it was time to pack up.

"They were good," John said to Kirby.

"Yes, but I believe they will perform even better once they settle down into coming here for practice and relaxing into the various songs."

"I think Brendan's right," McCrae said. "They are a good bunch of boys with some pretty good talent. We still have time on our side for the concert."

"Yes, you're right," Kirby said. "We must ensure they each bring a collapsible chair next time they come so they have somewhere off the ground to sit."

John laughed as he thought about what he had said to Kirby previously about the former tenant taking all the chairs. Duggan, McCrea, Kirby, and Cooper gathered near John's desk.

"I guess one of the things we will need to do is work out what will happen on the day of the concert and have a full rehearsal of what you want to be done," Duggan said as he looked at John and Kirby.

"Yes, Ken, I'll have a good idea by the time you come here next so we can start kicking it around and see what works," John said as he turned off his recording equipment. "I've got to sit down with Barry here and work out what pomp we can add to the concert that is doable along with exactly what you want the boys to do when the Army members do their bits."

"Have the Americans and others been given a list of songs we'll be singing so they can practice their musical support?" McCrae asked.

"Yes, I've been keeping our military people in the loop with a list of songs and I've also had help from the musical director of the Australian National Boys Choir. He's been finding the music for the songs so we can go through them. I'll send you all a copy of what I have so it will make it easier for you."

"Excellent John, thank you," McCrae said. "Well Ken, we should get the boys back now so they can go home."

"You're right there Ron."

Duggan and McCrae organised for the boys to re-board the waiting bus and take the chairs and keyboard with them. Cooper and John waved them off and then re-entered John's work area.

"I bet that was hard for you," John said to Cooper as he put an arm on his shoulder and gave a gentle squeeze.

"Yes, but I had to chase my own demons away. The last thing I did with Blake and my boys was to stop them from singing *The Lion Sleeps Tonight* to try and get them to board the bus and get to the airport on time. To see the Brighton boys all file in and take up positions where my boys once stood and sang was gut-wrenching. Even more so with their normal chatter and play. Maybe this is why I wanted to be here this afternoon."

John bit down on his bottom lip and nodded as he realised the emotional gulf Cooper had just crossed.

"Barry, you are most welcome here anytime, you know that. If you want to film these Brighton boys as they rehearse and then do their concert, please do."

Cooper wiped some tears from his eyes and looked at John.

"We need to sit down as Ken suggested and actually work

out the program of events and what is missing, if anything, for the concert."

"I've had some ideas on this but you are quite right. Who do you want to involve in our planning session?"

"I'll get a couple of the parents of the St Dominic Savio's together as we used to plan all our boys' concerts. Collectively we should have some good contacts and ideas of how to stage this important day."

"Alright, I'll leave the organising up to you. We can all meet here if you like, as long as ..."

"We all bring collapsible chairs," Cooper said, and both men laughed.

Cooper picked up his camera equipment and left leaving John alone in his workspace. John went to his desk and turned on the computer. No emails from work, this gave him some breathing space. He typed an email to both Andrew Jackson and Phillip Boyce and told both men he had inadvertently missed out on involving a British Army band or singer for the concert and needed someone to contact. John then leant across to his poster, wrote 'Brighton boys' first performance' circled the words and then ticked them. He then added a date. John looked at his watch and realised the time. The main news bulletins were due to start in a few minutes and he needed to see if he was being shown on BBC1 TV and how.

John locked up his workspace and made it into his lounge room with moments to spare before the news bulletin began. He was just getting comfortable when the front door opened and Melanie entered carrying some groceries.

"Hi love, I may be on TV shortly. It's only just started," John said nervously.

The first item was about the United States of America and the British Government discussing their troop withdrawal from Afghanistan. The second item was about the former St Dominic Savio's and the fight of a newcomer resident to honour the boys and youths who died in the horrific bus crash that shook the nation ten years previously. Melanie quietly put her shopping down and stood watching the report with mouth agape. Her husband had made national news with his community project. At the end of the report, the announcer said details of the upcoming concert and how to donate monies would be placed on the channel's website.

John jumped up and punched the air. He went to Melanie and gave her a strong hug and kiss.

"Yes, yes! This should get the mayor on the side now."

"Or make him show his true feelings."

"What do you mean?"

"I can't work out why he seems to be hedging with you rather than coming straight out and saying he backs you 100 per cent. By the way, I want your autograph."

"Autograph? What for?"

"Now you are a TV celebrity you're famous."

It was Melanie's time to hug her husband and kiss him.

"I want you to know I'm very proud of you for sticking by the boys the way you have. Well done."

John then told Melanie about his media day and the first rehearsal by the Brighton boys. He explained the pained expression on the face of Barry Cooper as he filmed the new choir singing the old songs and then playacting with their military salute medley.

"You know love, it was almost breathtaking listening to the two boys sing their duet," John said.

"Why?"

"Once the duo arced up I heard the St Dominic Savio boys harmonise and sing with them. It was truly cathartic to hear the two choirs back the duo. I only wish I could have recorded it."

"Well, this tells me our boys are happy with the ones from Brighton and joined them to show their solidarity with what they are doing."

"That's probably more correct than you know. When I played *The Lion Sleeps Tonight* from our boys" CD the Brighton boys cheered and clapped them at the end as if our kids were actually there."

"How remarkable is that? Come on Mr. Sutton let's get some dinner so we can unwind together in front of the TV."

The couple picked up the shopping and headed to the kitchen.

"You know Mel, the way our boys sang today it was as if they were really enjoying themselves."

"Well let's hope they don't become too complacent. This concert of yours will help them go to a place where they can sing to their heart's delight. You know; a place without time."

"Mmm, I hope so."

Chapter Fourteen

John couldn't sleep. Something about Father Kirby's boys didn't sit right with him but he couldn't put his finger on it. The boys looked and acted like schoolboys. They sang reasonably well, and they acknowledged the St Dominic Savio's boys. He retrieved his laptop and went through his emails. Phillip Boyce had sent him one with the name and contact details of one of his British counterparts – Captain Courtney Stevens. John was impressed. He made a pot of tea and read Captain Stevens' biography. Stevens was serving with a Territorial Army Regiment nearby but was also an accomplished singer and musician in her own right.

Boyce said the Territorial Army was similar to Australia's Army Reserve. He said Stevens had entertained British troops in the Middle East and also been part of a couple of national tours by some big bands. John copied Stevens' email contacts and wrote her an email explaining what he was doing with his concert and inviting her and her Territorial Band to take part with Andrew Jackson and Phillip Boyce.

No sooner had he sent the email than Melanie walked into the kitchen and kissed him.

"Couldn't sleep again?" Melanie asked.

"No. Something is bothering me about the boys singing in the concert and I can't work out what it is."

"Didn't you say they looked and sounded alright at their rehearsal?"

"Yes, and to me they were great. They carried the songs well, they had good voices but something, I don't know what is lacking."

"Surely the boys' teachers or Brendan would have picked them up for not being up to par?"

"Well yes, so I could be completely wrong."

Melanie reached for the teapot and made herself a cup of tea. She held the cup to her mouth with both hands and sipped gently with her eyes closed. Melanie really savoured her first tea of the day.

"So who were you sending emails to so early in the morning?"

"Ahh, this is good news. Phillip Boyce has given me the name and contact details of his Army Reserve counterpart near here. Her name is Captain Courtney Stevens and she is apparently a well-known singer."

"Army Reserve ... and you don't know her work?"

"Yeah, they're the same as our Territorials. No, I haven't come across her before. I'll check with Mitchell when the office is open. If anyone should know her it will be him."

"Good luck then."

"Thanks. I think it must be time for some breakfast. Would you like some toast?"

"You must have read my mind thanks."

John made toast for he and his wife while Melanie grabbed the butter and jam from the refrigerator.

"What about you? Do you have much on today?"

"I have two possible new starters today who are brand new to piano. One's a 10-year-old boy and the other is a young mother who is keen to fulfil her dream of playing the piano."

"Good luck! You'll now have people from both ends of the maturity scale to deal with."

"Well you know, teaching a child is easier than adults as their minds are more open to learning, so we'll see."

Melanie walked closer to John and put her arms around him and then nibbled his ear.

"I hope you find what it is the boys are lacking so it can be fixed. I hate seeing you restless."

"Thanks. I'm not a music teacher so I really can't say it's the boys' singing and musical attributes. I guess from an older male perspective they seem to be lacking a spark of some kind."

"Well let's hope the teachers can provide whatever spark it is the boys need to make this concert a real winner. After all, we have 45 souls depending on this concert."

"Yes – I agree."

Melanie went and showered and left John to clean up the breakfast dishes. *A spark*, he thought. *Maybe that's what they need – someone to gee them up. Mmm if that's the case, what would happen if they got geed up and how do you gee up a teenage boy?*

John finished washing and wiping up the cups and plates and headed off to the shower. Melanie was out and was now getting dressed. By the time he was out of the shower Melanie had dressed and was on her way to work.

John went to work in his former church surroundings and got stuck into a number of recordings his boss had sent him. It was a quiet morning and John was really looking forward to seeing the choir return for their next rehearsal. He enjoyed the sounds of the boys as they skylarked and practised their songs. He stood somewhat in awe when they sang. All the time he was mentally comparing Father Kirby's choir to what the choir waiting to move on would have been like. He had spoken to two members of the original choir for this former church but not long enough to get a grip on their personalities. John turned his mind to his work and made the old sandstone building reverberate with sound as he toggled the switches on his recording panel to get various sound effects.

The phone rang and brought John back to reality.

"Hi John, it's Caroline," the artist said. "I've been able to tee my mother up to come and have a look at your workspace. When's a good time to come over?"

"Hi, Caroline. Any time this morning would be great."

"Thanks, John, we'll be over within the hour to explain to you what's needed for the boys."

"Thanks, Caroline – see you soon."

John got up from his desk and went to check there was plenty of milk and biscuits for his guests. He had to cast his mind back to what Caroline had said about moving the dead choir on. Apparently, something had to be done to convince them to go rather than just hold a concert on the premise they'll automatically 'see the light' and then move on.

It wasn't long before John heard a car pull up out the front of his workspace. He started making his way to the door when Caroline and her mother entered. While Caroline looked at John, her mother seemed to be nodding her head and looking all around the interior of the building. Her gaze fell on the boys' plaque at the door and a large smile enveloped her face as she ran her hands over the boys' images.

"Hi John, I'm glad you were able to see us. John, this is my mum, Margaret Hill, and she can assist us with the boys."

John looked at Caroline's mother quizzically.

"We don't have the same name," Caroline said. "After Mum and Dad separated, I decided to use my mother's maiden name."

"No probs, I understand."

John noted Mrs. Hill was slightly smaller in the frame than Caroline, and had wavy dark brown hair and a large smile.

"Hello Mrs. Hill, Caroline has told me you may be able to help move our boys on."

"Good morning, John, I hope so. I feel the presence of a large number of spirits in this church. A lot are very young and the rest older. They all love singing. It was the first thing I heard when we pulled up in the car. We'll have our work cut out for us but I am sure we can help you."

"Thanks, Margaret. The boys had beautiful voices and were apparently a good choir before their untimely demise. You said 'we' so who did you mean?"

Mrs. Hill looked John up and down and took her time in answering. "I have a couple of friends that have helped me move on other spirits caught on Earth without knowing where to go."

"How come?" John asked.

"Like your boys, they too died too quickly to say goodbye and were set to wander the Earth for all time until my group and I stepped in."

"What happened?"

Before Mrs. Hill could answer, Caroline asked if she and her mother could sit down.

"My apologies ladies, I should have been more gallant. Please come over to my breakout area and grab a seat. I'll organise a cup of tea if you like?"

"That would be very nice John, thank you," Mrs. Hill said rather formally as she and Caroline moved to the breakout area and sat down.

John made a pot of tea and brought it out on a tray with milk and sugar. He went back into his tearoom and retrieved some biscuits. Mrs. Hill sipped her tea and looked around.

"You know John, this would have been a beautiful church in its day," the older woman said. "It gives off a lovely warm feeling in here."

"I agree. Melanie liked the warmth of the stonework, and I loved the harmonics which is why I set up my studio here."

John felt Mrs. Hill really wasn't listening to what he was saying. Every time he spoke the middle-aged woman would start looking at him and then divert her attention around the room.

"Mrs. Hill, I get the feeling you are hearing more than my voice at present," John said to test his theory.

"When Caroline and I first arrived here I could hear what seemed like a boys' playground – you know with lots of different boys playing games. Since we entered your workspace, the noise changed to individuals singing various songs. Now the boys are assembled and are singing some beautiful hymns. This place is truly amazing."

Caroline could see the frustration building up in John. She looked at him and smiled as she sipped her tea.

"You know John, you are a lucky man in some respects," Caroline said.

"Why's that?"

"You have a beautiful boys' choir on tap and you don't have to feed, clothe or house them."

The three laughed as they each realised Caroline was trying to make light of the moment.

"You know, I'm very thrilled to be part of the boys but I am also quite keen to help them. After all, it was they who asked me for their help, not the other way around."

Mrs. Hill put down her cup of tea and searched John's face.

"Well, John there are a few steps we have to go through to actually help the boys and their teachers move on. They are not too involved but must be done so the boys can find their eternal rest."

John nodded and put down his cup of tea ready to listen to Caroline's mother.

"I'll have a couple of friends of mine with me in the church on the day of the concert," Mrs. Hill said. "The first thing we'll be doing is going into a trance so we can centre our energies on the boys. Then we'll be inviting the boys' spirits to come to us so we can talk to them."

"But they're already here," John said.

"Yes, but we want them to come close to us so we can talk to them – sort of as close as you and I are now."

"Okay."

Mrs. Hill looked around the workspace again and then centred on John.

"When the boys come closer to us we'll be telling them we have the authority to send them on their way. We sort of use a special incantation for this. It probably sounds like a magical spell being said but it's not. It's explaining to the spirits their bodies belong here but they are now dead and they must move on to the light."

"Alright, I get all this so far. What happens next?" John asked as he took another sip of tea.

"Next we must visualise the white light for the boys to move to before the boys are told to move to the light where they will find peace."

John sat amazed at what Caroline's mother had told him. He had never really dabbled with spirits this way before and to have someone tell him how to expatriate spirits was mind-blowing.

"Will we see the light your friends visualise?"

"No, as they will be visualising the light in their minds and in discussion with the spirits directing them to go to it."

"Phew – the last thing I need during the concert is a beam of light to appear within this building and a group of spirits being seen to walk into it. I think it would be rather off-putting."

Both Caroline and John laughed at the mental picture he had just painted. John felt comfortable now that he had a group of people lined up to actually assist the St Dominic Savio Boys and Youth Choir complete their time on Earth. He would miss them and their antics with the light in his tearoom. Then again, the boys would be going to where they should have gone ordinarily once they died.

"John, never you mind. My friends and I will move the boys on for you. It will be a pity as they sound really great," Mrs. Hill said.

"Mum, I'm sure John will move on with his life. I guess John in one respect you really haven't had much of a go living here quietly with Melanie at all, have you?"

"What do you mean?" John asked.

"I think I'm right when you told me you heard the boys here the very first night you inspected this old church. Since then you've been leading a team of people to help the boys realise their dream of having one last concert for their parents."

John smiled as he thought about what Caroline said. She was right of course; life had been centred on the boys since he took ownership of his new workspace.

"I really think it interesting how so many people have come together to help the kids," John said. "Some knew them, and a lot did not. Either way, these boys have generated a lot of unity and love within the district and village. I'm sure the week after we hold the concert this place will revert to what it should have been – a quiet haven perched on a hill."

"You're right, John. Then again, think about what the boys have done in bringing people together. You'll record the concert so there will be a lasting reminder of what people did to help our choir on its way. It's just that we can't tell anyone."

"That's right Caroline," John replied as he thought about what Blake first said to him.

Mrs. Hill and Caroline stood and started to walk to the door when they were met by two people in Army uniforms.

"Oh, I say, we have the Army involved too. This will be a nice concert," Mrs. Hill emphasised.

John said his goodbyes to Caroline and her mother and then welcomed a diminutive female Army Officer and a tall, broad-shouldered Sergeant Major after they made way for the women to exit and leave.

"Hi, I'm John Sutton. Are you …"

"Hello John, I'm Captain Courtney Stevens and this is Sergeant Major Trevor Gilchrist. We're both Territorial musos – you know, part-time soldiers who assist with a Cadet band."

John was excited as Captain Stevens seemed animated and had a rich timbre in her voice. Her blue eyes sparkled and her gaze was wide. He was looking forward to hearing Captain Stevens sing. In contrast, Sergeant Major Gilchrist had a steely stare and a hand grip that could easily be mistaken for someone who bends metal rods with his bare hands – not a musician. John shook hands cautiously with him and smiled. He liked the Sergeant Major.

"Hello Courtney, Trevor – thank you for stopping by. We have a lot to talk about," John said as he motioned for the soldiers to join him in his breakout area.

"I hope this is not an inconvenient time for you," Stevens said.

"No, I'm pretty free. Those ladies who just left also have a part to play in the concert so we had to meet and see how we can help each other. Please grab a seat. Would you like a cup of tea?"

"We thought you'd never ask," Gilchrist said.

John cleared the coffee table; made a fresh pot of tea and refilled the biscuit tray. The light in his tearoom blinked on and off a few times.

Ahh, so you like these two, do you, boys? John thought. The light blinked once more. *So do I. Let's see what they can do for us.*

John joined the two soldiers and poured the teas.

"I guess I should start," Stevens said. "You know Captain Phillip Boyce and Robert King from Australia. Well, both of them have been in contact with me to say you are having a special gig on Remembrance Day here and you need some local help. So, here we are. What do you need and how can we help you?"

For the next fifteen minutes, John told the two musicians what he had in mind for the concert. He detailed how two local schools had combined to create a boy and youth concert and how the Americans under Captain Andrew Jackson had offered to play.

"All this is very fine," John said. "However, I think this whole event needs someone like you."

"If you have the Americans, why would you need us?" Stevens asked.

"Good question, but I think you have a lot to offer. For instance, the American band will be good to play inside here. The choir still needs some sort of help on a couple of levels and I seek your advice."

John outlined the lack of a sense of discipline within the choir. Also, how he wanted to really draw the crowds from the local railway and bus marshalling area to the church in an enthusiastic way and lead them to the concert.

"So John, from what you are saying you need help to enthuse this new choir but promote some sort of discipline in them," Gilchrist said. "You also need a way of leading the crowd from the main marshalling area in the village up here to the church. Yes?"

John looked at the Sergeant Major and saw the man's eyes had narrowed and his gaze had turned into a stare.

"Yes, you have it in a nutshell, except, it would be tremendous if you could also join the Americans here for the actual concert too. Is all this asking too much? I'm looking for your guidance here."

Stevens had a glint in her eye and nodded to her Sergeant Major.

"John, in essence, you need a marching band to lead the choir and the masses from the train station and bus stop in the village to inside here. Yeah?"

"Yes," John agreed.

"Then you would like us to join the Americans and play in the concert. Yes?"

"Yes."

"Hmm the only thing I left out was the discipline of the choir – this could be the tallest order but one that is not without possibilities."

John sipped on his tea with his eyes never leaving Stevens as she spoke.

"All this is a big ask I know but what I am providing …"

"What you are providing John, are some fantastic opportunities for my good Sergeant Major and me to explore. For instance, we have a marching band that can do exactly what you require and lead the people Pied Piper-like from the village to here. I can see where the Americans would set up here and we could fit around them and meld our musical talents. After all, we both play each other's music!"

"Excellent."

"The next bit is tricky. What do you think we can do discipline-wise Sergeant Major?" Stevens asked with a smirk.

"Well ma'am we have a Cadet training weekend camp coming up soon where we'll be taking our lads through their marching paces," Gilchrist said. "There's plenty of room in the barracks for John's choir and their teachers to stay separately if they wanted to join us. We could get together several times for some marching practices as this would also give the choir a chance to try out their singing while they march – I mean walk with us," he said with a smirk.

"You know John; we have some pretty good choristers among the Cadets too. They could certainly add to your boys."

John was in awe as his mind quickly thought over all that had just been offered to him. He closed his mouth and picked up his cup of tea – it was empty.

"I think this calls for a fresh pot – what say you?"

Both Stevens and Gilchrist laughed and nodded their heads. John got up and refreshed the pot of tea and brought it back out to his breakout area.

"The hard thing may be selling the concept to the choir's

teachers," John said. "However, I think I have a way around that."

"What are you thinking?" Stevens asked.

"Well, the Parish Priest who used to be the Priest here before this church was decommissioned is the one organising the choir. I'd be pretty sure he'd go along with it all."

"When do we get to meet the Priest and your choir?" Stevens asked.

John looked at his watch and laughed.

"I'd say within a short while – are you able to wait?"

"Sure but why is he coming here?" Stevens asked.

"Well the whole choir, their teachers and Father Brendan Kirby are due here for a rehearsal this afternoon. This would give you time to observe the boys and their teachers before you make any offer if indeed you still want to."

Gilchrist smiled and became animated moving his right hand around.

"It mostly falls to me to help shape up the youth before they become Cadets. Their musical tuition is done by schoolteachers and sessional musicians who are part of the band. You'll find I'll have no problems with your choir."

"I am so glad the way all this is coming together," John said. "If this all comes off we'll have a choir and parade this village has never seen before."

"Maybe so, but whatever the teachers, choir and Priest decide, we're behind you a hundred per cent," Stevens said.

"This has been a day like no other. Would you like me to show you around while we wait for our charges to arrive?"

"That would be great thanks, John."

"Great. Grab your cuppas and come outside and I'll show you what we're trying to achieve."

The trio moved towards the exit when both Stevens and Gilchrist stood rooted to the floor. They both looked at the plaque of the choir and nodded silently.

"They look a happy bunch," Stevens said.

"Yes – apparently they were."

Chapter Fifteen

Barry Cooper beat the boys' bus by two minutes to Sutton Hall. His eyes nearly popped when he saw Captain Stevens and Sergeant Major Gilchrist standing next to John in the graveyard. This was the first he had seen any military personnel in uniform at the old church. He was keen to get to know the pair as he knew they must be playing a part in the upcoming concert.

"Hi Barry, let me introduce you to Captain Courtney Stevens and Sergeant Major Trevor Gilchrist from the local Territorials. They have offered to help us with our concert."

"It's great to meet you," Cooper said as he shook hands with the pair.

"Barry is the father of one of the boys from the St Dominic Savio choir that used to sing here and is my right-hand man in helping me pull this event together," John said.

"You're too kind John. My boy Blake loved this church and his choir and I know he would have loved the concert John is helping to make happen."

"Nice to meet you," Stevens said.

"Likewise," Gilchrist said as he craned his head to look over Cooper's shoulder at the approaching bus. "It looks like we have company."

The four turned to look down the hill as the Brighton boys' bus and Father Kirby's car approached. The noise level increased dramatically as the bus approached the car park and then came to a stop. The bus door opened and Ken Duggan stepped forward. He waved to John and the others before directing the boys off the bus and into the former church. A hush came over the boys as they started filing past Stevens and Gilchrist. A couple braced their shoulders back in a gesture resembling a soldier straightening their backs ready to march, and then they smiled. One of the boys then stopped and shook hands with the Sergeant Major.

"Hello, Mr. Gilchrist – good to see you here," Cameron Hancock said with a large cheesy grin.

"And you too Cameron. I'm looking forward to hearing you sing," Gilchrist said as he returned the youth's smile and had a small chortle.

"Ahh, it's good you know one of them," Cooper said.

"Yes, I've known Cameron's parents since before he was born. His father was in the Territorials some years ago."

Once the boys had filed into the former church John introduced Stevens and Gilchrist to Duggan, McRae and Father Kirby.

"I'm really glad you are here to see and hear the boys sing," Father Kirby said. "They need to sing in front of strangers and with you in uniform – it's even better."

"Brendan, I think we should start the boys off on our military salute while we have our guests here," Duggan said. "This should allow them to spice up their singing and check how they are going."

"Good idea Ken, let's get cracking."

The six adults went into John's workspace. The boys decided to play a game and all stood to attention in their respective rows. Their eyes followed Stevens and Gilchrist as they entered the workspace and sat down.

"Very good boys, you look excellent," Duggan said.

"All present and correct, Sir," one of the boys said with a smirk.

"Okay, you can relax now. With us today are two members of our local Territorials who have come to listen to you sing. Captain Stevens, would you like to do the introductions please," Duggan asked.

Stevens and Gilchrist stood up.

"Hello boys, I'm Captain Courtney Stevens and this is Sergeant Major Trevor Gilchrist. We're Territorials, you know, part-time soldiers, attached to a Cadet band. Mr. Sutton has called on us to see if we can help out with the farewell concert. We arrived at the right time to meet you and hear you today by the look of things."

Both soldiers sat down and McRae started playing the military melody salute they had been rehearsing. Duggan raised his hands and the boys and McRae worked in unison to bring their songs and skits to life. Stevens and Gilchrist both nodded and quietly clapped their way through the various melodies associated with each military service. At the end, all eyes were on the two soldiers as the boys looked for feedback.

"Well done boys, that was quite marvellous," Stevens said. "I loved your cadence with your melodies and your various harmonisations. I'm pretty sure Sergeant Major Gilchrist here also loved your skits."

Gilchrist nodded and a large smirk broke out across his face. The boys were waiting for the "but" about their performance.

"Mr. Duggan, I know these songs pretty well as I sing them at benefits. Do you mind if I join in with the boys for a practice?" Captain Stevens enquired.

Duggan laughed and looked at John and McRae and raised his hands to restart the practice.

"Okay, boys you have the military seal of approval now let's see how you go with a professional singer among you."

McRae started the keyboard and the boys cranked up their rendition of the military salute. Stevens joined in low-key at first and then became animated and took centre stage. The boys sang even harder to harmonise with the female Captain while glancing every so often across to Gilchrist who was quietly clapping along with a huge grin on his face. At the side of the old church, Cooper filmed each of the songs. John had placed a couple of microphones strategically in front of the boys to record their voices.

At the end of the performance, all the adults stood and clapped loudly. The boys had really pushed themselves and it showed in the way they had sung and acted out their skit. The acceptance and pleasure of the adults were written clearly on their faces as they all lit up with large smiles and sang out 'bravo, bravo'. The boys looked at each other and then laughed. A few gave each other high five hand slaps.

"Boys, that was truly fantastic. We should have Captain Stevens sing with you more often," Duggan said with a large smile. "Okay, while you are still on a high, let's have a crack at The Lion Sleeps Tonight."

Stevens sat down and was quietly congratulated by Gilchrist. McRae started playing The Lion Sleeps Tonight and several boys began making animal noises. More of the lads slowly acted out animals in front of the choir before the first refrain began. Gilchrist's gaze intensified as he watched the boys perform and quietly nodded his head as he mentally summed up what he was watching. After the song, the adults gave a round of polite applause but the boys' attention was on Gilchrist. They had seen him watch them intently and nod as if he had mechanically worked out how to better their performance.

"Very good boys," Duggan enthused. "The sopranos and altos started well on cue but the tenors and base were a bit late. You must listen to Mr. McRae's key change and start singing straight away. Are there any other comments from the audience?" Duggan asked as he looked around the room. Most adults gently shook their heads. Gilchrist stood up and the boys seemed to flex.

"Mr. Duggan, may I assist for a moment please?" the Sergeant Major asked.

"Sure thing Sergeant Major."

"Oh oh, look out. Here it comes," Hancock said to one of his fellow choristers.

"Thank you. Boys your singing was fine to my untrained ear but I certainly go along with what Mr. Duggan has just said. Acting is one of my strengths. You there, third from the left in the first row, what sort of animal were you?"

A 12-year-old boy looked sheepishly at Gilchrist and then Duggan.

"I was a monkey, sir."

"Alright, your second from the right in the second row – what sort of animal were you?"

A 14-year-old boy checked his position and then looked at Gilchrist.

"I was a lion, sir," the youth said as he cleared his throat.

"Okay boys, listen up. Your audience has to pick out what you are automatically and not second guess. You must really metamorphose or change into the animal you are acting. Watch me."

Gilchrist got down on his hands and legs and prowled the stage. His sleek, lanky frame and shoulders moved fluidly as he morphed into a lion who was about to pounce and he let out a huge 'roar'. The boys laughed at first and then fell silent as the soldier sat on his haunches and scratched under his arms and became a monkey at play. He gave a large grin with his teeth clenched together and let out a series of noises similar to a monkey. Gilchrist stood up to a round of applause and a series of 'whoop whoop' calls from the boys and he bowed to them in acknowledgement.

"Okay, boys. If you are going to play being a lion or a monkey then don't. I'm sure Mr. Duggan wants you to be a monkey or a lion not just playing around. Okay, the two boys I spoke to earlier, come out and give us another try."

Gilchrist stepped back and the two boys went to the front of the choir. Not a sound could be heard at first. Both boys looked at Gilchrist and then Duggan before resuming their respective poses. The difference in performance was quite noticeable as the boys morphed into their chosen animals with increased intensity and made their respective noises. Gilchrist clapped loudly.

"Bravo boys, bravo," Gilchrist said enthusiastically. "Acting like a jungle animal takes a lot of confidence. Don't be afraid as you step forward and take the spotlight. Just remember, it is not you slinking around out here, it is the animal you represent. Make them work for you."

The choir nodded and patted their chums on the shoulders as they went back to their places. Duggan nodded enthusiastically as he looked around at the other adults and resumed his place.

"Okay boys let's take a five-minute break," Duggan said. "Please go out to the car park and get some fresh air. See you in five minutes."

The noise in the workspace suddenly intensified as the boys relaxed and started filing outside to the car park.

"Trevor that was great, thank you," McRae said as he rose from behind his keyboard. "It's amazing what an outsider can achieve with the boys rather than those who are with them all the time."

"I agree," Father Kirby chimed in. "I haven't seen the boys so animated or in such good form before. I think we need the Territorials here more often. Better still, if the boys perform this way when you are here now, imagine what they should be like at the concert."

John started laughing and placed one hand on the shoulder of Father Kirby and the other on Stevens.

"You know Brendan, Courtney and Trevor may just have an

offer the three of you will like about an upcoming activity, but I'll leave it to them to discuss it with you."

McRae and Duggan moved closer as Stevens and Gilchrist discussed their upcoming Cadet Camp where their band would be doing a lot of rehearsals and marching practice.

"John has discussed how he would like the Cadet band to lead the way from the railway station to here on the day of the concert, sort of Pied Piper-like," Stevens said. "This camp we're holding shortly would be a great place for your boys to independently practice their routines like we're doing today and then join in with our boys in some marching and other fun activities. What do you think?"

McRae, Duggan and Kirby all looked at each other and then at John before looking back at the two Territorials.

"We'd have to discuss it with the boys and sound out the parents and schools before we could make any decision," McRae said.

"You know Ron, I think this would be a really fantastic way for our boys to bond more with each other and also the Cadets," Duggan said. "If we're going to help lead the multitudes from the village to here, we have to learn to put the right foot in front of the other so we don't look out of place. I'm sure Trevor would be our main teacher here."

Gilchrist smiled broadly.

"Yes, this is where my role kicks in to assist with the soldier instruction of the Cadets," he said. "I'll email you the camp's particulars, timings, costs and gear lists this afternoon."

"Fantastic," Duggan said. "This would give us the information to help argue our cases."

Father Brendan, McRae and Duggan again looked at each other and the two Territorials and nodded their heads. They agreed to get back to Stevens within three days as this would allow the school time to discuss the opportunity and for notes to go home to the boys' parents.

"Do you have any US or Australian flags," Gilchrist asked.

Both McRae and Duggan said "no."

"My suggestion is you could follow what the American youth choirs do when they perform a mixed armed forces medley like yours," Gilchrist said. "At the beginning of each melody a boy from the choir or if you like, we could arrange a Cadet from each of the three armed service organisations, could bring out a flag representing the particular service – Army, Navy and so on. The boy or Cadet stops in front of a flag holder waves the flag and then places it into its position. He salutes it before marching off stage. This action adds more pomp and circumstance to the songs. If we supplied a Cadet from each of the various services, Army, Navy, and Air Force, this would allow you to continue singing unhindered. Just thoughts."

McRae looked and Duggan and then at Father Kirby with amazement.

"Gents this sounds pretty good as we're performing on Remembrance Day and the handling of flags would be better done by the children in uniform," McRae said.

"And allow our boys to concentrate on their singing," Duggan quipped. "I'm all for it. What do you think Brendan?"

"I think it's a brilliant idea and would certainly add to the whole performance. It's up to you and your schools."

"Okay, we'll sort it out once Trevor sends us his email this afternoon. Alright, what are we playing next?"

McRae looked through his notes and then quickly said "Soldiers Cry is next on the program."

Stevens and Gilchrist looked at each other and smiled without saying a word. This was one of Stevens' favourite and moving songs.

The boys started trickling back into the workspace. They had been outside in the car park with some playing chasings; others throwing balls at each other and the rest sitting and talking. Their neat worn uniforms had started showing signs of play with shirts hanging out, some long socks were up and others down. One lone boy walked to John's workspace and looked closely at the proposed memorial.

"Mr. Sutton is this all there is to remember the boys who used to sing here?" the boy asked.

"Hi, yes, they were all burnt up in a very large truck and bus accident. Who are you?" John asked.

"I'm Bryce Harrison, and if this is all there is for the boys' parents to remember them by, I'm glad to be assisting."

"Me too," John said as he rubbed his hand through the boy's golden yellow hair.

Duggan took the cue.

"Okay boys hopefully the fresh air has done you some good," he said. "We're going to try our new song Soldiers Cry. Thanks Mr. McRae."

The keyboard came to life with a soft song similar to a hymn. Duggan raised his hands and then started conducting the boys as they tried to pick up on the chords and sing.

"No, no stop there," Duggan said. "This is not a pop song, it's a sort of tribute to our fallen soldiers so there has to be more reverence in your voices."

"Perhaps I can help you here Mr. Duggan," Stevens said.

Duggan nodded as Stevens stood and walked closer to the boys.

"This song is actually called *Soldiers Cry (Oseh Shalom)* and was made famous by a boys' choir like yours in Ontario, Canada called The Amabile Boys Choir," Stevens said. "It's a song about peace and asking for God's help to bring peace. Therefore it is sung more gently and with feeling."

John had been checking his CDs and finally found the Saint Dominic Savio songs he had compiled.

"Captain Stevens, Mr. Duggan, I think I can further help set the scene if you like?" John asked. "The boys who we are remembering with our concert sang the song this way."

John then played the song and turned up the volume. Cooper stood in awe as he listened to the song and heard the voices of boys past. The boys in the Brighton choir nodded their heads and the adults could see most of them silently singing in unison with John's recording. Duggan noticed what was happening and asked John to stop the music.

"Thanks Mr. Sutton. Okay, boys, how about we try a different approach. I noticed most of you singing quietly as the other choir sang. Let's see how you go as a combined choir with you singing in tune with the Saint Dominic Savio boys."

The Brighton boys nodded among themselves and smiled.

"Mr. Sutton, if you please."

John restarted the song and turned the volume down to

allow the Brighton boys' voices to be more heard. The boys had other plans as they had begun to harmonise with the Saint Dominic Savio boys and let them lead. Duggan looked at McRae and then to Stevens as he made his decision.

"Okay, thank you Mr. Sutton. Thanks, boys. I thought you were going to join the other choir not just vocalise with them?"

"Sir, I guess the other boys sounded so good it was great to give them a boost rather than for us to take the limelight," Cameron Hancock, the boy who greeted Gilchrist said.

The other boys agreed and asked if the song could be played in full with the other choir louder.

"Alright, let's see how we sing with the boys from Saint Dominic Savio. Thanks Mr. Sutton."

John played the song again and turned the volume up this time. The result was electric. The voices of the Saint Dominic Savio Choir rang out crisp and clear. They were in turn harmonised by the Brighton boys beautifully. John's workspace had filled with nearly sixty boys and youth voices with a song that was so moving Cooper, Gilchrist, Stevens and John all reached for their handkerchiefs. Once the six-minute song was over the adults gave a strong and enthusiastic round of applause. The light in the tearoom blinked a few times and John smiled knowingly.

"Well done boys, that was terrific," Duggan said as he wiped a tear from his eye. "I haven't heard you sing with such emotion like that before. Cameron thanks for your suggestion I think we should stick with it. Phew, how do you top that?"

"I think we should go straight on with *Hymn to the Fallen*," McRae said.

"Thanks, Ron, I think you're right. Can you give us the intro please?"

Stevens closed her eyes for a few seconds and then spoke quietly to Gilchrist before standing up and walking over to John. McRae played the introduction to the hymn and watched as Gilchrist picked up a microphone. The choir started harmonising the music. The boys with the higher voices started intoning their parts as all eyes fell on Stevens. She joined the boys and picked up on the melody and raised her voice so it filled the workspace. The boys instinctively but quietly formed a half circle around Stevens to give her centre stage. Duggan looked at McRae who raised his shoulders in an '*I don't know*' move. There are no words to the hymn just soft music with voice harmonisations. *Hymn to the Fallen* was made famous by Welsh mezzo-soprano Katherine Jenkins in the first decade of the 21st Century. After the song, the boys clapped Stevens and patted her shoulders as a sign of 'well done'.

"Well, Captain Stevens, that was tremendous," Duggan said. "The boys had been practising the hymn for only a week, but you certainly added a whole new dimension to it. Say the word and the lead is yours. What do you think boys?"

The choir closed in on Stevens with lots of clapping and hollering by the boys.

"Well that's done – you are now the lead for that piece," Duggan said.

"Mr. Duggan, boys, thank you for letting me join you," Stevens said. "*Hymn to the Fallen* is a particularly solemn piece of music and I thought you may need a boost with some of the notes. I hope you didn't mind?"

The boys cheered and clapped again and looked at their teachers who nodded in agreeance.

"Well I don't think there will be any resistance to the camp," McRae said as he joined Duggan.

"No Ron, I think that's a given now."

McRae looked at his watch and said it was time to leave as the boys would be running a bit late. Cooper packed away his camera and John turned off his recording system. The group filed outside to the car park and saw the bus waiting for the boys.

"Well team, this was quite a day," Father Brendan said. "If it gets this emotional during rehearsals imagine what the concert is going to be like."

Cooper shook his head. "I was frozen in my place when the boys decided they wanted to harmonise with the Saint Dominic Savio choir," he said. "What a moving rendition of that song! I'm so glad I captured it on film."

"Well, I'm certainly glad I've been sound recording as we go as that song will go down well as a lead on an album," John said.

Duggan looked at John and computed what he just said.

"Do you think our boys here are good enough to go on an album?"

"Yes Ken, I think they are shaping up to be a good choir. I believe with Courtney's added voice and the US band backing you, this farewell concert will be a winner."

Stevens nodded in agreement.

"These boys of yours are good," she said. "They seem to take in what you say and also improvise. They're thinkers, not just followers. This will also set them apart from other choirs."

The two teachers rounded up the boys and got them to board the bus. Stevens, Gilchrist and Father Brendan drove off too. Cooper stayed with John as all the guests departed.

"You know John, this concert is shaping up to be something incredible, thanks to you," Cooper said as he touched John on the elbow. "I believe my boys would be so happy the way this is all turning out."

"Ah Barry, your boys were very good and if these current lads keep singing the way they did today, they will be too. I think today we saw an injection of energy from the Brighton boys even they didn't see coming."

"Yes, I agree. Well, I'd better be off too so I can edit what's needed with this film and add it to the files."

"Alright Barry thank you, I'm glad you're here as you are a real link to what we are all trying to achieve."

Cooper drove off and left John to the solitude of Sutton Hall. He walked back inside his workspace to clean up and the light in his tearoom went on and off.

"I thought you boys would approve of what happened today," John said aloud. "We're assembling a good team and it will be a concert to remember."

John checked his work computer and decided the work his boss had sent him he could complete in the quiet of tomorrow morning. It was time to lock up and head to Sutton Hall and await Melanie. He needed some quiet space and time.

Chapter Sixteen

John wanted a special sensuous evening with Melanie. He started organising the dinner table with two candles when there was a knock at the front door.

"Damn, who's this," John thought to himself. He opened the door to find Neville Davies filling the door frame with an A4 piece of paper in one hand and a small plastic bucket in the other.

"Hi Neville, come on in," John said as he shook the big man's hand.

"Hello, John. I can't stay long but I wanted to let you know the moment I knew," Davies said.

"Know what?" John asked.

"Ah sorry, I should better explain myself."

"Come on in, please. Let's go into the lounge room where we can talk."

Both men then went to the lounge room where Davies gave John a piece of paper from the local Council.

"I only got this in the mail today so I came straight over. Council has approved your application to have a memorial seat built in the graveyard outside. This means the boys' memorial has the go-ahead."

John's face lit up like a Christmas tree. He couldn't see any impediment to the memorial but it was really great to have the official sanction to do what he wanted to do – especially on part of his property.

"This is fantastic news, Neville. Thank you for your support and help in getting this through."

"After what the Mayor said at our meeting here I was determined to ensure he was held accountable."

"Excellent – now the real question is who pays? No doubt on the day of the concert the old church and grounds will be overflowing with people. I'm sure they'll each donate towards the memorial, and this should help enormously."

"There is something else I wanted to tell you," Davies said rather sheepishly as he patted the small bucket. "You know my eldest son Paul was in the St Dominic Savio Choir. He was aged 14 when he died in the bus crash. Well, his younger brother Gabriel was only four at the time and dearly loved Paul. They'd always be playing wrestling or games together."

"So this would make Gabriel around the same age now as when Paul died."

"Yes. Well, Gabriel has started a pound line for you in the village and this has started to gain some momentum."

John shook his head as he tried to compute what Davies was trying to say to him.

"What's a pound line?"

"Oh sorry, it's where someone starts a collection for a charity and draws a series of continuous looped lines in chalk on the pavement."

"And Gabriel is doing what with the lines?"

"Well, he has a pretty good voice and has taped a photo of Paul to a power pole. Gabriel stands in front of the pole. He drew the lines and then placed ten one-pound coins on them to start things moving. He started singing some of Paul's songs and within a very short time passers-by had started filling the lines with their pound coins."

"Wow, this has taken off then."

"Yes. Here is the first day's taking in the bucket. Gabriel will be back on Saturday and a few of his classmates said they would play their instruments to accompany him while he sang."

Davies looked at John who was in semi-shock from all that he had just offloaded onto him.

"Neville I can't believe what I'm hearing. Gabriel's busking will now be the end of the mayor unless the Council donates towards the memorial too."

"Yes, it could be – especially if he refuses any groundswell of support from the children of the village and district and through them their parents."

"Okay big man, what has Gabriel earned so far for his troubles?"

Davies smiled as he raised the bucket and gave it to John.

"So far Gabriel has raised forty pounds for one afternoon's performance. He even wrote you a note saying how much he had earned."

John pulled the top off the bucket and tears welled up in his eyes as he read Gabriel's note to him.

Dear Mr. Sutton,

Thank you for helping my brother Paul be remembered by your special concert and memorial seat.

I have started to help too and will keep singing until the concert to assist you in my own way.

Your friend,

Gabriel.

John poured the money onto his coffee table and started making a quick count. He got halfway through and had to wipe tears from his eyes as he thought of the selfless act Gabriel was performing for his brother.

"Sorry Neville, I never had brothers or sisters and this kind act by Gabriel has just blown me away. I'm sure this is going to get momentum and I am pleased he is doing what he's doing but is he okay on the street by himself?"

Davies started laughing.

"Yes, because he's singing in front of my brother-in-law's butchery. You know, O'Grady's – it's the one with the large canvas awning out the front. John's been keeping an eye on him to make sure he's okay."

"This is excellent Neville. Please tell Gabriel I am thrilled by what he is doing and will drop down on Saturday to add my coins. Tomorrow I'll start a special bank account for the seat donations with Gabriel's money as the first deposit."

"No problems John. I best be off now so I can pick up some veggies for tea. Oh, one last thing. Gabriel has cousins around the same age as him in Wales and they want to help too, so you'll have some Welsh messages coming your way soon."

"Wow, I am impressed. Please thank Gabriel and his cousins. I'll keep a look out for any Welsh traffic."

John saw Davies to the door and then went back to the lounge room and re-read Gabriel's note to him. He picked up the phone and first rang Albert Miller from the Brighton Post and told him what Davies had said to him. He then rang Barry Cooper and Father Kirby to appraise them.

"This is fantastic," Cooper said. "I'll be there on Saturday to film one of his performances and the shoppers' reactions."

"Thanks, Barry. I think this has the potential to turn into a great news story so it's worth watching."

"I agree, John. I'm glad you spoke to Albert as I'm sure he'll organise some sort of Media response."

Father Brendan took a different attack.

"So my young Gabriel is singing for his supper, is he?" he started saying.

"And his brother, Paul," John added.

"Yes, and his brother. Well, I think we can give him some extra help. I'll check with Ken Duggan as I'm sure he could rouse up a few extra teenage singers to join in. I'll see what I can do; after all, we only have a few weeks to the concert."

The village tom-toms were now fully engaged and John was sure there would be a good turnout of people to help Gabriel. He turned his attention back to dinner and Melanie. After setting the table John started preparing the meal when he heard the front door open and Melanie walk down the hallway.

"Hi love, have a good day?" John asked as he kissed his wife.

"Hello, my husband. I had a fantastic day. Everything just

seemed to go so well. Mmm, what's all this about? The table is set nicely, candles, wine glasses out and a nice meal is cooking. Don't tell me the concert has been cancelled or something?"

"No my love nothing like that. I thought it's time we brought the restaurant to us and dined at Chez Suttons – this time on the inside!"

Melanie laughed and gave her husband another kiss.

"You're very thoughtful – thank you. I'll go and get changed and give you a hand."

John believed everything was under control and he was looking forward to some quiet couple time with Melanie. He was mistaken as he had lit a fuse by telling Cooper and Father Brendan of what Gabriel was doing. The first phone call was from Ken Duggan just as John had started serving the meal. Melanie was non-plussed and took over the serving from John while he took the call.

"Hi Ken, what's happening?"

"Brendan just rang me about Gabriel Davies busking in the main street of the Village to raise money for the memorial seat. This is pretty fantastic for a lone teenager to do. I couldn't see any of ours doing a lone act like this. Also, we've got permission from the parents of our joint choir to go on the Cadet Camp next weekend and maybe if we helped Gabriel out it would be a good public opener for the boys."

"Okay, this is great news about the camp, Ken. I think it will be a real eye-opener for the boys as they learn some military skills and have a weekend together with you and Ron. What did you have in mind for Gabriel?"

The two men discussed some ideas for a number of the boys

in the joint choir to assist the lone busker and add strength and support to his singing. Melanie had put the dinner in the oven while John took the phone call from Duggan. She was just about to retrieve the meal when the phone rang again. An excited Barry Cooper rang John to discuss Gabriel's busking which caught John by surprise as it was John who had apprised Cooper of the event.

"John, I've had a call back from Albert and he will be sending a photographer down to the village to take a photo of Gabriel."

"Wow, Albert must be short of news," John said as he raised his shoulders to Melanie in an act of 'sorry about the call'.

"It gets better. Do you remember you had Monica Ryan from BBC1 come out and do a story on the concert?"

"Yes."

"Well Albert was in touch with her and she'll probably be there on Saturday as well."

This message took John by surprise.

"This is just a lone teenager busking in the street. Why is there such news value in it?"

"Ah, you see it's not just a teenager singing that's the story; it's the fact he's raising money for people to remember his brother and the other boys who died in that terrible bus crash that became national news. This is also a first by the community to do something real rather than just a plaque on a wall for a memorial to the dead choir."

John told Cooper what Duggan was planning and the pair went into overdrive as they nutted out a Media Release that could be issued on Friday. John was also keen to call another meeting of people with specific tasks and roles for the concert to ensure all was in readiness for the big day. Cooper agreed to organise the meeting. Throughout the phone calls, Melanie had sat patiently at the dinner table. She had opened the bottle of wine John had been chilling and poured them both a glass.

"I'm sorry love. I wanted this to be our night," John said as he walked around to Melanie and bent over and kissed her while she sat at the dinner table.

"I know – our boys were calling and you had to solve the issue now. John, I'm very supportive of what you are doing for the boys who used to sing here. Our time will come."

"You know my sweet," John said in a tone just above a whisper as he started kissing Melanie's neck. "We could have dinner later and go straight to our desserts now."

"Whatever are you suggesting?"

"Mmm, we could enjoy some love-making."

"This is probably the best thing you have said all day. The dinner will keep until we're ready."

"You know it would be about now in the movies when the stars would be reaching for their cigarettes," John said.

"Don't even think about it. Our togetherness should satisfy you."

"It does my love," John said as he arched himself up on his elbow and caressed Melanie's face before he started kissing her again. "It really does."

The couple later found dinner never tasted so nice.

In the morning John was first up and sat at the breakfast bar with his laptop working out what he wanted to achieve with his next meeting of the major players for the concert. He outlined a sequence of events for the concert itself and then started electronically ticking off the ones that were organised or in play. John checked his emails and found a long list of re-recordings to do for his boss which had to be done that day.

"Damn," John said to himself. "Mmm, fancy work getting in the way of my favourite hobby, the concert! This will be a long day."

Chapter Seventeen

Gabriel Davies rose early on Saturday morning – he was on a mission. He was keen to start his pound line and get into position opposite his uncle's butcher shop. The dark-haired teenager scoffed down his breakfast; said goodbye to his parents and then walked into the village. Gabriel had packed his brother Paul's portable music stand in his backpack; took some copies of the various songs he had been practising and had a laminated photo of Paul with his fundraising message ready to tape to his stand.

Today was going to be different for the teenager. He had already completed the hard yards by singing alone on the street and raising a third of a small bucket in cupro-nickel pound coins for the upcoming Remembrance Day concert. Within thirty minutes Gabriel knew the streets of Brighton would be bustling as shoppers and tourists milled around, did their shopping and enjoyed the various sidewalk cafés. Although Paul had been dead for a decade, Gabriel often thought about the brother who was so kind to him when he was a youngster and loved playing games with him. Gabriel was shattered when news reached the family of Paul's demise. It was some years before reasonable normality resumed in the Davies household. Gabriel was the one who returned joy to the family with his love of music and song. The Davies had moved to Brighton from Wales but still had strong family connections there. Both Paul and Gabriel's singing voices had lilts in them when they sang as their Welsh background permeated through their vocal cords to the delight of all who heard them sing.

The Suttons' upcoming concert gave Gabriel the out he wanted and a street stage he needed to perform for Paul to show the world he too missed his brother. Village newcomer John Sutton was providing a vehicle for the families of the village and surrounding district whose sons died in the flaming bus crash to not only say goodbye but also have a memorial to visit. Gabriel was keen to add his energies to the memorial too, for his brother's sake. He wasn't in a school choir but loved to sing and could keep a tune well and would often join in with his cousins from Wales on family visits. Often his parents would find him singing as he worked around the family home listening to both English and Welsh music. Singing was his way to help the memorial be built and paid for.

Gabriel was aware members of his school's choir would be in Brighton today to lend him a hand. Classmate Cameron Hancock also told him not to be surprised if Gabriel heard an Army band in the area. This last message was cryptic to Gabriel and he was concerned any bands playing when he was trying to sing would direct crowds away from him. No sooner had he set himself up outside his uncle's butchery when a young butcher in a blue and white apron and white coat came out to see him.

"Hi Gabe, I'm Tommy Hanks. I work with your uncle," the young butcher said.

"Hi Tommy, glad to meet you," Gabriel said as he shook hands with the youth.

"Your uncle wants you to know we're all with you and has asked me to help start your day with these five one-pound coins."

Gabriel was chuffed. He knew his uncle was keen to assist but this was excellent. Hanks bent down and placed the coins along the beginning of the chalk pound line Gabriel had drawn.

"Tommy, please let my Uncle Patrick and all the crew know I appreciate what they are doing."

"We know and we're looking forward to today's singing. Go get 'em champ."

Hanks walked away with a big smile on his face leaving Gabriel to his power pole; music stand and pound line. Gabriel sang several songs with little success at first. Crowds seemed either to not hear him or were more interested in their shopping or socialising. John and Melanie visited to see Gabriel and hear him sing. They placed two one-pound coins on the pound line and then introduced themselves to the teenager.

"Hello Mrs. and Mrs. Sutton, I'm glad you could drop by," Gabriel said as he took a swig of water from a water bottle. "I hope you liked my present the other day."

"I'm glad you mentioned that Gabriel," John said. "What you are doing is worthwhile and your singing is brilliant. You should be in a choir or a band – you're a natural and I know Mel and I are very pleased with what you are doing. Just have a look at this bank book I have started in the name of St Dominic Savio Memorial Concert – with your first contribution."

"Thanks, Mr. Sutton – I appreciate what you have done."

"We'll drift over to your uncle's shop and watch and listen for a while over there out of your way. You should have some support here soon."

"Yeah, so I've heard. I'm looking forward to it. Well, I better get back to it then."

John and Mel started walking to the shop window of the butchery when they saw the BBC1 TV crew stop their car nearby. Monica Ryan and her crew were just starting to alight from their station wagon when John noticed Albert Miller and a photographer walking towards them from the opposite direction.

"This should be good," Melanie said.

"It gets better," John replied as he looked up towards the end of the main street. "I can see a crowd forming near the jeweller shop and wait … there it is. I can now hear one lot of the choir coming our way."

Melanie swung around to see the footpath filled with people and the gentle strains of a choir approaching from the north. Ryan's TV crew stood on the roadway and filmed the approaching crowd and then turned their camera on Gabriel who was singing a pop song. Both Ryan's crew and Miller swung around to see a second crowd forming up in the south and the high-pitched singing of a second younger choir approaching. Gabriel saw what was happening but kept singing. He was on a mission. His singing began to get louder as he tried to be heard over the top of the two choirs. Shoppers started pouring out of shops and onto the sidewalks on either side of the main road to see what all the commotion was about.

They stood in awe as they heard the two choirs approaching Gabriel and started walking over to the youth.

Cameron Hancock and his teenage choristers from Brighton High School were the first to reach Gabriel. The sandy-haired youth gave Gabriel a pat on the shoulders and a copy of the songs for his music stand and continued singing. The teenagers formed up on the right-hand side of Gabriel and continued to sing as they watched their junior partners from Brighton Public School slowly join them. In the crowd which had swollen to around a hundred people, stood Ron McRae and Ken Duggan as they watched their young charges perform. Once the combined choir stopped singing a rousing cheer went up and loud applause ensued. The combined choir then started singing *The Lion Sleeps Tonight*. Gabriel started clapping to the tune and beckoned the crowd to do the same as the choir burst into its now favourite song.

Barry Cooper wasn't going to be kept away from the event and had positioned himself on a shop's first-floor balcony to film. He had commanding views of the choirs from both directions as they sang and walked towards Gabriel and then performed jointly.

The junior boys swung into the rhythm of *The Lion Sleeps Tonight* and acted out the various animal parts without fault. After the song, Gabriel's pound line had to be extended to make room for the extra pound coins being placed on it.

While there was a break in the singing a distant, energetic drum band could be heard approaching from the south. The crowd started straining to see up the main road. The drumming became louder and louder and shoppers started leaving Gabriel to see what was happening. Brighton was usually a quiet village. Commotion of this sort – street singers and a drum band – were unheard of.

"Didn't I tell you not to be surprised at a band would be appearing today," Hancock told Gabriel as a large smile appeared on the youth's face.

"What is it?"

"You'll see. We'll be with them next weekend on a camp ready for the concert."

"What the ...?" Gabriel started asking but was drowned out by the cacophony of the crowd as the background noise increased substantially.

Slowly but steadily the Cadet Band marched its way along the sidewalk to the strains of *Men of Harlech* – the 15th-century marching song made famous by the seven-year battle of Harlech Castle. The boys in the band were finely turned out in their army uniforms and well-polished drums. Gabriel knew the song as it was one of his father's favourites and started singing it as the band approached. It was now Hancock's turn to enthuse the crowd to join Gabriel. The crowd members started singing gently and then more enthusiastically as the band neared and took up position alongside the senior choir members. The combined choir harmonised with the band and Gabriel. When the song was complete the crowd erupted once more into rapturous and enthusiastic applause 'well done, well done,' being yelled by shoppers.

John was buoyed by what had taken place and was about to step forward and make an announcement when Melanie stopped him.

"See what the boys do first, it's their time to shine."

"You're right love. Let's see what happens."

Hancock grabbed Gabriel and took him to the Cadet band and introduced him to the bandmaster. He then turned around and faced the crowd.

"Ladies and gentlemen, my name is Cameron Hancock from the Brighton Boys and Youth Choir," the teenager said as looked around the crowd. "Joining us is Cadet Colour Sergeant Timothy Park of the Brighton Army Cadets and his lads. It's our pleasure to help out our friend Gabriel Davies here who is trying to raise money for the stone memorial to be built at the old St Dominic Savio's church as a tribute to the 45 members of the boys' choir who died in that fiery bus crash ten years ago.

"The new owner of the property, Mr. John Sutton has organised a special Remembrance Day concert in two weeks at the old church. He'll have an Army band from America, an Aussie soldier who used to be in a youth choir and of course, all of us. Please help Gabriel and the members of the boys' choir that can only be here in spirit today."

The crowd applauded wildly and then quietened to see what would happen next.

"Mate, I know you know this next song," Hancock said to Gabriel. "We're going to sing it twice so give it all you have – we'll back you."

Gabriel winced and then his face lit up as the band struck up the chords for *Land of Hope and Glory*. The teenager took the lead and the crowd came to attention. Men doffed their hats in respect of one of the unofficial national anthems used across the United Kingdom and joined in earnest. Cafe patrons enjoying their sidewalk breakfasts joined in too and stood to attention at their tables.

Gabriel poured his heart and soul into the song and started with the chorus: *"Land of Hope and Glory, Mother of the Free. How shall we extol thee, who are born of thee?"* It was almost like singing *God Save the Queen* as all movement along the shopping strip stopped and virtually everyone joined in. After the early 20th Century song, the crowd again applauded wildly. Hancock went to the front of the choir and the band asked whether the crowd would like to sing it again and a mighty roar rang out. Colour Sergeant Park started the band again and virtually every bystander along both sides of the road sang the song in unison with shopkeepers standing in their business doorways alongside their customers. Again the crowd clapped and cheered at the song's rousing conclusion. Traffic had come to a standstill as drivers and their passengers wanted to see what was happening and then joined in.

"Okay mate, you're on your own now," Hancock said to Gabriel as he winked. "See you at school on Monday."

"Thanks, Cameron, I really appreciate what you are doing."

"No problems."

"Thanks, Tim – you really added to today."

"Catch you soon Gabriel."

The band started playing *The Lion Sleeps Tonight* and then began to march north along the main sidewalk. The full choir kept singing but made its exit south along the footpath leaving Gabriel still singing where he started. The crowd clapped and started to disperse with quite a few people patting the lone teenager on the shoulder and adding coins to the pound line before walking off.

Both John and Melanie had tears streaming down their eyes as they watched the crowd break up and depart and the traffic started flowing again. John looked up to the first-floor balcony of the adjoining shop and saw Cooper still filming. Monica Ryan and Albert Miller moved in to interview Gabriel for the next five minutes and then they also left. The Suttons went over to Gabriel and gave him a group hug.

"Gabriel that was quite a moving performance you and the team did today," John said. "I'm so looking forward to Remembrance Day as it will bring this nation to a stop – not just our village and surrounding districts."

"Thank you. This has been quite a morning," the teenager started saying as he fought back tears. "It was great ... to have the others here too. I know Paul would have loved that."

Melanie put her arm around Gabriel to comfort him as the teenager cried freely. It had been quite an emotional surge for him to have his classmates back him from his school – also for the junior boys and the Army Cadets to join in.

"No one cared about Paul and what happened to him and the others until you two came on the scene," Gabriel said as he disentangled himself from Melanie and blew his nose. "You've stirred up this village as I've never seen."

"Well, John is helping right something that should have been put to bed quite some time ago," Melanie said. "We're just trying to be good neighbours."

"I know if Paul was here he'd thank you for what you are doing."

John put his arm on the boy's shoulder and squeezed gently.

"Gabriel, we all have parts to play to help Paul and the others be remembered," John said. "I never knew your brother, but there's no mistaking he'd be very proud of what you have been doing for him too. Are you okay?"

"Yeah, I'm fine thanks. I get a bit teary when people show so much support for others. Well, I better get back to raising some money."

Gabriel shook John's hand and Melanie kissed the youth before the couple left the teenager. Cooper joined the pair after congratulating Gabriel.

"Wasn't that a fantastic show of support for Gabe," Cooper said.

"I'll say. I saw Duggan and McRae among the shoppers, and I'll bet they were pleased with their boys," John said as he slipped his hand into Melanie's.

"The crowd was just so enthusiastic and supportive. You know, I haven't seen such a large pound line as Gabe's for some time. It seems to take a major disaster to shake money from people."

"I think you're right there. Well, it will be interesting to see how the BBC and the Post cover the event."

"That's why I'm going home now. I'll bet our phones are going to ring off the hook with enquiries about the concert."

"You sorted out a concert ticket line so they should be the ones taking the calls."

"Ah yes, but the locals who know me will ring my home and still want to try and book through me."

Melanie nodded and looked around.

"You know who was missing today?" she asked.

"Well Brendan couldn't be here as he had some church business to worry about," John said. "Our two Territorials weren't here either. Okay, I give up, who?"

"The mayor – this would have been a great opportunity for him."

"You're right Melanie," Cooper said. "I somehow don't think he's long for office."

"Why what makes you say that?" John asked.

"Well, he has shown no real leadership in the cause that has united the Village and surrounding districts. How long he retains the Mayoralty will be interesting."

"I think you're right Barry. Fancy a spot of tea here somewhere?"

"No, I better get home otherwise Coral will have a lot of phone calls to take."

"Okay Barry, see you later."

John and Melanie stopped off at a sidewalk café and ordered morning tea. All around them the chatter was about the morning's singing event. The boys' actions were definitely the talk of the town.

After the Suttons left Gabriel, the boy's Uncle Patrick came out of his shop with Hanks by his side carrying a small bucket. The huge beaming smile said it all. O'Grady was a bear of a man. He was as tall as he was wide and had a vice-like hand grip but a very soft heart. O'Grady put his left hand on the teenager's shoulder and shook his right hand vigorously.

"Gabriel your mini-concert today was an outstanding success," O'Grady said. "I haven't seen so many people come to a stop and sing *Land Of Hope and Glory* outside my shop before," the big man laughed. "Then again, people have never stood outside my shop and sung the song!"

"I had some great help from Cameron and his choir and the Cadets – they were terrific."

"Well, let me tell you, business picked up extraordinarily today as a result of your singing. After the choir and the Cadets left my shop was filled to capacity a couple of times over."

"Yeah well, it's a pity it took something like Mr. Sutton's Remembrance Day Concert to make it all happen."

O'Grady saw the youth in front of him holding back his emotions and put his arm around the boy's shoulders.

"I watched Paul grow up and I'll never forget his fondness for you and his wonderful personality. Nothing will ever bring him back lad, but you have lit a fire in people that will help us all remember Paul and the others after this concert. I'm looking forward to visiting the special memorial seat at the old church and just having some quiet time with your aunty as we think about and remember your brother and all the other boys."

"Thanks, Uncle Patrick, I appreciate your support," Gabriel said as he hugged his uncle.

Hanks had started filling the bucket with the pound coins and looked up at his boss.

"I think we'll need another bucket boss, this won't hold all the coins here!"

Gabriel smiled as he bent down to help Hanks place the coins in the bucket.

"I'll organise another bucket," O'Grady said as he went back to his shop.

Within minutes a second young butcher, a couple of years older than Gabriel carried out a bucket, introduced himself and helped the other two boys pick up the coins. Both buckets were full to capacity and were taken into the butcher's shop. Gabriel packed up his music stand and poster in his backpack and went into the shop.

"Thanks, lads," O'Grady said to his young charges. "Gabriel, what do you want to do? Do you want a lift home with all this cash where you can count it out?"

"Any chance of a lift to the old church as I'd like to give this lot directly to Mr. Sutton if that's okay? You know, he's even started a special bank account with the money I have already raised."

"Done! The crew will look after the shop for me. Come on through the shop to the rear car park."

Gabriel walked through the shop with the other butchery staff slapping him on the shoulders and congratulating him. The drive to Sutton Hall only took a few minutes. Gabriel pointed out to his uncle the site where the stone memorial would be erected.

"What a fantastic view," O'Grady said as he alighted from his car. "This is the perfect spot for the memorial."

"Yes, it's a view I'll take with me when I grow up and move on."

"Don't grow up too soon – there are a lot of us that want to enjoy you reaching manhood."

"No probs."

The duo walked around to Sutton Hall and was met at the door by Melanie.

"Hi Gabriel, come on in. Hello, I'm Melanie," she said to O'Grady."

"Hello Melanie, I'm Gabriel's Uncle Patrick and I thought it better I give him a lift seeing he has a lot of loot to give your husband."

"That's very caring of you. Please come on in, I know John will be very glad to see you."

The three made their way to the lounge room where they saw John watching TV and taking notes. He looked up and saw his guests and stood up to greet them with Melanie making the introductions.

"I'm really glad you two arrived just now," John said as he pointed to the lounge for O'Grady and Gabriel to sit down. "The BBC has been running snippets of Gabriel and the choir singing ever since I arrived home from watching you sing."

"That's pretty quick," Gabriel said. "I didn't think about the interviews with the BBC and the Brighton Post."

John checked his watch and smiled.

"Well, now it's on the hour there should be a news update."

All four people watched the television intently as the commercial break came on and a news update appeared. Gabriel's item was first.

"Heading this update – traffic came to a standstill in Brighton today when a youth choir and Army Cadet band joined a lone teenage busker singing on the village sidewalk. Fourteen-year-old Gabriel Davies started a pound line to raise funds for a memorial seat to commemorate the deaths of the 43 boys from Brighton who died in a bus and truck accident a decade ago. He was joined by the Brighton Boys and Youth Choir and the

Brighton Cadet Band who entertained the crowds. Gabriel said his brother Paul was among the boys who died in one of the biggest national disasters to strike the United Kingdom since the 1966 Aberfan mine disaster. A Remembrance Day Concert will be held in the former St Dominic Savio Church at Brighton to raise funds for the memorial seat. In other news ..."

John slapped his hands on his thighs in a sign of jubilation and turned to see the faces of O'Grady and Gabriel. Both looked slightly stunned.

"Well gents you have made the national news today so there will have to be a follow-up in the nightly bulletin too," John said excitedly.

"I think this calls for a cup of tea," Melanie said. "Who's up for it?"

The three males all put their hands in the air and Melanie went to the kitchen to make the teas.

"I did the singing to help raise funds for the seat so mum, dad and I had somewhere to remember Paul," Gabriel said meekly. "I didn't do it for me to be a national song headliner."

"Whoa, sunshine!" O'Grady said gently as he put his hand on his nephew's shoulder. "Without you doing what you did today and the other boys joining in, the Suttons wouldn't have got the free advertising they just did for their concert on national TV and perhaps beyond."

John grinned and nodded, and his face looked strained as he carefully thought of what he was going to say.

"Gabriel, you did what you did for Paul and this is quite a noble thing," John said. "I helped you along the way to not only give you some notoriety as to what you were doing with your pound line but also to assist the other families who have lost sons. Today was a major victory for all those families when they saw and heard you all this morning in the Village giving support to the sons who were so cruelly taken away from them a decade ago.

"Tonight in the comfort of their living rooms they will see and hear you again along with millions of other Britons. This will help swell support for the Remembrance Day Concert and also hopefully pay for all its logistics, including the seat. Guy Fawkes may have only lit a fuse under Parliament, but today you ignited the hopes of millions of Britons who are looking for a happy way to celebrate this wonderful country of ours. We've been at war too long overseas and had too many domestic disasters. Your joyful message has captured the missing spirit we all thought was lost across the UK. I'm very proud to know you and see a youth selflessly do what you did today. If I was in the Army I'd salute you. Instead, you'll just have to let me shake your hand."

John extended his right hand and the teenage boy grabbed it and then hugged John. Gabriel sat with his head bent down as tears trickled down his cheeks. O'Grady put his arm around him and hugged him.

"It's alright mate, we're all so proud of you," O'Grady said. "Anyway, don't you have something to give to Mr. Sutton here?"

Gabriel wiped his eyes and nodded. He reached over to the two buckets and gave them to John.

"I think the crowd was more than generous today," he said with a glimmer of a smile.

"Ah, feel the weight in these will you?" John asked. "While we're waiting for Mel and our tea how about helping me count your riches?"

Gabriel and O'Grady agreed and helped John open both buckets before tipping them on the floor. The lounge room carpet became a sea of cupro-nickel as the pound coins covered the floor space. Each of the three males started counting coins and placing them in rows of ten. Within a few minutes, the final count was in with £160. The looks on the three males said it all. They were surprised to see so much money. Gabriel was doubly surprised as he had never raised so much money before either.

"What do you think of this?" O'Grady asked his nephew.

"I knew there was a lot, but I didn't realise the crowds had been so generous," the teenager said with a smile slowly enveloping his face.

"Well this puts your real count to £200 which is a princely sum for the seat," John said. "Thank you, Gabriel, for what you did today, including the media interviews. I was told you knew one of the boys from the Brighton choir. What's his name?"

"That was Cameron Hancock – we've been best mates since we started school."

"It showed today with the way he worked with you and introduced you. I was impressed. I guess my real question is why you are not in the choir with him?"

Gabriel winced and took a deep breath.

"I wanted to be in the choir, but mum and dad seemed rather fazed by it after what happened to Paul. That's why I sang alone."

"If there was an opening for you to sing as part of the choir for the Remembrance Day Concert, would you do it?"

"I'd jump at it but my parents would have to agree first."

"Okay, leave that to me. I think I have a way to approach the subject."

"You know my family comes from Wales, right?"

"Yes, I do and you showed it today by your magnificent voice."

"I have several cousins in Wales, and they have just joined a couple of boy choirs there. I've kept them in the loop as to what I've been doing for Paul, and they are keen to help out at your concert – not as the main event but as support to you."

John thought about what Gabriel said and envisioned the whole of his former church grounds awash with young singers.

"Let me work on the actual program as to how we can use them effectively but keep me informed of how they are going; their singing and preparations. Also, what songs could they contribute and how the hell would they get here and back home again?"

Gabriel started to laugh.

"Okay – leave the logistics to me and I'll keep messaging you so we can see if it is a workable thing or not having them here."

"Gabriel if the other Welsh boys are anything like you, they will bring the house down. Okay, here's my business card with my email address – keep me informed."

O'Grady nodded and a giant smile enveloped his face. He knew what Gabriel's cousins were able to do as he often went to Wales to meet his wife's family. Melanie brought in the teas and biscuits and was amazed at the rows of coins on the coffee table.

"You boys did well today. I've never seen so many pound coins before. Well done."

O'Grady finished his tea and told John he had to return to his shop. He offered to drive his nephew home, but Gabriel begged off by asking John whether he could see inside the former church.

"No problems mate. It's the least I can do for you and then I'll drive you home."

"Thanks."

John escorted Gabriel and his uncle to O'Grady's car and waved the butcher off. He then took Gabriel inside his workspace. Gabriel entered the building slowly and took in everything he could see. He noticed the wall plaque of his brother's choir and touched it gently with his hand.

"Mum loved this photo of the boys. They all seemed so happy then."

"You're the same age as Paul was then and you are a happy person. The Brighton boys who come here are all happy – especially when they sing. You can see now why I wanted to do something for your brother and the others as this is just about all there was to remind people they existed."

"You know; I have played Paul's CD probably a million times and sang along with it over the years. I can sing his songs in my sleep."

"What was Paul's favourite song and did he sing solo at any stage?"

"Apparently he would take the lead when the *Make Me a Channel of Your Peace* was sung during services here."

Gabriel walked over to the end of the nave and looked to the rear of the church.

"You know Gabriel, I just happen to have a copy of the music for that song. Do you know its background?"

"No."

"Do you remember being taught about St Francis of Assisi?"

"No, saints weren't my strong points."

"No probs. St Francis wrote *Make Me a Channel of Your Peace* as a prayer in the 13th Century. That's a long time for a prayer to be around huh?"

"Wow, thank you –I never knew its background."

John slowly looked around and then back at Gabriel.

"There's no one here except us souls. Would you like to try it out?"

Gabriel shook his head at first and then bit gently down on his lower lip. He tilted his head towards John and then nodded.

"Alright, I'll give it a go."

John told the youth he wanted to record him singing because he knew what a fine voice he had. He set up a microphone in front of Gabriel and instructed him how to stand. While the youth readied himself John went to his console and found the music for *Make Me a Channel of Your Peace* sent to him by Robert King, the Musical Director of the Australian National Boys Choir. John played the music through once and then cued Gabriel to sing.

Gabriel was a natural. He followed the musical key changes and knew when to start and when to stop. The moment he began to sing John knew a special career awaited the boy. Gabriel sang with such finesse and passion it brought tears to John's eyes knowing the youth wasn't singing to him but to his dead brother. The teenager had a commanding presence about him and could easily take centre stage and sing with gusto. After the song, John stood and clapped. He watched and laughed as the light in his tearoom blinked a couple of times. Paul was happy with his brother's performance!

"That was fantastic Gabriel. It was and I'm not just saying that. My full-time work here in this building is to re-record material from all styles of music so I have a pretty good idea of what sounds great for CDs. Would you like to try another song?"

"Alright, Paul's other favourite is a song the Welsh Rugby Union players sing before games. It's called Calon Lân."

"I don't know that one, what does it mean?"

"Ahh, not up on your Welsh songs, eh?" Gabriel asked with a smirk.

"No not his one."

"This is a song about asking God for a pure heart to go to heaven."

Now it was John's turn to be gobsmacked as Gabriel's words sank in. He was sure Gabriel's brother Paul was now in the act of pushing to have a say in the farewell concert.

"Okay mate, let's have a look among my Welsh instrumental recordings. Yes, yes, I found it. Let's give it a try."

John donned his headphones and adjusted the sound levels and then started playing the music and a giant smile covered his face.

"Alright Gabriel, I'll set the music and give you the cue, ready?"

The teenager gave John the thumbs up as his breathing changed and the look on his face became full of concentration. Once Gabriel started singing the song John became an emotional train wreck as he heard the teenage boy fill the old church with a beautiful voice that filled the building with overpowering joy. The music trailed off and John stopped the recording. He played Gabriel's performance back through his large speakers. The youth was surprised at how good he sounded with orchestral backing in the old church.

"It sounds like a proper recording already, wow. Thank you."

"I have a present for you and your family," John said as he placed a CD in a plastic cover. "Your first recording on a CD – I'm sure your parents will love it."

Gabriel's face lit up and he beamed a huge smile before starting to flush and turning red with embarrassment.

"This place sounds so fantastic Paul and the others must have really liked singing here."

"You know Gabriel there are some places you can walk into and feel uncomfortable without realising why. When Melanie and I arrived here and took over the place we felt nothing but warmth and happiness. This is truly a place gifted for the song. Please consider singing here on Remembrance Day as I'm sure Paul and his choir would have wanted you to."

"I'll think about it and ask my parents. This CD may smooth the way for me after all and of course, my Welsh cousins – they loved Paul too."

"Okay mate, I'd better get you home. You've had a long day already."

As they walked out of John's workspace the lights in the tearoom blinked a couple of more times.

"I must get that fixed one day," John said as he smiled knowingly at the youth.

Gabriel saw how John reacted and then looked at the lights. The boy had a quizzical look on his face as he evaluated what he had just heard and saw then smiled.

"Do you think Paul and the other boys will be watching the concert from heaven?"

"I have no doubt your brother will be here with the other boys in spirit ensuring all goes off well."

"Hmm, that will be great."

"Come on let's get you home."

Chapter Eighteen

The phones at Sutton Hall, the concert hotline and Cooper's home rang consistently for two days after the boys' choir and Army Cadets teamed up with Gabriel in the village. John and Cooper were run off their feet taking enquiries and sorting out any issues.

"I'm damn well glad we set up the concert hotline," John said to Cooper over the phone.

"I knew we could get to a stage like this but not so dramatically. We should have all tickets for both inside the former church and the outside viewing area, sold by the end of this week the way things are going."

"That's great Barry. I've been in touch with Peter Brown and our memorial seat is now complete. He wants us to go over and have a look before he arranges transport here."

There was a moment's silence on the phone as Cooper took in what John had just said.

"Can you make it this morning John?" Cooper said with a noticeable change in his voice.

"Sure Barry; how about I meet you at the stone mason's in an hour?"

"That would be great, thanks, John."

The pair rang off and then the import of what John had just said to Cooper hit him like a bolt of lightning. "I forgot Barry was one of the dads of the boys killed on the bus. Note to self: be more understanding."

The hour went quickly, and John drove across the village to the stone mason's yard. He was greeted by the sight of a large factory with various headstone shapes in the front yard yet to be inscribed. Cooper was waiting inside the office foyer as John walked in.

"Morning Barry," John said with a measured tone.

"Hi John, this is an interesting place, I've never been here before."

"I guess not. It's not the sort of place we would usually go to unless someone has died," John said as he put his hand on Cooper's shoulder. "Will you be okay with this?"

Cooper looked melancholy and nervous.

"Yes thanks, I'll be fine."

"Okay."

A dark-haired man with silver streaks; large hands and broad shoulders walked into the foyer from a rear door.

"Hello gents," Brown said. "I'm glad you could come over. This has been a labour of love for my staff and me – I can tell you. Once we got Caroline's designs we went straight to work. You know it has been highly unusual."

"What do you mean?" Cooper asked.

"Well usually, projects like yours have all sorts of issues from sourcing the stone, having the right design and then actually having the stone arrive in good order."

"So what was so unusual about this stone?" John asked.

"Well, once Caroline gave me the designs, I was able to source the stone from Wales within 24 hours. I had the piece of stone here two days later and without blemish or fault."

John and Cooper were quite chuffed about the good fortune.

"How did you go carving the stone and the designs?" Cooper asked as he blew his nose.

"I'll show you in a few moments. I think you'll be quite pleased. The seat is in eight panels. There are three curved back plates joined to three bottom plates to sit on and of course the sculptured bookend pieces. Underneath the seat is four stands to hold and spread the weight. I'm sure this thing will outlive the pyramids the way it's built."

Cooper and John looked at each other and then Brown and laughed. "Come on through the factory and I'll show you what I've done."

Brown opened the door leading to the factory floor and the three men made their way through into a large metallic warehouse-like area. It was full of different pieces of stone being made into various graveyard pieces depending on the person's religious beliefs. Standing on a platform about shin high was a beautifully carved stone seat. It was grey, rounded in a semi-circle with two ornately carved book-end style reliefs. One had a young boy singing and the other a youth. Around the boys were some birds in flight. Cooper stood rooted to the ground when he saw the seat. He bit down on his lower lip, took several deep breaths with his eyes closed and then slowly caught up with John and Brown.

"Are you okay mate?" John asked Cooper as he touched his friend's shoulder.

"Yes thanks, I'm fine. It's seeing the final product of how Blake and the other boys will be remembered – that's all. This is beautiful and something the other parents and I are, and will be immensely proud of. Peter, you've done an excellent job here."

"Thanks, Barry," Brown said as he shook Cooper's hand. "I was given some fantastic designs by Caroline and had three talented men working on the project. That's them over there," he said as he pointed to where three men wearing raised face shields, leather aprons and gloves stood among a collection of stone works watching them.

Cooper and John walked over to the men, introduced themselves and thanked them for their work.

"Once we knew what the project was we couldn't wait to get cracking with it," one of the men said. "We sort of all knew the kids this seat is about. The three of us ..."

"Make that four," Brown chipped in."

"Well, the four of us had all seen the boys growing up in the village. That bus crash occurred so quickly it seemed to take the life out of the village. Hopefully, this can now bring about some joy."

Both John and Cooper thanked the men and then made their way back to the seat.

"When will you have the concrete poured for the base?" Brown asked John.

"Now your work is complete I'll check with the concreters as I think it should be this afternoon or tomorrow."

"Excellent as this means you'll have the seat in place for the weekend. I'll organise a special cover for you so Father

Brendan can lift it to officially reveal it to the public at your concert."

"You're a marvel Peter, thanks," John said. "I'll be in touch once I know about the concreters."

Cooper and John made their way out of the factory and back to their cars. John was looking forward to returning to Sutton Hall and having a cup of tea. Cooper was in a hurry to tell his wife Coral about the seat and then put the word out on the bush telegraph to the other boys' parents.

John returned to his workspace in the former church and walked over to his desk. He put a second tick next to the image the artist had drawn of the seat and then wrote the word 'complete' next to it. The weather had picked up outside with the wind starting to howl and the clouds getting ready to make a good dump of rain. The wind's noise could be heard in bursts as it raced across Sutton Hall and down onto the village.

John decided to play Gabriel's songs *Make Me a Channel of Your Peace* and *Caolun Lân* as he checked his computer. It was usually dead quiet within the workspace except when John cranked up his music. Within seconds of the music starting the wind died down and the sun started breaking through the clouds, sending a shaft of light through one of the stained-glass windows. John was taken aback by the change in noise and the appearance of the light.

"Mmm, so you all love Gabriel singing huh?" John said to himself. "Well, so does Father Brendan. I dropped off a copy of Gabriel's CD to Brendan last night and he was most impressed, especially with the advent of teenage Welsh choirs joining in. Let's see how it plays out from here."

No sooner had he stopped talking to himself than a shadow filled the entrance door. Neville Davies filled the doorway blocking a lot of light going into John's workspace.

"Knock, knock," Davies said loudly as he stood waiting for John to acknowledge him.

"Ah Neville, come in, how are you?" John asked as he saw the man was bursting to tell him something.

"I have some very good news," Davies said. "Council held a no-confidence motion against the mayor last night and he only just scraped through to hold his position."

"Well, that would have certainly rattled his cage."

"More than that – he was told to come aboard with support for your project here or step down. I think you'll be hearing from him today somehow."

"Now this is interesting news."

"I'll say. I don't think he reckoned on how much sentiment you have stirred up in this village and surrounding district with your concert in a fortnight and the memorial seat. It really has the whole village abuzz."

"I think this calls for a celebratory cup of tea. What do you think Neville? Are you up for it?"

"Yes – thanks, I don't mind if I do. I've been on the run all morning."

"Mate, come on into my special break-out area and I'll organise a nice cuppa for us both – I think we've earnt it. However, before I do, tell me what you think of these songs."

Davies sat down in John's breakout area while John prepared and cued Gabriel's songs and started playing them. He then went to the break-out area and grabbed two cups of tea and a plate of biscuits. John went to rejoin Davies and noticed the man's eyes closed and he was nodding slightly as Gabriel's two songs filled the church. John quietly put the biscuits and teas on the coffee table. Two small tears slowly ran down the cheeks of Davies as he heard his youngest son sing his eldest son's two favourite songs. The man was transported back in time when the church was in full swing and Paul was one of the man choristers who used to sing in it.

"You looked like you were deep in thought there, Neville."

"Sorry, John," Davies laughed. "I thought for a moment I heard Paul singing and not Gabriel – the two sing very much alike."

"Did you like my CD of his two songs?"

"Yes. My wife and I initially burst into tears when he heard it and then almost squeezed the stuffing out of Gabriel as we congratulated him. We knew he had a good voice but between your recording and the upcoming concert, there has been a real change in the boy. His singing is fantastic, I'm so proud of him."

"Are you proud enough to let him sing in the concert on Remembrance Day?"

"Yes and I've told him to liaise with his cousins in Wales and their choirs. They will be here to back Gabriel and Paul – just wait and see."

John nodded enthusiastically and thanked his guest profusely.

"You know John, I must be hearing things. When I walked into here I thought I heard could hear Paul talking with a group of boys here. I must be hearing things."

Davies shook his head and John smiled.

"I think there is a lot of the boys' energy still here Neville which is why in one sense I'll be sad when the Remembrance Day concert is held but also very happy."

"What do you mean?"

"Well for me, it will be a happy day that we have achieved the concert with all the various bits and pieces to make it work. Also, the fact that you as parents will have a memorial seat to sit on and actually remember your boys is good. The sad part is what it must mean by having the concert as in one sense it's a farewell concert."

"You're right, but let me tell you, you have brought this village and its surrounding district together like you wouldn't believe. You never knew our boys, yet you helped us with the seat and a special concert so none of us could forget them. I can tell you, we're all pretty thankful."

"Thanks, Neville – my goal has always been to help the boys. Now tell me more about what happened with the mayor."

Davies detailed how Council members had witnessed the news items about Gabriel's busking and being joined by the choir and Cadet band. He said others had also been shopping when they witnessed firsthand what the boys did in the village. The majority of Councillors said the mayor had not moved to support John's effort. They said as the concert is likely to attract national attention they wanted an assurance the Mayor backed John to the hilt or to move on. Davies laughed when he said the mayor was almost caught short-handed when a motion of no-confidence had been raised in his leadership; however, he scraped over the line by one vote.

"I'm impressed by the Councillors," John said. "Please thank them as I have not been political in any of my actions."

"They know that and that's why they back you."

John looked at his watch and gasped.

"We'll have to finish up and move out of the way Neville as the school choir is due here any minute – sorry to rush you."

"That's alright. Do you mind if I sit up in the back and watch and listen to the boys, please? I'll keep out of their way."

"No problems at all. Use the chair next to mine at the desk. I'll introduce you to the teachers first."

"It's okay, I know both Ron and Ken – we're in the local lodge together."

"Lodge? Are you all freemasons?"

"Yes – how do you think you got the seat so quickly and cheaply? Peter Brown told us what was going on and we assisted in the background. In a sense, we were an unseen force."

"Wonders will never cease. Thank you for that story. I've organised for the concreters to be here tomorrow to lay the slab for the seat. This means the seat should be ready to attach on …"

"In a few days, Peter will be here to drop off the seat."

"Excellent. Thank you. I think I can hear the bus now."

A series of shrill and deep base noises could be faintly heard in the background as the combined choir made its way up the hill in the bus followed by Father Brendan in his car. Barry Cooper's car was 100 metres ahead of the bus. John and Davies watched from the car park while the convoy made its way to them.

"Just made it," Cooper said as he alighted from his car. "Hi, Neville, interesting times in Council I hear."

"Hello, Barry. I think a little purge now and then is good for democracy, don't you?"

"Oh yes and sometimes well deserved."

The three men laughed as the bus came to a stop and the boys started to exit. The junior school students were first and they milled around while their teachers and the senior boys made their way off the bus. John scanned the boys and found who he was looking for and walked over to him.

"Hi Gabriel, I'm glad you made it," John said.

"Hi Mr. Sutton, hi dad. My parents talked with Father Brendan, and I got the green light to be here – thanks to your CD. Cool huh?"

"Well done mate," John said as he messed up Gabriel's hair. "I'm really glad you could make it."

Davies laughed as he and his son exchanged looks and then giant smiles. Cameron Hancock was standing next to Gabriel and broke into a smile too. He rested his arm on his mate's shoulder.

"He's also allowed to come to camp this weekend. Don't worry, we'll look after him."

"Great news Cameron, thanks for all your support."

Duggan and McRae made their way through the throng of boys and shook hands with each of the adults. Father Brendan had been talking with a couple of the junior boys and then joined the adults.

"I see Gabriel is now part of the choir," John said.

"Well you know, John, God works in mysterious ways.

After you gave me the CD I spoke with Gabriel's parents and convinced them to let the boy join in."

"I'm really glad he's here. He's an asset to you all."

"Ah yes, they are all assets."

The two teachers then shepherded their choir into the old church ready for rehearsals. John asked if he could say a few words to the boys before they started and both Duggan and McRae agreed. Davies made his way to the chair next to John's desk and Cooper set up his camera to film the boys.

"Hi guys, it's really good to see you all again," John said. "I was enthused and appreciative of what you did on Saturday by joining forces with Gabriel here and helping him out. Brighton will never be the same again. You were fantastic. When you were joined by the Cadets you stopped all traffic with people leaving their cars to join in the singing. I've never seen such support before in a village or town. Well done. I'm looking forward to hearing about your camp later as we now begin the march towards our Remembrance Day concert."

The boys applauded and John turned to go to his recording suite as Cameron Hancock made his way to the front of the choir.

"Mr. Sutton," Hancock said loudly, and John stopped in his tracks. "On behalf of the boys and I, thanks for your words. None of us has to be here or take part in your concert. We're all doing it for the same reason as you – to make sure the community never forgets the original choir that used to sing here."

Father Brendan and the other adults applauded, and the boys joined in.

"Thanks, Cameron, I appreciate that."

"Okay boys we have a lot to get through today as this is your final rehearsal before you go camping with the Cadets," Duggan said. "You've all got the program, so we'll start at the top. Mr. McRae if you please."

For the next two hours, John's workspace was full of song and music. During the breaks, some of the boys went outside to play while others sat in groups on the floor of John's workspace and talked.

"What do you think about the boys' singing?" he asked Davies.

"Absolutely first class – I don't know what it is about this place, but the boys' voices sounded so professional. When you added the full orchestral backing, I was more than surprised."

"The next time you see the boys they'll be here for the Remembrance Day concert. They'll join with two combined bands and two former boy choir singers. It should quite an exciting performance."

"Yes, and don't forget we now have one of the largest Welsh boys choirs assembled also playing a part."

"I am so looking forward to it."

Two hours went fast as the boys and their teachers tweaked the various notes, refrains and performances. Before long the boys were heading back on the bus to return to their schools.

"You know John, there was a standout voice there today," Cooper said as he waved off the bus and Father Brendan.

"Whose was it?"

"It was Gabriel's. When he sang the other boys seemed to work closely with him rather than compete. It was exciting to hear and see him in action."

"I agree," said Davies. "His solos should bring the house down."

"I'm with you gents. Today we didn't see a collection of boys singing. I believe today we saw a choir."

Davies and Cooper agreed and shook hands with John before they too departed leaving him alone. John walked back into his workspace and locked up. This had been a long day and he had dinner to organise for Melanie.

Three days after their rehearsal at the former St Dominic Savio Church, the Brighton boys again boarded a bus but this time it took them to the local Army Cadet Force band barracks. The usual chatter and banter gave way as the bus approached the large barrack complex. The bus was stopped at the front gates by a security guard and a tall Sergeant Major in woodland fatigues boarded the vehicle.

"Good evening, ladies," Sergeant Major Gilchrist barked with a friendly smile and sent the boys into fits of laughter. "Welcome to Brighton Barracks. This will be your home for the next two days and two nights. We're going straight to the drill hall where we'll get you sorted. Thanks, driver."

The boys looked at each other and then around at their teachers who raised their shoulders and smiled. The bus went past a major parade ground and a series of accommodation and office blocks. The moment the first boy alighted from the bus when it stopped outside the drill hall Cadet Sergeant Major Park raised his baton. The Cadet band sprang into life and played the *Colonel Bogey March* as the boys braced up and pretended to march into the drill hall.

"Come on boys that's our cue," Gabriel yelled out.

He and Hancock started whistling the marching song and the other boys joined in. It was a stirring rendition as one group of boys saluted the other with their prowess. The choir formed up near the Cadets and was joined by both Gilchrist and Captain Courtney Stevens as they whistled and hummed to the music.

"I'll bet John wishes he was here," Duggan said to McRae in a light whisper."

"Yes, I think he would have loved to have recorded this."

"Ah, and don't forget Barry, he would be over there near the doorway filming."

Both men laughed quietly while their boys whistled and hummed accompanied by the Cadets. At the conclusion, the choir gave three cheers to the Cadets and the Cadets responded the same. The ice was more than broken. Gilchrist welcomed the boys and their teachers to his barracks and gave them a brief history of the Cadets while a barbecue was being organised for their dinner.

"We have more than 1200 Cadets throughout the United Kingdom in bands," Gilchrist told his civilian guests. "The boys and girls here can play a range of instruments and get to travel around the country and overseas. Twice a year we have what is called a Concentration of Cadets where more than 500 of the little beasties gather for a week to extend their musical learning."

"Sounds pretty good," Hancock said to Gabriel.

"Yes, but are they also taught how to sing?"

Gilchrist heard the boys talking and answered them – albeit for all to hear.

"Two of your comrades have just asked whether we also encourage and teach singing. The answer is yes but Cadets must first learn a musical instrument. You all know Captain Stevens here and have heard her fine voice. Did you know she is also a fantastic flautist? If we encourage her during the weekend, she may even accompany us with her flute in our training."

Stevens smiled and nodded. After the barbecue, the Cadets and choir practised working together for a couple of their songs. They were then given time to help the choir stow their bags in their barrack block before returning to the drill hall.

"Do you blokes play any games?" Gabriel asked Park.

"Games? Do you mean like tip football or something?"

"No. Games inside the drill hall here?"

"No."

"Hmm, I think I have a way of my team getting to know yours."

Gabriel spoke to Gilchrist and Duggan and offered to run a no-contact physical game for the group. Gilchrist agreed and let Gabriel organise it.

"Okay team, we're going to play a game of musical chairs without the music," Gabriel said loudly to get everyone's attention. "I need you all to grab a chair and form a circle and sit down."

The Cadets looked at Gilchrist while the choir looked at Duggan but both men told their groups to join in. Gabriel got the group of more than 60 to move their chairs close together in a circle. Everyone had a chair except him. He then said he would count to three and everyone had to move to their left and sit down. If he got to an empty seat before anyone else, then the person left standing was the next "in" and so on. Gabriel emphasised it was a fast-moving game and not for the faint-hearted. He counted to three and the boys sluggishly moved.

Gabriel darted between two Cadets and sat down first. This left a Cadet standing. The Cadet glared at Gabriel, grimaced and nodded. He yelled a count to three and the boys started picking up on their speed at darting between chairs. The game went for fifteen minutes before a stop was called. The adults noted how sweaty each of the boys was from the fast-action game. Gilchrist called on Park to organise a tarpaulin from the store room and to spread it out on the drill hall floor.

"Okay gents that was a great game, thank you, Gabriel. Now we need a quiet game before lights out. Sergeant Major Park organise our tarpaulin will you."

Park nodded and asked all the boys to stand on the tarpaulin close together. He told them the object of the game was to put as many people on the smallest amount of tarpaulin as possible. After the boys closed in together, Park then told them to step off the tarpaulin. Two Cadets folded the tarpaulin into two-thirds of its former size. Park ordered the boys to stand on the tarpaulin with no feet touching the outside floor and everybody within the shape of the ground cover. Both the Cadets and choir pushed and lifted each other so a number of the smaller boys were sitting on the shoulders of the older ones to make space.

"This should be interesting," McRae said as he watched the boys all dismount and move off the tarpaulin. Two Cadets then folded the cover by another some more and a series of groans and moans could be heard from the boys as they struggled to hold each other and stand on tiptoes. Hancock looked at the ceiling and noticed there were a series of dual metal supports running across the hall at intervals. Each of the supports had large continuous metal piping in the shape of joined 'w's connecting them.

"I've got it, Gabriel," Hancock said to his best mate. "We'll form a sort of pyramid and pass all the junior boys to the railing above and support them from below."

"Done."

Park gave the order for the boys to regroup on the floor cover and Gabriel and Hancock organised a series of human pyramids. The senior boys faced each other in pairs and had the junior boys climb their backs and reach up to the ceiling. The primary school boys loved the challenge but looks of heavy concentration bordering on being scared soon showed on their faces. The Cadets followed suit and were soon hanging from the metal rafters.

Gilchrist called a stop when the pyramids were complete and asked the boys to slowly get down.

"Well done team, for this is what you are now. You are no longer a group of Cadets and a boys' choir, but a team. Good initiative on the pyramid and raising the little ones to the top. Don't try this at home. I somehow don't think your parents would like it."

A haughty cheer went up among the boys with the Cadets and choir congratulating each other. The boys were then organised to go to their respective barracks for the night. Over the next two days, the Cadets showed the choir how to march and sing on the move. They were now ready for the Remembrance Day concert.

Chapter Nineteen

John, Cooper, and Bailey watched as the flat top dual cab truck made its way up the hill to the former church. On the rear of the truck was a six-seater curved stone seat with two ornately carved book-end-style facades.

"Caroline, you did a great job with your design of this seat," Cooper said to the artist.

"Thanks, Barry. It was a labour of love. I'm looking forward to seeing it locked into position on John's new concrete slab and then the job is complete."

"She's a beauty, Caroline," John said. "I have no doubt this seat will be here long after we're all dust."

"I think you're right. It was built to last."

Four workmen used a small hoist attached to the truck to lift and position the seat in place. They then bolted it down with a series of brackets to the supports and slab so it was unmovable. The whole operation took about an hour. The crew leader for the workers approached John after he checked all the supports to ensure they were tightly in place.

"I guess we'll all see this seat this Sunday on the news," the leader said.

"Yes, it will get some top billing when it's unveiled by

the former parish priest here," John said. "I'm sure the Remembrance Day concert will also get some good prominence in the news."

John thanked the crew and they drove off. He then lifted the lid off his plastic cooler box and produced three glasses and a bottle of champagne.

"I think this calls for a special toast, gang. What say you?"

"I was wondering what you had in the box," Bailey said. "Yes please, a glass of bubbly will shake the cobwebs away."

Cooper laughed as he also took a glass. John poured the champagne and the three of them went to the seat and sat down. They toasted each other and the seat and then sat back to enjoy the view and the quiet of the day from their perched position overlooking the valley.

"You know John, at first I didn't think your project was going to get off the ground," Cooper said with a pair of moist eyes.

"It was initially a pipe dream and then it gained such momentum it couldn't be stopped."

"You're right John," Bailey said. "These boys had such love for them in this village that it stirred the emotions here when you said you wanted this memorial seat for the boys. I still remember the looks on the parents at our first meeting in your workspace. They were so excited that someone was doing something for their boys. I understand you've had tremendous support across the board for the concert too."

"Yes, it's been a very wonderful project. The support has been just overwhelming. Take this seat for instance. Caroline did the wonderful artwork for free, thank you. Neville Davies teamed up with Peter Brown and the local Masons to raise money for it and had the seat sourced and organised within days of my request. The seat is almost paid off. We have an outstanding choir to help us this coming weekend and the military will be here in force too to support us – not to mention the Welsh teen sensations yet to make themselves known here."

Cooper sipped some more champagne and wiped his eyes.

"I somehow wish the boys knew what we have done for them."

"Oh, don't worry about that," John said carefully. "I have every feeling your boys have been behind us 100 per cent. How do I know? Well by the way so many things have fallen into place; the Brighton choir for example and how their singing picked up once they heard your boys. Remember how the Brighton boys listened to yours and then harmonised with them as a kind of salute?"

"Yes – that was very moving."

"We now have every bit of available space here at Sutton Hall sold out for the concert. Everything is in play and lined up ready to go. I'm so looking forward to the concert."

"Hear hear," Bailey said as she raised her glass in salute.

John then opened his cooler box again and took out some pâté and biscuits, a spreading knife, and some paper plates.

"You've been waiting for this moment for some time, haven't you?" Bailey asked with a laugh.

"Yes, and I wanted to share it specifically with you two as I think the three of us deserve a little reward for our work."

"John, when do the Americans and Australians arrive here?" Cooper asked.

"The concert is on Sunday so they should both be here on Saturday for rehearsals with the Cadets and Brighton boys."

"Good, it will be great to film them all together."

"What about the Welsh kids?"

"They should be here about 3.30 pm on Saturday."

"Where will you fit them in?"

"The boys have a special coral stance they want to use and will only be outside the old church while Gabriel and Cameron take centre stage inside. It should be fantastic."

The trio nodded enthusiastically and had their special celebratory morning tea in the graveyard before fitting a cover over the seat. They were about to leave when Bailey noticed a car driving toward them.

"This should be interesting," Bailey said. "It's the Mayor."

The trio walked towards the mayor's car and waved to him as he alighted and returned the wave.

"Ah, the seat is now here!" Butler said as he scanned past the trio and saw the covered bench seat.

"Good morning, Mr. Mayor," John said. "Yes, as you can see I've kept my promises all the way. The seat is fully in place, and everything is set for this Sunday's Remembrance Day concert."

"Oh yes, I see. Well done. Look, some time ago we spoke about Council or the Tourist Association erecting a special acid etched photo of the former choir here. Do you remember that?"

"Mr. Mayor, I remember a lot of things but I never remembered your Council or your Tourist Association saying they would do anything specific with this project. Oh, by the way, you do know I've been guaranteed national coverage through BBC1 for the concert?" John asked as he started pushing home his imaginary dagger.

Butler swallowed hard and lifted his eyes from looking at John's shoes to his face.

"Well, that will be good for ..."

"It will be great for this community and village and put us on the map as I said it would," John interrupted. "I'm even thinking of doing up some brochures and posting them out to the various tour companies for them to come and view our lovely village from here and spend time at this special memorial."

The mayor's face changed from light brown to a very dark red as he realised John could be setting himself up in direct competition with his own Tourist Association.

"You'd need to come through my Tourist Association and possibly Council for this as you'd be making it a commercial concern."

"Mr. Mayor, I'm glad you brought that up as I have been speaking to our local Member of Parliament, the Member for Brighton Pavilion, and I am under the impression from him I don't need either Council or your Tourist Association permission as the tours would come here of their own free volition. I'm not out to make money from the dead."

"Brighton Pavilion, huh?" Butler started to flounder as he realised he was having the carpet pulled from under him. "Mmm, the Council has asked me to contribute your memorial seat – that is if you would like it."

"What did you have in mind?"

"Come and I'll show you," Butler said with a noticeable quiver in his voice as he walked to the rear of his car and opened the boot. He pulled out a plinth and stood it up. Cooper, Bailey and John looked on in earnest as they saw on top of the plinth were mounted the acid-washed photo of the St Dominic Savio Boys and Youth choir; their names and a description of the choir and how they met their fate in the bus crash. Bailey and John held back from saying anything until Cooper had said something first.

"Graham this is pretty good," Cooper said. "It's a good likeness of the boys and all their names are spelt correctly. What do you plan on doing with it?"

"I was hoping it could be erected on the concrete slab here in front of the bench. However, if John has something else in mind Council could probably put it somewhere in its offices."

John decided to put the mayor out of his misery.

"Barry, Caroline will you help me lift the cover from the seat, please? Graham, let's have a look at how the plinth would fit in. Will you position it at the front of the concrete slab please?"

The trio then lifted the cover off the seat while the mayor positioned the plinth. Butler's eyes widened when he saw how beautiful the memorial seat looked.

"Barry, as the parent representative here, what do you think?" John asked.

Cooper's eyes had begun to well up when he saw the memorial seat and plinth in position. He sat on the right-hand edge of the seat, and he did the same for the middle and left-hand side.

"This looks as it should be," Cooper said with measured tones. "I sat in the various positions to view the village and surrounds and check what could be seen on the plinth. This would be a tremendous addition for here if it was allowed."

"There are no strings attached," Butler said. "If John is prepared to have it here on this property, I will arrange for Council workers to come this afternoon and bolt it in place on the top of the concrete slab."

John looked at Cooper and then Bailey and both nodded.

"Mr. Mayor, your Council's plinth will be a welcome addition to this memorial. Thank you."

"I'm, err sorry it took so long to get back to you about the plinth but I had so much Council and Tourist business lately it's been hard to keep up."

"So I understand," John said as he looked Butler straight in the eye. "How's your Saxon Museum coming on?"

Butler drew his chin in and narrowed his eyes as he took in what John said. He was in shock.

"You know about it?"

"You of all people should know you can't hide things in this village. We've all been watching your progress. No doubt your finds will be the next big thing for this village."

"Well they will be but, just for now, let's just keep it under wraps."

The three residents nodded their heads in unison. The mayor had eaten his humble pie; it was time to move on.

"It would be a privilege to have you officially open this site with Father Brendan on Sunday," John said with a smile. "This site will be complete when your Council workers affix the plinth. Then after Sunday, it will become a beautiful setting for the parents of our boys from here and tourists to come and sit down and take in the sights of our lovely village."

"Thank you, John," Butler said as he shook John's hand and then Cooper's and Bailey's. "Is there anything you need for the concert?"

"No, I think I have everything covered. My record company has done a contra deal with a company to install some large TV screens inside and outside the old church."

"What do you mean by contra deal?"

"My boss has said he will produce some music for several artists for free if the company supplies and installs the screens. It's like bartering."

"That's good."

"The MP for Brighton Pavilion has assisted with the Territorials supplying lighting and a generator for outside. Seating is being covered by the local schools and I have some Explorer Scouts and Senior Girl Guides running barbecues and drinks stalls."

"What about the music?"

"The Americans and the Australian have rung in to say they'll be here on Saturday for rehearsals along with our new choir and Cadets. A huge contingent of Welsh teenage boys will sing here also and complete our largest-ever ensemble for Brighton. I also understand your mother wants to play a part?"

The mayor had listened intently up to now but John's last comment threw him.

"You've got Welsh singers coming here too, wow – this

is turning out to be the biggest event in this town in living memory. Have you been in touch with my mother?"

"No, but I understand from some of the parents who are helping out; that Veronica and other seniors, will be here to assist with some craft stalls."

"I didn't know that. However, it doesn't surprise me as she is always knitting things like toilet roll covers; little dolls and slippers. Well, it seems you have all bases covered."

"I think I have – however, if I find I need something I think you can supply I'll have no hesitation in contacting you."

"Okay, thanks, John. Well, I must be off so I can organise the Council workers to come here today and then get back to my real work."

"Thank you, Mr. Mayor, I'm sure all the parents of our former choir will appreciate the plinth and your assistance," Cooper said.

"Hear, hear," John said.

Butler left the plinth with John and then drove off with Cooper following him.

"Well Caroline, now we're alone I need to ask if everything is okay with your mum and her friends. They play a very significant part on Sunday and need to be here."

"I spoke to mum before coming here today and she and her friends have all been heavily thinking about this Sunday," Bailey said. "They should be fine. They've done this several times and moved spirits on. These dead boys would have died with pure hearts …"

John shook his head when he heard Bailey's last words.

"What's up?"

"Oh, nothing it's just that one of the songs the Welsh boys will be singing is Caloun Lân which is a song about ..."

"Pure hearts going to heaven. These are the sorts of words my mother and her friends will be using in their mantras. Well, the spirit world is certainly working hard in unison with this one."

"Can I ask you again how your mother and her friends will move the boys on to the next spiritual plane?"

Bailey smiled knowingly and thought for a few seconds before answering.

"Mum and her friends are used to going into trances daily as they meditate. Tomorrow will be no different. However, they also have to centre their thoughts on the boys and invite them to come close to them."

John was listening very closely and cocked his head to his left shoulder and scratched his right ear. "So you just don't tell the boys to move on and call them to you?"

"No, the boys must be asked, you know, invited to be with mum and her friends. Once the boys are there the ladies will tell them they have the authority to send spirits away. The boys will be told mentally their bodies are dead but their souls will live forever. The women will then tell the boys they are forgiven for anything they may have done while alive. They may have to say this several times to make it effective."

John had straightened his head and was nodding slowly as he took in every word Bailey told him.

"Then there are two remaining things mum and the others have to do. They have to ask the boys for their forgiveness for anything others may have done to them while they were alive. Lastly, the women must visualise a bright white light and ask the boys to go to it because it is there they will find peace."

"I can't believe the help we are getting from seen and unseen forces – it's truly amazing. Thanks for your double check on things, I'm just doing the mental checks for Sunday as there will be a lot going on and I still have my part to play."

"Don't worry, I'll organise my mum and her friends. Leave this job to me."

"Done and thank you – there is a lot most folks don't know about the unseen world."

Bailey smiled and nodded before departing. John walked into his workspace and placed the plinth and cooler box down next to his desk. He wrote the word 'plinth' on his notice board list and then ticked it. After a few seconds of deliberation, he wrote 'releasement' and also ticked it.

"Okay boys, this completes the list for the outside for our little concert," John said in a loud voice. "We have the concrete slab, the memorial seat and finally the plinth. Now your parents can come and talk with you any time they like from Sunday. We also have a way mapped out for you to find eternal peace."

John started checking his emails when he noticed his tearoom lights blinked a couple of times in succession.

"Thank you, I thought you'd approve of what's been done – now, for the concert!"

Within an hour a Council works van arrived and a Council engineer visited John to retrieve the plinth from him so he and his crew could bolt it to the concrete slab. Over the next two days, John had work crews; soldiers and community groups setting up their facilities ready for Sunday's concert. Sutton Hall was becoming a major entertainment venue.

* * *

Melanie arrived home early just as the last workers were leaving Sutton Hall for the day. She made her way into John's office and stood there for a few seconds taking in the sight. A raised platform had been erected at the front of the former church, ready for the bands and choir. Plastic outdoor seats filled virtually every available piece of floor space including the platform. Two large screens had been erected on the top left and top right of the hall so the bands and choir could be seen from any seat. A number of speakers dotted the walls both inside and outside the old church. Two very large screens had been erected outside the building and stacks of chairs waited to be used by the overflow of people. Melanie was astounded. John was sitting at his desk wearing earphones and adjusting the various volumes of a musical piece he was re-recording and didn't notice his wife enter. She walked over to his console and stood looking at him. John looked up and almost fell off his chair when he realised Melanie had arrived.

"Hell, you scared the heck out of me," John said.

"I tried to get your attention, but you seemed too involved with your work. This place looks amazing with all the various bits and pieces here."

"Now you know why you've hardly seen me these last couple of days. I've been pretty flagged overseeing what goes where and the various work crews that have been here."

"I knew you were busy but this takes the cake. I guess the real question is; are our performers ready?"

"Well, I'm very sure the boys from the choir and the Cadets are okay. I have no doubt the Americans and Aussie will be okay on the day and Gabriel assures me nothing will stop his Welsh friends from being here."

"Is there much more to do for preparation?"

"The Territorials will be here again tomorrow to dig a hole for a generator and lay a cable to power up everything."

Melanie winced and cocked her head as she took in what John said.

"How big a hole do the soldiers need?"

"Not very big. They have to dig the hole to put a 6 KVA generator in and then run leads for about 50 metres so the crowds will hear the speakers and not the generator."

"Okay."

"Also, some of the community groups still have some stalls to set up. Lastly, we'll have security guards patrolling the place tonight and tomorrow to ensure none of the equipment is pilfered or damaged by anyone."

"Hmm, your parents' group and you have been busy. I guess it's time we went out for tea then?"

"Yes, sorry love, I've had no time today to prepare anything for us."

"No problems as this will give us some couple time to catch up with what's happening."

John locked up his office and went out for tea with Melanie. It was good to just sit and talk with the love of his life and share what they had been doing.

During the night John was again restless as his mind went into overdrive mentally ticking off things he would need for the concert. Eventually, he got up and made a cup of tea. He checked the kitchen clock and saw it was 4 am. It was still pitch-black outside. For the next hour, John sat at the breakfast bar and worked on his laptop checking and double-checking every arrangement for the concert. His mind mentally travelled inside and outside his office space looking for missing things. He was a spectator at the concert and had followed the Cadets and choir from the railway station up to the former church. John looked at everything from the roadway: to the outside buildings, temporary toilets, lights, seats, stalls, screens, and speakers. Finally, he breathed a sigh of relief as he realised he could personally do no more except orchestrate others. Gentle footsteps could be heard as Melanie padded her way into the kitchen.

"Hello, my darling," she said as she kissed John. "Finding it hard to sleep?"

"I just had to mentally check everything to ensure there was nothing else left to do."

"Is there?"

"I don't think so. All I think we need now is the Territorials with their generator and the community groups with the last-minute installation of their stalls and goods."

"Great," Melanie said softly as she tugged the sleeve of her husband's pyjamas and kissed him.

All day Saturday John was talking to an army of volunteers as they worked around the former church festooning it with flags and lights and setting up their stalls. The real break came at lunchtime when the local choir, Cadets, Americans, and a lone Australian made their way to John's working space.

"At last we meet John," Captain Andrew Jackson said with a heavy American drawl. "My band and I are looking so forward to tomorrow's performance here."

"Same here," Captain Phillip Boyce said as he introduced himself. "Andy and I haven't been here for a long time and I'm excited to sing here again."

"Well let me tell you," John said as he introduced the choir and Cadets to everyone with a huge smile on his face. "You will have a fantastic group of energetic and professional young people to perform with. Already, these youngsters have grabbed national headlines."

"Yes I saw that in the news," Boyce said. "Well done guys. It will be great to get a feel for what we all can bring to this fantastic opportunity."

For the next three hours the Cadets, choir, band, Boyce and Jackson filled the old church with voice and music. Cooper filmed the performances while John recorded each of the various songs. Those not singing or playing sat and watched the others and acted as the readymade audience.

It started small and slowly the hills and valley surrounding the former church started to echo with the strong stirring voices of teenage boys. The Welsh choirs had arrived in style. The local lads and the bands poured out of John's workspace to cheer on their Welsh counterparts as the tourists formed up in four small groups making a rectangle around the former church. Hancock and Gabriel stood in the grass in the middle and started to sing Caloun Lân at the top of their voices in

Welsh. Hancock sang the first few verses before Gabriel joined in.

"*I don't ask for a luxurious life, the world's gold or its fine pearls: I ask for a happy heart, an honest heart, a pure heart.*"

When it was time for the chorus, the rest of the Welsh boys joined in and within seconds had found their collective voice as young men. Their song echoed throughout Brighton as they poured their hearts and energies into it. When they had finished, the local boys gave their counterparts a series of rousing cheers and went out to meet them. Davies and a couple of other parents of the Welsh boys made their way to John.

"Did I not tell you they would be here?" Davies enthusiastically asked, pointing to where the Welsh choir was being greeted.

"I am still shocked by the power and depth of the boys' singing. They are just fantastic," John said. "Tell me something. Why did they stand in four groups and sing and not one?"

A smile pushed its way across Davies' mouth before he answered.

"My boys have formed up like a number five domino with groups in each corner and one in the middle. We found this gives a great presence to the boys' singing and allows the audiences to be enveloped in the kids' songs."

"So how many boys are there?"

"We brought 115 boys from Wales and with Gabriel here, this makes the number of children 116. It will give Brighton a presence they have never had or heard before."

"And no doubt will ever feel, see or hear again here. Phew,

I am taken back by what you have achieved with them – well done."

One of the parents with Davies signalled to his boys and they re-formed into their four groups. He then started playing a ghetto blaster with the music for *Sosban Fach* – a nonsensical Welsh song that showed the power of the teenage boys' voices. The Welsh teens swung into the song straight away and the other boys harmonised with them. The impromptu concert received rapturous applause from all the bystanders.

At one stage Peter Allan, John's boss leant in towards John's ear.

"Mate, I'm so impressed with what I've seen and heard today I think we have a winner here for CDs after the concert."

"Thanks, Peter. Now you can see why I've been a bit slack with some of my work recently. It'll pick up again next week after all this is packed up."

"No probs. You're the toast of the village as people get ready to come here tomorrow. I'll bet you have more than you can handle."

"I do not doubt that. At least we can entertain them, water and feed them and give them some really good views."

"I'm looking forward to seeing this special memorial seat."

"All in good time, my boss."

Chapter 20

John had fielded several Media calls on Saturday as pre-records for Sunday. The national newspapers, radio stations and virtually all TV channels broadcast stories of the Remembrance Day service at the former Saint Dominic Savio Church on both days of the weekend. Two TV channels; three newspaper reporters and two radio Journalists interviewed John on Remembrance Day. Throughout the solemn broadcasts of the various Remembrance Day services links were made to Sutton Hall.

John was impressed with the way the local British Legion had run the village service. Scouts, Girl Guides and community members participated in large numbers to remember the wars British Defence Force members and those from other Commonwealth countries had participated in and died in. He attended the Brighton cenotaph where the local service was run.

"It was on this special day at 11 am on the 11th of November 1918, the German guns in World War One fell silent and the Armistice was signed," President of the Brighton British Legion Craig Youll, told a packed cenotaph. "We also call this Poppy Day to remember those who so gallantly lost their lives in the fields of Flanders where the poppies grow."

Speeches from former serving members of the armed forces were made followed by the laying of wreaths. It was a moving ceremony for anyone to watch. As soon as the service was over John darted home, parked his car in the garage and locked up. He checked with each of the various groups organising the stalls, barbecues and security that all was well. Melanie had stayed home to prepare some cakes for one of the stalls.

"Well, all we can do now is wait," John said.

"It will be fine, as long as the rain holds off it will be a great concert," Melanie said as she spread chocolate icing over her cakes.

"You're right. I think regardless of the weather, there is nothing more we can do. It will be a success."

Buses and trains had made their way to the railway station to drop off the crowds so they could walk to Sutton Hall. No vehicular traffic was allowed up the road leading to the former church and no public parking was permitted. The concert was set for 3 pm and the choir and Cadets were in position by 2 pm at the railway station and played a few airs. Crowds had already started forming both at the station and around Sutton Hall as they began the countdown to the concert. At 2.25 pm the Brighton Boys and Youth Choir formed up behind the Brighton Army Cadet Force Band. On the stroke of 2.30 pm, Cadet Sergeant Major Tim Park struck up the band and started to march towards Sutton Hall. The band played *Men of Harlech* and the choir joined in and sang loudly and proudly as they marched along behind their mates in the band to Sutton Hall. The crowd clapped initially and then joined in the singing as they followed the choir and band. It was easy for the crowd to fall into step with the cadence of the band as the boy soldiers had rehearsed this song many times and the rhythm flowed easily.

Police in cars with flashing lights were stationed at either end of the procession and led the way slowly through the village to the former church. Robert Kitchen had pre-positioned six *kneelie* buses along the road leading to Sutton Hall. Each of the buses was parked inwards on the grass facing toward the road. Groups of girls from the local schools and community organisations had joined forces and stationed themselves at the front of each bus with candles. The girls had felt left out from activities and sought permission to show their feelings at the last parents' meeting. John and the parents quickly agreed. When the girls heard the band and choir approaching, they lit their candles. Slowly the procession made its way up the long hill. Each time the crowd approached a bus the driver flashed its lights and made it kneel as a sign of respect. It was Kitchen's way of saying sorry for what one of his buses did a decade ago when it ploughed into the side of the truck carrying LPG bottles and exploded, wiping out all aboard in both vehicles.

Crowds at the top of the hill watched in awe as the procession made its way past the buses and covered the memorial site. They clapped and cheered as one by one the buses knelt as the band processed past them. TV crews stood on top of their parked outside broadcast vans filming the whole event. The first police car peeled off to the side at the top of the hill and the Cadets and choir marched into the former church to an eruption of noise as the audience stood and clapped. They were soon followed by the crowds and the girls. The former

Saint Dominic Savio's was overflowing with people sitting on every available chair both inside the building and out on the lawns. The moment the Cadets entered the building Captain Andrew Jackson stood up. He took the salute from Park before the Cadets and choir joined him on the raised platform. The crowds kept their applause going as the boys found their seats and settled down. Jackson introduced himself and the various performers. He told the gathering the concert would be held both inside the former church and outside when some special guests arrived and then began the concert. The band launched straight into the specially adapted salute to the military medley to capture Remembrance Day. The medley was initially written to honour America's armed forces but was adapted by Jackson and his band to salute the armed forces of America, the United Kingdom, and Australia.

At the beginning of each song about an armed force – army, navy, air force, marines, and coast guard – Cadets brought forward flags from each of the three country's armed services; swung them around to allow the air to flutter the flags and then placed them into special holders on the floor to the sides of the band before saluting them. The moment Cadets carrying the flags entered the front of the band men and women who had served in the various armed services stood up and saluted. It was their way of showing support and also paying their respects to their respective service.

After the medley, the audience gave a standing ovation with most of the crowd covering the outside grassed area following suit. John was beside himself as the raw emotion and energy overflowed from his workspace and throughout the grounds.

He looked up to the choir stand and noticed Margaret Hill and her friends quietly sitting with their eyes closed and their mouths moving as if they were in conversation. Bailey was sitting near John and turned to look at her mother and then John and nodded.

"Ladies and Gentlemen," Jackson said. "This next song is quite stirring as it tells the story of the war from both a soldier's perspective and that of our mothers. *Soldiers Cry Oseh Shalom* has started to become the call for peace around the globe."

Once the choir started singing several girls brought out pairs of old army boots and placed them on the raised platform in rows. They then imitated crying scenes as each pair of boots represented a loved one killed in action. Emotion ran high throughout the song with most people reaching for their tissues and handkerchiefs. It was time for more solemnity and Gabriel stepped forward. The bands began playing *Make Me a Channel of Your Peace* and both Jackson and Boyce joined the teenager on stage. The variety and richness of the three voices were overpowering and had the audience on their feet in a clapping frenzy at its conclusion.

"You know whenever the boys sang this song here no one clapped like this," Father Brendan said to Butler as they both also joined in the applause.

Jackson introduced the next song *The Lion Sleeps Tonight* saying it was the last song sung in the former church by the Saint Dominic Savio Boys and Youth choir. He said it was their favourite song and had become a favourite of the Brighton choir. John watched for the cue. The boys acted out their animal noises and waited for the key change in the music. John then played his special recording left by Blake. The Brighton boys harmonised while the voices of the Saint Dominic Savio Boys and Youth Choir took centre stage at their one last concert. Cooper had managed to get every parent of the former choir along for the concert and they filled the front of the former church. The moment John started playing his recording a murmur went up among the families as they realised who was singing.

"That's our boys, that's our boys!" could be heard loudly as one by one the families stood and applauded amid tears of joy as their boys were feted by a backing they never had before. Eventually, the whole audience was on their feet again clapping as they realised there had been a change of choir. The crowd outside did the same as calls went up it was the Saint Dominic Savio Boys and Youth choir singing.

"Ladies and gentlemen," Jackson said. "By special agreement with the Brighton Boys and Youth choir, they just harmonised to the boys who we salute today. They have grown to appreciate the level of competence of the choir that sang here. Initially, the boys from Brighton were going to sing this song as they had practised it with the Cadets here for some time. However, in a salute to the Saint Dominic Savio Boys and Youth choir, the boys from Brighton harmonised for them instead."

The crowd gave a standing ovation to the boys from Brighton which lasted several minutes. Jackson looked at Boyce and then at Stevens. The female Captain took centre stage and harmonised while *Hymn to the Fallen* was played.

The song had a calming effect on the whole audience. Next both Jackson and Boyce stood up.

"You know ladies and gentlemen it has been more than a decade since Andrew and I have sung here with the Saint Savio boys," Boyce said. "With your indulgence, we'd like to sing with them one more time."

The parents of the dead choir looked at each and all seemed to wince as *Panis Angelicus* started being played. The voices of Blake and Richard were heard from John's recording and a hush descended on the audience. A whisper started from the front rows and made it to the rear of the church and outside. Both Boyce and Jackson gave strong performances and harmonised well with the two original choristers who were no longer physically around.

"It's Blake and Richard from Saint Dominic's." Again the parents stood in unison at the song's beautiful conclusion and applauded enthusiastically with tears flowing down their cheeks. The crowd outside was also on its feet when it realised what had happened and how the former boy singers had given a special tribute to the choir they sang with as children. Dark clouds threatened to bring a storm across the whole of Brighton as the concert continued. The outside light dropped in intensity and zephyrs started racing across the hillside and building in intensity. John could see the noticeable change in outside light and looked at Margaret Hill and her friends. Margaret caught his eyes and gave the thumbs up.

John had been wearing a special set of earphones that allowed him to speak with a series of key people during the performance. He got the message from Davies he was waiting for and nodded to Boyce and showed him his right hand with his index finger closed on his thumb – the sign the Welsh boys were arriving. Boyce asked for total silence as the audience was about to be given a special treat. The former church fell silent, and a hush descended on the huge outside audience.

A series of boys' voices could be heard lifting from the valleys and encircling hills as the Welsh teenagers made their way to the grounds of Sutton Hall. The boys formed up in four groups and Gabriel and Hancock donned bright orange safety visor vests so they could be easily seen by the crowds. They left the former church and walked outside to the top of the hill overlooking the surrounding valleys. Both boys were wearing special earphone microphones John had given them so their voices could be enhanced and picked up inside and outside the former church on large loudspeakers. The teenage pair took centre stage on the lawns as the Welsh choir stopped singing. John cued *Caloun Lân* and started to play it. Hancock began singing the first refrain and was then joined by Gabriel. The Welsh boys joined in the chorus and the applause from inside and outside the former church was almost deafening as the choir found their joint timbre. While the singing was in full swing, calm descended outside as the little puffs of wind stopped racing across the hilltop and the clouds began to part. Shafts of sunlight broke through the cloud lines and streamed through the front stained-glass windows of the former church and illuminated the floor with various vibrant colours. John was astounded and looked up at Hill as she and her group was waving to no one in particular. John nodded. The boys had gone. He had managed to keep Blake's secret as much as he could and it had paid off. The boys had now entered their eternal home and finally left Earth. Melanie watched John as he was looking at Hill and nodded as tears slowly trickled down his cheeks. She too understood what was happening and a giant smile raced across her face.

The Welsh boys sang with such passion and enthusiasm all audience members both inside and outside Sutton Hall rose to their feet and cheered and clapped wildly. Cameras placed outside the former church captured the boys singing and relayed it to screens inside John's workplace and outside to large screens for the people on the lawns. When the boys' singing had stopped and the audience regained its seats, not a dry eye could be seen anywhere. Boyce took to the stage and wiped his eyes and proclaimed he had never heard such beautiful singing before. He then introduced the Welsh choir's next song *Sosban Fach*. The Welsh choir came together and ringed the outside walls of the former church and held hands. They then broke into their favourite rugby song. Again the crowds found it hard to contain themselves and cheered, clapped wildly and whistled at the song's close. The boys took a bow and then quietly moved to the side area of the crowd while Stevens took a turn to gain control on centre stage.

She had the crowds singing and clapping along to the World War Two songs, *Pack Up Your Troubles* and *Bless Them All* as she led the next part of the singing. At the conclusion, the Brighton Boys and Youth choir stood up and walked outside the church. They joined the Welsh boys while Jackson started the music to *Rule Britannia* and the whole audience was on its feet joining in. The singing could be heard right down to the village as the outside and inside audiences sang in unison. Jackson was forced to play the song again due to the calls of *'more, more'* being hurled at him by the crowds.

The finale came with Jackson inviting the girls who held the candles next to the buses to stand around the stage. More than forty girls aged from nine to 16 stood up and went to the front. Jackson thanked the girls for their strong support of the Saint Dominic Savio boys and asked them to lead the audience in the final song. The moment *Land Of Hope And Glory* started, virtually the whole audience was on its feet and came to attention. The girls started singing and were quickly joined by the boys, Jackson, Boyce, and Stevens. The final ovation was long and boisterous as the audience called for another round of *Land Of Hope And Glory*. The band and singers obliged with Gabriel and Hancock taking the lead to play and sing the song again to rapturous applause from all choirs and singers. At the end of the ovation, John took centre stage and thanked everyone for their fantastic support of the choir who once sung in the hallowed place they all now occupied. John had a long list of people to thank – especially the boys from Brighton and the military folk and the teen sensations from Wales. He asked Father Brendan to say a few words and then asked everyone to join them outside for the special unveiling of the memorial seat and plinth.

It took ten minutes before the inside crowd had emptied the former church and made their way out to join the outside crowd at the seat. Both Father Brendan and Butler lifted the sheeting covering the memorial seat amid huge cheers and clapping. Butler then moved to the covered plinth. He called on Cooper as a representative of the Saint Dominic Savio boys' parents to help him. Together they lifted the cover on the acid-etched photo of the boys and a large cheer erupted over the hillside. Butler called John forward and explained how John had set the whole concert and memorial seat project in motion. Raucous cheers and clapping ensued as the crowd showed their appreciation of John.

Jackson sidled up to John and whispered in his ear with John breaking into a huge smile.

"Ladies and gentlemen," John said in a loud voice. "Captain Jackson has just informed me his band and Captain Boyce will be playing some of their latest hits outside here for the next hour so please join with them and support our allies. Also, our teen choirs and Cadets will be joining in too."

The crowd broke up as the American band moved its chairs and equipment outside of the former church and started playing a series of modern songs. Gabriel, Hancock and other members of the choir joined in singing along to the tunes. Melanie caught up with John and gave her husband a big kiss.

"Well done my darling. What a wonderful concert. I'm sure our boys loved it."

"It was fantastic, and I can't wait to hear the recording and make the CD of it. It should be a top seller. Now there's one person we need to speak with … ah there she is now."

John waved to Hill and the middle-aged woman joined him and Melanie. The smile on her face said it all.

"Well, how did we go? What happened to the boys?" John gushed out.

"They've all gone – every last one of them," Hill said with a continuous smile. "I told you they'd go when they were shown the light."

"You're not telling me they left when the sun broke through this afternoon are you?"

"As a matter of fact, yes. My friends and I had taken them through the releasement procedure and had each imagined a source of white light. We then directed the boys to the light and that's when the sun broke through – just as they were leaving. It was beautiful as this was the time the Welsh boys sang their first song about becoming a pure heart and going to heaven. It was very moving."

"That's unbelievable. It sounds like a miracle with the sun and all."

"I have a special message for you two from Blake," Hill said with a lowered tone.

John and Melanie looked at each other in puzzlement and brought their faces closer to Hill's.

"Blake said to thank you for arranging one last concert for them. He said to please call them after him and Richard. He said you'll know what he means shortly."

Melanie went red and John's eyes widened as the penny dropped as to what Blake meant. Twin boys would be nice. They would have a great place to grow up and a fantastic environment to learn to sing and play the piano. Hill wasn't finished yet and grabbed both Melanie and John's shoulders to pull them closer to her.

"He also said don't tell anyone."

Acknowledgements

A big thank you to my wife, Yvonne; my sisters, Liane and Nerida; Robert Hodge, and Sue Jones for their work in helping to edit *One Last Concert* and assisting me to bring it to life. I truly appreciate your efforts and guidance.

To the former British Army soldiers and civilians who worked with me within the Army Reserve and provided the necessary contextualisation – thank you.

About the Author

Christopher J. Holcroft is the author of six books. His background is in communications, media training, complex public information planning and implementation, and journalism.

He was a member of the Australian Army Reserve for more than 43 years. His overseas deployments have included Bougainville (1999), East Timor (2001), and Iraq (2006). He is now a Commander in the Australian Navy Cadets as Director of Communication and Media

For more than 36 years, Christopher has been involved in scouting, including Venturer Scout Units in both Victoria and NSW. Christopher was presented the Silver Wattle Award by Scouts Australia in August 2008 for his outstanding service to Scouting. He was later awarded the Silver Koala in 2016 for his distinguished service.

Christopher holds a Masters degree in Organisational Communication from Charles Sturt University and a Bachelor of Arts degree from the University of Technology, Sydney, where he majored in Journalism and Communications Technology. He is also a Justice of the Peace.

He is married to Yvonne and the couple has three sons. They live in NSW and enjoy outdoor recreational activities including camping, abseiling and scuba diving.